PLAIN SIGHT

M. E. Delaney

This is a work of fiction. Long-standing institutions, agencies, and journals are mentioned but names, characters, businesses, places, events and incidences are either the products of the author's imagination or used in a fictitious manner. Any resemblance to actual persons, living or dead, or actual events is purely coincidental. The text should not be taken as a replacement for clinical advice, diagnosis or treatment.

For Clark

I came in from the wilderness
A creature void of form
"Come in," she said, "I'll give ya
shelter from the storm."
-Bob Dylan

1

We met in a ditch.

I had almost arrived. The neon pie advertising my destination blinked in the distance. I scrolled a flood of new emails while navigating wormy pools in the sidewalk, the remnants of last night's downpour.

At a gaping hole in the sidewalk, I stopped. Shovels full of cement and earth had been ripped out of my path. Orange cones and sagging yellow tape detoured pedestrians into a puddled, low-lying trench.

I glanced at my watch and searched for an alternate route. To my right, a wire fence. To my left, more fence, and a road stripped of concrete by the still present, hulking machinery. Their massive steel consumed the watery roadway, adding a harshness to the gloom.

I cringed at the thought of backtracking. I preferred to be timely. I launched myself into the detour, stepping across uneven pallets and chunks of concrete, muttering at the creators of this mess and their questionable code compliance. At the bottom, I sloshed through a wide, brackish pool.

I headed upslope toward the intact sidewalk. My feet slipped out from under me. I lurched forward then back, arms flailing. I hit the ground, hard, first with my lower back. Whiplash, my head smashed into concrete.

Pain. Then nothing.

I regained consciousness, face up in the soup.

The solitary head of a passerby loomed over me, blotting out the paltry sunlight.

"Are you okay?"

Mortified, addled, "Yes. Just a klutz. I'm fine, thank you."

I heaved my six-foot frame into an upright position and hesitated in the slop. Where was I? Where was I going?

Eyes bored into me. I scanned the area. A woman across the ditch, standing on a wooden plank, stared. Hers was the face that had just before, leaned over my pathetic, supine self. We glanced at each other. I forced a weak smile and waved. She smoothed her side part and looked down at her phone.

I flicked globs of mud off my sport coat and jeans and wiped filthy hands on tissues unearthed from my pocket. I felt it again. Her, watching me. We made eye contact.

She smirked, slid gloss across her lips from a narrow tube. "That was hilarious."

One of my students? A former student? I searched my memory. I did not recognize the features.

Physically striking, with an easy, earthy sensuality, she was tall, wore a white T-shirt, jeans, and black Converse high tops. Strands of blond, wavy hair lifted, shining, aloft in the breeze.

My mind formed an image of that mouth, those white teeth and full lips drinking from a glass of lemony iced tea.

"You lurched this way and that way, then flipped backwards." She mocked my fall with exaggerated arm movements. "You should have seen your face."

"I'm glad you found it entertaining."

"Most fun I've had on the way to work in months. I'm Alex Argyle." She bowed. "At your service."

"Pleasure to meet you, Alex, I'm Simon Brust."

We shook hands and scrambled out of the gully, side by side.

"You really should see someone. You hit your head pretty hard."

"I'm fine. Late for a meeting."

"Yeah?" She shrugged. "I'm late for work. Seriously, you were out cold. Could be concussed, start seizing, veer into traffic."

"I'm obviously a lummox, so I suppose the veering into traffic is entirely possible." I gave her a short salute, embarrassed, not wanting to socialize, and turned away, in the direction of the coffee shop and my colleagues.

Halfway down the block, I could no longer ignore the pain in my ankle. It must have twisted in the fall. Also a little dizzy, I headed straight for a bench and sat down.

I was pondering my capacity to make it the next two blocks to the coffee shop, my transportation options, how I was going to be able to work and take care of Mother with an injury when the woman from the ditch appeared. What was her name? Alex something.

"We meet again," she said.

"No coat? It's freezing out here."

"Not a fan of coats. Too confining. And I work just up the block." She poked a silver ringed thumb in the direction of the coffee shop. "At the Brash Barista and Books."

"That's where I'm headed."

"Best coffee in town. Don't miss the scones. So what's this big meeting about, Simon Brust?"

"Dissertation committee. I'm a professor."

"Well, professor, you look a little nuts all covered in mud. That fancy jacket can't hide what happened to you this morning."

"They already know I'm a little off," I said, woozy, head and ankle pounding. I hoped a joke might hide my deteriorating condition.

"You alright? You look pale."

"I'm fine," I lied, and vomited the toast I had for breakfast onto the sidewalk. I wiped my mouth with the back of my hand, grabbed for the muddy tissues in my pocket and stooped to sop up the mess.

"You're not fine. You should see a doctor. There's an urgent care around the corner."

"Really, I'm good." I stood to throw away the tissues and instantly became dizzy and nauseous. I sat back down.

"You can't even get up. Come with me, I'll take you."

"Don't you have to work?"

"I wouldn't miss this. Besides, they won't fire me. I bake the scones and do their marketing."

Resistant and humiliated, I hobbled down the block next to, I remembered, Alex Argyle.

White lights and the stench of urine, poorly masked by chemical cleaners, greeted us at the clinic door. Squinting in pain and from the glare, I pulled insurance card and driver's license out of organized rows in my wallet and handed them across the counter at check-in.

We sat not talking on mauve, patent-leather chairs at a 45-degree angle from each other in the waiting room. Under our weight, air forced from the cushions sounded like deflating balloons. The commercial carpet, an emerald green. Rumpled magazines formed stacks beside us on small wooden tables. The color palette must have come highly recommended, by a decorator, to create a calming ambience.

I, however, was distinctly on edge. I texted a colleague, *Roberto, I don't think I'll be able to make the meeting*. I didn't mention my current predicament. According to my watch, it was already half over.

"Alex, you don't have to stay. Please, you've been more than helpful. I can handle it from here." I wanted to be alone in my misery.

"Oh, I don't mind. I'd rather watch you try to walk than serve angry customers."

I bounced open palms on the arms of the chair, "Excuse me. I'm going to wash up."

Alex peered into her phone as I dragged my aching foot to the restroom, grateful for the privacy of a locked door. While scrubbing hands with hot water and pump after pump of pink soap from the dispenser, scraping grit from under each nail, I caught a glimpse of my reflection in the mirror.

Disaster. I wiped splattered mud off my face with a wet paper towel. My thick swoop of light brown hair was matted in the back, emphasizing the thinning patch at the top of my head. I cleaned off the dirt, clump by clump, working around a tender lump, a gift from the concrete. Grey water ran down my neck, vanishing into a starched, white button down.

I collected a long line of toilet paper, folded it over itself, and blew my prominent, crooked nose, the victim of multiple sports injuries. My eyes, rust and black, like the bark of ponderosa pine, gazed back at me in the mirror. They were my father's eyes.

I wasn't exactly handsome. Not ugly, either. Unremarkable. I straightened my shoulders, usually hunched from poring over data, typing, and the avoidant concavity of low self-esteem.

2

I lingered in the solitude of the urgent care's restroom, trying to come to terms with the impact an injured foot would have on my ability to rake Mother's leaves, clean her gutters, shop for her groceries, and get myself back and forth from campus until someone on the other side of the door jiggled the knob.

I hopped back into the waiting area and sat down. Alex didn't acknowledge me. Her eyes were trained on the screen of her phone. I caught a glimpse of the page she was reading as I sat down. Yale logo. She googled me? Probably making sure I wasn't a felon. What would she learn from googling my name? I was an immunologist at Yale? Definitely. I was up for tenure next year? Probably not.

She hit the home button on her phone and surveyed me head to toe, amusement in her eyes and in the corners of her mouth.

"You look a little fresher."

"Really? I feel as squalid as before."

She laughed, watched me for a long moment then opened her phone again. My fingers drummed the arms of the chair.

A business-like medical assistant in electric blue scrubs opened the door to the clinic's inner sanctum and beckoned me down a dim hallway. Almost to the door, I turned, waved goodbye and pantomimed a thank you to Alex still ensconced in mauve.

Two hours later, my grade 2, right ankle sprain was wrapped, booted and my head, examined.

"You have a concussion," said the physician, blandly. "You need to rest with your foot elevated. You shouldn't be alone tonight."

"I live alone," I said, attitude detectable.

"Please contact someone who can stay with you. You shouldn't be alone in the event that your symptoms worsen. And, no alcohol for the next 48 hours."

"I'm a physician. So, I'm in good hands."

"Oh, yeah? What's your specialty?"

"Immunology. Studying how cancer hides from the immune system."

"That must keep you off the streets. Where?"

"It does. Yale. M.D/Ph.D. program."

"Do you teach or do research?"

"Both. Can't quite give up teaching. The students anchor me. Without them, I'd be lost in data."

"Well then, Dr. Brust, you know you shouldn't be alone tonight. If your headache worsens or you vomit again, please have someone drive you to the emergency room."

"Will do," I said, with no idea who of my friends, all working late at the lab, would have time to babysit a concussion. "How bad is the sprain? Maybe you already told me."

"Grade 2 and yes, I did tell you. You got your bell rung. Get some rest and wear the boot. Drink lots of water. No driving for four weeks."

"Right," I said, with a firm nod.

I hobbled out of the examination area toward the door to reception. Grouchy, awkward in my new boot, I carried one soggy sock, a ruined loafer, and several pages of instruction pertaining to my new diagnoses. I wasn't calling anyone and would be fine on my own, I mumbled, as a plane of emerald came into view. Alex stood, hands in pockets, slouched against the wall, near the door.

"You're still here?" I said, with a mannerly smile. I didn't want to be rude. She was nice. More than nice. But I wished she would go away. I didn't want anyone to see me like that. Especially not her. I needed time alone to collect myself and to process the situation.

"I thought you might need a ride. My car isn't far. I park for free in the lot at Hard Rain Brewing Company. I've done some contract work for them."

"I appreciate the offer, but I don't want to trouble you. I'll get a Lyft."

"Okay, professor, just making sure you're not a menace to society with that head injury of yours."

"Ah, just doing your civic duty. The fine professionals here at the urgent care have determined I'm not a danger to myself or others. Thanks again for encouraging me to get treatment. Sprained ankle. Concussion. You were right. And for waiting. It's very thoughtful."

"No problem. That boot really suits you, by the way. Goes with the muddy look you're sporting."

I absorbed her features. Salient jaw line. Chin with dimple. Cute little upturned nose. Her eyes were the color of the Caribbean, the sort of color that changed with the weather or the shade of clothing. Against today's white T-shirt, her eyes were mangrove green, clear and bright.

"Dapper, no?" I laughed, for the first time all week, maybe for the first time all month, as I modeled my footwear.

"Take good care of your noggin." She glided languidly toward the exit.

I thumped over to an expirating mauve chair, head and ankle throbbing, nauseous, and ordered a Lyft. Twenty-five minutes. Sweat exploded across my scalp. The stench of urine niggled. It sent me reeling, back to the bathroom. I hovered over the toilet. Nothing happened. I gave up and returned to reception.

In a flash of red, a 1980s convertible Mercedes Benz 560SL pulled into the patient drop-off area near the entrance door. Alex's hair glimmered in the light. She slammed the door shut and jogged into the clinic, found me, and waved for me to follow.

Sick, sore, eager to be home, I limped out of the clinic and into the car's paper and garbage strewn interior. I half-noticed unopened mail flung across the back seat. I canceled the Lyft and, against my better judgement, accepted the brief ride home.

I forced myself to socialize, "Nice car."

"Thanks. My ex bought it for me."

"So, how do you like working at the Brash Barista?"

"I like it. Fast pace. Great for networking too."

"How so?"

"I'm building a clientele. The CEO at Hard Rain Brewing Company comes in on her way to work a lot. She always asks for me because I'm the only one there who can make a cappuccino the way she likes it. Dry. That's pretty much how I got the contract gig for them. She wanted someone to spruce up their home page. I finished it a couple weeks ago."

"How'd it go?"

"I nailed it. It's perfect."

While she chatted about how she preferred to use neutral tones and organic shapes for the background of her web pages, I sat in the front seat concluding that taking a ride from someone I just met was clear evidence of brain damage or of personality change brought on by a blow to the head.

"Turn left on Monarch," I said, as we approached a tree-lined neighborhood near the university where long blocks of stone mansions graced expansive lawns.

"This is the type of neighborhood I love to wander at dusk. You know, when lights are on but curtains aren't closed. You can catch a glimpse of the inside."

"That's mine," I pointed, grateful to see the vine-covered turret of my home.

I opened my wallet and removed a couple of bills as Alex pulled up to the curb. "Please take it. I don't know how else to thank you for your kindness."

"I don't want your money. I just like helping people. And there's something about you, Simon Brust. You're...odd, for sure, but in a good way." She handed the money back to me. I let it fall on the seat as I heaved myself and my belongings out of the Mercedes.

"Need a hand? Your place is stately, by the way. Enormous. Space for a big family."

"It's just me. I own the top floor. I think I can manage from here." I shut the car door.

The passenger-side window slid open. She unbuckled her seat belt and stretched across the front seats.

"Any chance it's designed by Henry Austin?"

No one had ever asked me that question. I bent down and leaned toward her. "It is. He actually lived here in the 1860s. It's one of the reasons I moved into the building. I like his work. How did you know?"

"I like it too. The shape of the turret. Square. Dead giveaway. I study design. Know every one of his buildings in town."

I was about to ask what she thought of the New Haven City Hall building, but my ankle throbbed. I needed Motrin. I needed to elevate that foot. I needed a nap.

"Well, then, we have something in common. It was nice to meet you. Thanks again." I straightened and backed away.

"Hey. Professor. How *does* cancer hide from the immune system?"

I peered at Alex. "I don't remember mentioning my research." I told the physician about it, but had no recollection of mentioning it to Alex. I was certain I hadn't.

"You did," she nodded. "While we were in the waiting room."

I touched the lump on my head. "Wow. I really am concussed."

"So, how *does it* hide from the immune system?"

"It pretends to be something it's not."

3

I winced as I stepped away from the car. "Bye, Alex, I hope to run into you again sometime. Maybe I'll see you at Brash Barista?"

"I won't be there much longer." A thin, hooped earring brushed against her neck while the other swung free. "Starting my own business as a website designer. And a hacker. The good kind." She winked. "I'll pop by later and check on you."

"No. No need. I'm fine. Be well. Good luck with your new business."

I limped across the mushy lawn, up cement stairs, across the porch. I unlocked the towering wooden double door as Alex Argyle sped away in a red blur.

I struggled up the three flights of stairs to my home. Finally inside, I gimped across the hardwood of the living room, opened the French doors to my office and flopped into my ergonomic desk chair. I should have gone straight to bed.

I called Mother.

"Everything alright?"

"Terrible," she slurred. "The heat doesn't work. Could you come by and take a look at the furnace?"

"Yes, I'll come by tomorrow, after class. I teach in the morning."

"Could you come by now? It's supposed to be cold tonight. And I'm out of cat food. Would you mind picking some up on the way over?"

"I had an accident. Sprained my ankle. I'm in a boot and under strict orders to rest. I'll stop over tomorrow."

"I figured you'd be busy. You're always busy. Don't worry about me. If you're lucky, I'll freeze to death overnight. See you tomorrow, if I'm still around."

"Goodb," I said. The line went dead. She hung up on me.

I sat at my desk, staring at a tidy stack of ungraded labs. Red circles on my phone indicated twelve unheard voicemails and seventy-three new emails.

Guilt seeped into my mind and weaved its oily fingers through my chest. Images of Mother's face, blue and waxy, poking out from under layers of quilt sent me searching for my keys. With aching head and throbbing ankle, I grabbed my wallet, removed the boot and hobbled to the door and down the stairs.

I caught my breath at the bottom of the stairs, sweat bleeding through the cotton at my armpits, then hopped to my Land Rover, parked in the street. I opened the driver side door. How was I supposed to get up there?

I tried to scooch myself up and in but the seat was a few inches too high. I tried to push myself up, using the arm rest on the door and seat for leverage. My bad foot banged into the door frame. I grabbed the handle over the window with both hands and swung myself inside, maneuvering to land on the seat. I eased my foot into position, started the car and drove to the grocery store. I did it all over again before driving to Mother's.

"Hope you're hungry." I limped into her handsome but dilapidated bungalow, bearing cat food and rotisserie chicken. She weaved toward the cat food and ignored the chicken. Stanley, a sweet orange tabby, meowed at her feet.

"If it isn't the prodigal son. Looks like you found some time for me after all." She didn't ask about my accident. "Your clothes are filthy."

"I told you; I fell. I didn't have time to change. Came right over. Wanted to make sure you had heat tonight."

"Oh. Not sure what's wrong with the furnace. It can't get it to turn on."

After some poking around, while she sat on the worn leather couch, sipping an undoubtedly spiked, transparent beverage, I discovered the unlit pilot light. I relit the pilot and headed straight for the door, the smell of vodka screaming in my nose, grating at memories I'd long since tried to forget. My hand turned the brass knob.

"Have you heard from your father?"

"We talked a couple weeks ago, about cancer research, not much else."

"At least he talks to *you*. Stay. We could have dinner."

"I can't. Got a pile of work to finish tonight."

"Of course you can't. Tomorrow?"

"I'll try."

A heavy grief escorted me home.

The commute to and from Mother's reinforced the "no driving" recommendation. Not only was my vision blurry, but every time my unprotected foot pressed the brake or accelerator, shooting pain in my ankle convinced me that the urgent care physician had a point. Driving with the massive boot was impossible. Driving without it, excruciating.

I labored up the stairs again. Once inside my apartment, I changed out of dirty clothes, flung them into the washer, started the machine, and donned clean sweat pants, an old flannel shirt, and thick, dry, woolen socks. I turned on Bob Dylan, poured Don Julio Reposado from a squat bottle over rocks and lime, and scored labs until late.

Through concussion headache, fog and fatigue, one page after the next, I pushed myself to consider the logic behind each student's conclusions and to identify their missteps. I jotted feedback, in red, hoping to guide them toward the next level of understanding.

I showered before bed. Hot water stung scrapes and soothed aching muscles. Soap streamed down weary flesh. A question niggled. Why couldn't I remember telling Alex about my research? I remembered telling the physician. Was I so concussed that I had amnesia? Or was Alex lying? But why would she lie? It didn't make sense. I grabbed a towel, pushing away the thoughts.

Sheets. Pillow. Sleep.

My tongue investigated a loose molar. I reached inside my mouth, grabbed ahold of the tooth and pulled it out by the root. I examined the bone in my hand. Blood mixed with saliva left a sheen on my fingertips. My tongue searched again. Another loose tooth. Then another. And another. Teeth slid out of place, settling between lips and gums. They felt like gravel in my mouth.

I spit them into my palm as Alex slowly drove me up and down campus streets in the Mercedes, staring straight ahead.

Wonk. Wonk. Wonk. The alarm jerked me awake. I pressed snooze. Eight minutes later, it wonked at me again.

Resentful, groggy, I left the warm bed and limped to the bathroom. My head ached, the swollen ankle throbbed. Purple bruises dotted my flesh. As the toilet flushed, I remembered my feet slipping, the thud of my skull against pavement, the smell of the urgent care, and the mischievous grin of Alex Argyle.

In the kitchen, I poured milk over a bowl of corn flakes, stood on one foot and ate over the sink. I'd had a dream. Or a nightmare. The details were fuzzy but the thought of it raised the hair on the back of my neck.

I couldn't shake the residue of that dream. It haunted me the entire fifteen-block slog to the university. Even the crimsoning leaves of sugar maples, lining my walk, seemed to shiver a warning. I distracted myself by making a detailed list of the day's obligations.

While the fresh air and exercise eased the stabbing in my temples, it did nothing for the pain in my ankle. I arrived at the modern hallways of the Anlyan Center for Medical Research and Education with plenty of time before class to hone the day's lecture.

Rounding the corner to my office, I nearly collided with Dr. Genevieve Hale, barreling toward me. She stopped short and looked straight at me, tunneling to my core. She crinkled her forehead. I glanced away, at a placard on the wall behind her then down at the floor, trying to hide.

"Jeez, Sy. What happened to you? You look like hell. Wipe out on your bike again?" she said, dropping her pen while words blasted out of her mouth with an alacrity that matched her stride. She had just picked up the pen when two of several papers in her hand wafted to the floor.

Genevieve was the department chair and my former, sometimes current, lover. We dated seriously for two years, both agreeing against childrearing, marriage, and co-habitation. About four months ago, before she became chair, after weeks where we didn't even have time to meet for lunch, we decided to break-up. The relationship had become another number on each other's to-do list. Another burden. We didn't want it to be like that. No labels, no pressure, we agreed.

I didn't feel the loss of Gen because, afterwards, little about our interactions changed. We still went out for dinner with some regularity, had sex, and she was still the person I told when my mother said or did something despicable. Or funny. I considered her to be one of my closest friends and I liked knowing she was down the hall.

Everyone in the department still considered us a couple. The people who really knew us claimed that the dissolution reflected our stubbornness and fear of commitment. We joked that our breakup was just for appearances but neither of us made an overt gesture toward reconciliation.

Gen had a way of turning ordinary conversation into philosophical debates and was more direct than most. Her astute observations and attention to detail didn't make her a comfortable companion. She'd notice, for example, if I took too long to answer a question or ever so slightly raised my eyebrow or in any way varied typical patterns of behavior.

She'd demand to know the underlying reasons for the aberration and expected an immediate and entirely honest answer. Her annoying attunement to these subtleties generally uncovered a hidden truth I may not have recognized or may not have wanted to discuss.

What Gen made up for in vigilance and speed, she lacked in grace. More than once, usually after wine, I'd witnessed her spastic, unhinged elbow launch a glass of water clear across the room.

"Construction zone. Sprained my ankle. I'm fine."

She stooped to gather the papers. "I thought I was the clumsy one." She returned them to the messy collection in her hand, stood, and searched my face again. "You don't seem fine. You look a little pale. And...more uptight than usual. Are you sure you're okay? Can I get you anything?"

"A new ankle and a stiff drink?"

She laughed. I liked her laugh. It was hearty and genuine.

"I'm in my office if you need anything. Check with the other members of your committee about the meeting you missed yesterday."

"How do you know I missed the meeting?"

"Omniscience," she said, as if that was how she knew. I wondered, for a second, if it was true.

"Thanks for the unnecessary reminders and the outpouring of support."

My headache returned in full bloom.

Gen descended from generations of old money. Her parents were socialites and philanthropists. Photographs of the Hales made the covers of newspapers and magazines. Several buildings bore their name.

She spent the summers of her childhood sailing the coasts of France, Spain and Italy. Raised in country clubs, she attended the best schools. Her three siblings followed in their parent's footsteps.

From childhood, however, Gen struggled to understand the deference given to her family simply because they had money. She likened it to the data indicating that physically attractive people are presumed to possess positive characteristics not granted to less attractive people. Beauty, she would say, was something people were born into, much like her wealth. She didn't do anything spectacular to be wealthy, so she didn't think she deserved the special treatment.

She lived simply. Her home was well appointed but not ostentatious. She didn't require employment for subsistence yet Gen's internal drive and work ethic was peerless. Not only was she often the last to leave work, but she took on some of the most challenging research projects.

As we passed in the hallway, in the direction of our original goals, she said, "Hey, just something I've noticed, your walk, even with the injury, is a lot like your personality; reliable, slightly pronate, with an unexpected spring."

"That is the strangest thing anyone has ever said to me."

She laughed again. "Dinner later this week?"

"As long as you're driving."

She was so often courted by people aiming to get rich quick or to combine and protect family wealth, that she had become skeptical about dating. Her family played matchmaker. They disapproved of her decision to remain single. They disapproved of me. I wasn't rich enough.

She often said she was attracted to my commitment to curing cancer, my humility and dedication to the students. She said she appreciated my lack of fascination with her family name. I might have been the only one she ever dated that liked her for the person she was.

I ducked into my office and closed the door.

4

The space had white walls and floor to ceiling shelves, stacked with books and journals, organized by topic, alphabetized by author. I yanked open the desk drawer and fumbled for the bottle of Motrin that had rolled out of sight.

I squeezed open its top and poured three orange pills into my palm. I tossed them into my mouth, gulped them down with yesterday's coffee and flipped on my computer. In no condition to conduct a three-hour lecture and a one-hour lab for a group of overachieving first-year students, I collected articles and made notes for the day's Basic Immunology class.

Not all of the new students majored in pre-med. The ones who finished their bachelor's with degrees in liberal arts had catching up to do.

The purpose of the class was to review the elemental concepts of immunology. It was easy for the pre-meds. They usually skipped, except for the most neurotic, appearing only for exams. For the rest, it was their first exposure to the concepts and the data.

I *volunteered* to teach Basic Immunology because I liked knowing who was who and because watching ignorance give way to insight was one of the most gratifying experiences of my life.

It also fed my compulsive need to control the training new students received. I was comforted by the fact that all students in the department started out with my pedantic, picayune version of the basics. The fundamentals, after all, informed all other work.

No one in the department fought me for the class. They teased me for teaching "kindergarten." Most professors had no patience for explanation and expected the students to have knowledge beyond their years and education.

With my forty-pound head cradled in both hands, "just go home," I said to the walls, "just cancel." I couldn't. But I would shorten the lecture. I decided to start the class with a field trip to the same hall where I had earlier collided with Gen, to the placard honoring Dr. William Coley. I forced myself to stand, left the office and rode the elevator.

I made my way to the airy classroom and placed notes and articles on the desk next to my phone. "Good morning, everyone. Let's go for a stroll."

Eight students and I clogged the hallway. I pointed to the placard. "Okay. Who is this person and why are they in our hallway?"

"He's the Father of Immunology," said Lucas, an eager former philosophy of ethics student, fresh out of Columbia University.

"Correct. Why is he considered the Father of Immunology?"

"He discovered that infections in the body inadvertently fight cancer by kicking up an immune response."

"Exactly. Around 1891, as a surgeon in New York, he researched his theory by injecting cancer patients with streptococcal bacteria. The strep caused an immune reaction which reduced and, in some cases, eliminated the cancer. For decades, he injected patients with strep and other bacteria, named Coley's Toxins. The research we are doing here, today, was inspired by Coley."

We filed back into the classroom.

The Motrin proved ineffective. With headache and swollen foot, I taught, "The body's tissues and organs are composed of cells that are covered in markers called antigens. When patrolling immune system cells encounter antigens marked as unfamiliar or 'foreign,' they launch an attack and destroy the cell. Antigens recognized as familiar or 'self' components of the body are ignored by the immune system."

My phone buzzed. A text from Mother. *Could you bring me some coffee? I'm out.*

"Tell us about the immune system. Lucas, go."

"It has two branches, innate and adaptive. The innate immune system acts within hours of the appearance of suspicious cells. The adaptive immune system starts working four to seven days after the start of an infection."

"Good. Ling, please elaborate."

Pre-med undergrad at Harvard, Ling held a tuft of her hair near her eyes, pulling at split ends. She already knew the material, but I was pleased to see her studious face in class. Sitting in the way back near the window, she dropped her hands and sat up straight when I said her name.

"The innate system is made up of Natural Killer cells and macrophages, they're white blood cells, lymphocytes. The adaptive system is also made up of lymphocytes, T cells for example. They all protect the body from and help fight cancer."

The classroom and slides blurred. My foot begged to be elevated. I sweatily struggled to maintain my composure. The students didn't appear to notice until I pulled up the desk chair and sat down. They looked up from their laptops and stared.

Another text from Mother. *I need milk too.*

I lost my train of thought. What were we talking about? "Antigens, people. Why are they so important?"

"They kick off an immune response and attack cells marked as foreign or non-self," replied Jonathan, a promising student in a bow tie and desert boots occupying a seat, as always, in the front row.

"Say more, Shay." She rarely contributed to the discussion but from my position at the front of the class, I saw in her eyes the hungry assimilation of information.

"Because cancer cells are clever. And sneaky."

"Like your ex," said Lucas. Everyone laughed.

"I hope cancer cells are nothing like your ex, Shay," I said. "But please continue."

"They disguise their antigens so they look like normal cells. This allows the cancer to multiply. If we could prevent cancer cells from disguising the true identity of their antigens, we might be able to cure cancer."

"Preventing cancer cells from hiding. That's what we're trying to do," I said from my seat, in a delirious burst of enthusiasm. "As you all know, researchers in your department study both protein and carbohydrate antigens in an effort to block cancer-cloaking interactions."

I invited the class to draw on white boards known interactions between cancer and immune cells that resulted in the disguising of cancer cells until I was sure they knew the material by rote, would be dreaming about it in their sleep and telling their friends about it at the bar.

After class, I asked my research assistant, Hety Sullivan, "Could you get lab started?" I hobbled to the bathroom and splashed cold water on my face. I gulped burnt coffee from the lounge as fast as I could swallow and finished teaching. Blood pooled in purpling toes.

Lyft transported me from the university to Mother's house. I wasn't fit to walk back home to my car. I wasn't fit to drive. I wasn't allowed to drive.

Stanley rubbed his face against my shin and wrapped an orange tail around my calf. I bent down to scratch his ears and searched around for Mother. She was nowhere in sight. My footsteps creaked down the hallway toward her bedroom. Stanley trotted by my side. She was in bed, eyes closed. I watched her chest for the rise and fall of breathing. Passed out already.

Stanley and I let her sleep it off. We were famished. I scooped food into his bowl and refilled his water dish. Rummaging, I found cheese, mayonnaise, and mustard in the refrigerator. Grilled cheese sandwiches. I smeared the last of the butter on the last of the bread. No tomatoes or onions.

From my shirt pocket, I removed pen and folded paper and added these items along with coffee and milk to the list of groceries I intended to purchase and deliver despite the fact that she was fully capable of driving. She rarely left the house. She was busy. Drinking.

I pulled a frying pan out of the cupboard. The lid crashed to the floor. It must have roused Mother from her stupor because she shuffled into the kitchen, taking a slurp from the beverage in her hand.

"Hey, you're up." I tried to sound upbeat. Experience taught me that naps made her testy.

"With you banging around in here, how could I not be?" she mumbled through a yawn.

"Sorry. Dropped the lid. Hungry?" I slid sandwiches onto two plates.

"Did you bring coffee?"

"No. Sorry. Haven't had a chance to get to the store." She looked away and, for the rest of the meal, would not make eye contact. I asked her about her day and other items she needed from the grocery.

"The sandwich is soggy," she said. "You used too much butter."

"Probably."

She didn't ask about my class, my research, my ankle or my head. I no longer noticed – consciously. However, on some level, I knew that her words penetrated and clung to my self-regard like emotional cockleburs, influencing my thoughts, feelings, and behaviors.

On one foot, I washed the dishes, stacked them in a wooden drying rack and mopped the floor. She drowsily watched the news.

"Have you heard from your father?" she shouted from the living room.

"Not since the last time you asked."

"Don't get smart. Is he planning a trip to the U.S. anytime soon?"

"Not to my knowledge."

"Bring me my hanky."

I shuddered as I picked up the tiniest, unused corner of the lumpy ball of lavender cotton left on the table, between index finger and thumb, and delivered it to her open hand in the living room.

Pushing away a deep sadness, I watched houses and trees pass from the back seat of a Lyft as I was driven home.

5

My father, a physician and genetics researcher in Geneva, specialized in the study of acquired mutations - damage to genes that occurred after the ovum was fertilized, sometimes caused by environmental factors.

He left Mother and returned to Switzerland in 1994 when I was 15, freshman year of high school. My brother, Oscar, was 17 and my sister Alice, only 12. He detested her drinking which increased over the course of their marriage. When the opportunity for an academic appointment in his hometown appeared, he didn't hesitate to accept the offer.

Mute, standing in a line with our backs against the wall of their bedroom, my siblings and I watched while he packed one bag with noticeably few articles of clothing and some hand tools. He offered no explanations, no reassurances. I assumed he just wanted to be gone from her - and me.

We visited him in Geneva for two weeks every summer. It was uncomfortable and he worked most of the time.

As a kid studying in my room, I overheard horrible fights.

"You have so much potential. Why can't you just stop?" he would yell.

"I don't drink that much."

"Then why are you always drunk?" He'd storm through the house unearthing empty bottles of alcohol from their hiding places and line them all up on the counter. Thump, thump, thump.

"Maybe if you came home once in a while, I wouldn't have to drink. How come you're never home? You're having an affair aren't you? I bet it's that Suhana from Microbiology. It's Suhana, isn't it?"

"I've told you a thousand times, I'm not having an affair."

"Don't lie to me."

He'd lower his voice, the words more difficult to overhear. "I am exhausted by this conversation. Stop drinking or I'm gone." The door to the coat closet groaned when it opened. He was about to walk out of the house.

"Don't go. I'll quit. I promise." And she would, for a day or two.

I covered my ears with headphones, drowning out the noise, finding solace in music. Any music. All music. But I gravitated toward blues and classic rock.

When I was in fifth grade, she went almost one year without alcohol. Everyone was less edgy, more jovial. My parents' relationship improved, affectionate moments were witnessed, and the fighting nearly stopped. Gradually, she slipped back into denial, lies, and vodka.

After he left, I developed a fear of germs, salmonella in particular, an illness I learned about in biology class. I stopped eating meat and eggs, raw or not. My fears came with a handwashing problem that left dry, red patches between my fingers.

She'd pound on the bathroom door when I was deep into a scrubbing ritual, "Get out of there. Your brother and sister need to shower. And don't use all the soap." She threatened to send me to a therapist, so I told her I was better and switched the washing to the middle of the night.

From the computer in my room, I researched phobias and obsessive-compulsive disorder over the internet. I forced myself to stop washing. Response prevention. It worked. Both the fears and the washing subsided by the beginning of sophomore year.

Despite the daily use of alcohol, Mother maintained a corporate accounting practice with her father, Michael Barnes. For years, they were partners in a well-respected office in New Haven.

After he retired, the practice flourished. Grandpa Barnes joked that he should have gotten out of her way and retired sooner. "She's a go getter," he would say at family dinners. Over time, however, the alcohol consumption interfered with her reliability.

When she started being too hung over to make it to work until after noon, client details and relationships, the mortar of her business, crumbled. One by one, she began losing clients that had been with them for decades.

She closed the business one year after our father moved to Switzerland. Without work to keep her occupied, she took to drinking earlier in the day. Her capacity to attend to household duties dwindled and she became a ghost in the house, physically and emotionally unavailable.

My parents weren't officially divorced, though I suspected Father was dating other people. He didn't discuss his personal life. When I visited him in Geneva last summer, his flat didn't tell any secrets.

He lived in the Carouge neighborhood, on a narrow cobblestone street above a weaver's shop. Austere like his temperament, the flat was tidy and efficient. Despite his proximity to galleries and restaurants, he rarely wandered the neighborhood. He did, however, trek into the Alps as often as his schedule allowed. We planned to hike in and around the Matterhorn together at the end of spring semester.

To my knowledge, Mother hadn't been on a date since my father left the country. He randomly deposited money into her account. "Guilt money," she declared. She owned the house and didn't want for material goods. I suspected that he still loved her, but his anger and her ongoing alcohol use prevented him from crossing the ocean.

Alice was in middle school when our father left. She wore the vestiges of his departure in her relationships. Trusting no one, she moved from one unsatisfactory short-term relationship to the next.

She lived in Hartford, less than an hour from New Haven, owned her own realty company, and assisted in Mother's caretaking when she could. "Need a break?" she would ask every so often and pop over for a couple of days. We understood each other.

Oscar, a tax attorney, lived across the continent in Eugene, Oregon, and avoided the entire family unit. He married Yasmine, whom I hadn't met until their wedding, and had a three-year-old child I'd never held. He also avoided all mind-altering substances and became restless and irritable when in the company of those who partook. He remembered best Mother's slow decline into alcoholism and the events following the closure of her business.

She had been out of work for about three months and on a bender of the same duration when we found her the first time.

Oscar waited after school, hanging out with friends, to give me a ride home from soccer practice.

"I'm starving. Mind if we stop for burritos?" he said.

Full of fast food, we pulled into the driveway. From the windows in the door, we could see her bare feet and a portion of her calves, half concealed by a white robe.

"Is mom on the floor?" We shoved past each other and ran into the house.

Fetid pools of vomit, reeking of bile and alcohol, left a trail from the bathroom to the living room. We kneeled by her head, one on each side. Oscar shook her, "Mom. Mom." She didn't respond.

"Her lips are blue," said Oscar, the Eagle Scout. He tilted back her head by the chin and peered into her mouth. "Can't see anything blocking her airway."

I dialed 911.

"Your address, sir?"

My mouth dropped open but no words came. I stared across the room at Oscar.

"Sir."

"114 Orange Street," Oscar shouted from the floor next to Mother's limp body.

Sirens wailed into our placid neighborhood. Oscar and I, unskilled, applied CPR until two paramedics took over.

"How long has she been unconscious?" asked a third.

"I don't know. She was like this when we got home a few minutes ago," said Oscar, not taking his eyes off Mother.

"Has she passed out like this before?"

"I don't think so."

They hoisted her onto a gurney, loaded her into an ambulance, and sped off, sirens howling. We were alone to soothe ourselves and to clean vomit.

An hour later, after choir practice, Alice bounded through the door. The TV was off and we were both on the sofa, just sitting.

"What's with you two?"

We didn't have a plan for what to tell Alice.

"Where's Mom?"

"She wasn't feeling well. Went to see a doctor," said Oscar.

We distracted her with a movie, Forrest Gump. Oscar made popcorn. Hours passed. I couldn't study. We were about to watch another movie when the phone rang. Oscar and I raced to answer. I reached it first.

It was Mother.

"I was just dehydrated. I'm as good as new again. Can you send Oscar pick me up?"

Chipper, acting like everything was normal, she didn't say a word about what happened after she entered the house in her robe, hospital gown and slippers.

Oscar later told me that she apologized all the way home, swearing she wouldn't drink again, she was serious this time, she would start a program. He believed her. I wanted to. After two days of remorse, manifested in clean laundry and elaborately prepared meals, she was back to her old habits.

The next incident, occurring only a few months later, wasn't as severe in terms of Mother's condition but far worse in terms of what it did to Oscar.

That time, when we arrived at home after school, she was passed out and the vomit was the same but we were able to revive her with a good shake. "I'm so sorry. I'll take care of this," she said, sitting up. Stumbling drunk, she cleaned the mess.

Oscar started coming home early, foregoing time with friends, skipping Scout meetings to make sure Mother was upright. Like our father, but without the hostility, he pleaded for her to stop drinking, researched in and outpatient sobriety programs and took every opportunity to educate her on the options.

All senior year of high school, he called her during lunch and, sometimes, between classes. Convinced it was the solution, he also called our father, begging for him to return home and reunite with Mother.

Oscar had nightmares. I knew all about them because we slept in the same room. Once, I heard him holler "hurry" in his sleep.

"Oscar, you're okay," I said. It woke him up. "You were having a nightmare."

"No, I wasn't." He rolled over, his back to me.

Oscar hardened. Perhaps he realized that he couldn't help Mother, that she wasn't a willing participant in his efforts to keep her alive and sober. He graduated from high school and moved away to attend the University of Oregon. Detached. Silent.

Just like that, responsibility for Mother transferred to me. I threw myself into it. It was my chance to win the approval I went my whole life without. I studied diligently, earning A's, and took all advanced classes. I excelled in soccer. I cooked and cleaned around the house. I paid bills. I tried to be *good*. If I was good enough, maybe she'd stop drinking. Maybe my father would come home. I swore that I would never abandon her, like he did.

6

I tipped the Lyft driver and climbed the stairs to my apartment, clinging to the rail for support, my ankle puffy and sore.

Gen texted. *Dinner? I'll pick you up.*

I stood in the doorway, my fingers wanting to type yes, come over. Instead, they wrote, *Already ate with Mother. Made grilled cheese. She said it was soggy.*

Gen had mixed reviews about the way I handled Mother. On the one hand, she admired the selfless dedication. On the other hand, she wished I would defend myself, lay down some boundaries and confront her drinking and verbal abuse. She urged me to record her drunken rants and force her into treatment. I knew from a long history of data that Mother wasn't ready to acknowledge her addiction or to apologize for her behavior, regardless of any evidence.

I suppose you didn't tell her to make her own damn sandwich.

I didn't. Raincheck?

Raincheck. See you at the lab. Miss you.

She missed me?

You too.

I walked straight into my bedroom. Despite the piles of reading, lecture prep and nagging grant applications, I fell into bed and slept without dreaming until daylight pierced through haphazardly closed curtains, creating long rectangles on the floor.

I limped to the kitchen, made strong coffee and scrambled eggs. A list of unaccomplished tasks hounded every bite. But my thoughts were less foggy and the headache, less severe.

I pushed aside the empty coffee cup, plopped the purple ankle, sans boot, up on a chair and covered it with a fat, lumpy ice pack. I opened a recently published journal article I'd assigned for class. Cancer cells, it indicated, have the capacity to trick and deactivate immune cells.

By the end of the article, I felt almost like my old self. I performed the daily ablutions, strapped on the boot, packed my leather messenger bag for a day of grant writing and lab work and left my apartment.

At the top of the porch stairs, a familiar red car caught my eye. Alex?

She burst out of the driver's side and walked toward me. "Hello Professor."

"Good morning," I said, flooded with unsavory memories of orange cones and a slip and fall mixed with a twinge of happiness at the sight of her. "To what do I owe the pleasure?"

"I told you I'd check up on you. Thought you might need a ride. Doubt you're getting very far on one good ankle." Her lips curved into a smile.

How long had she been waiting outside my apartment? "Most people just *say* they'll check on you without actually doing it."

"I'm not most people."

She wasn't like most people. She was cavalier. Unflustered. Not a care in the world. Like nothing was a big deal. Like everything would work out fine. The opposite of me.

"It's not a long walk to work. My version of physical therapy since I don't have time for the real thing."

A grey mist pressed into the space around us.

She lifted her chin toward the sky, exposing a long neck and the same hooped earrings from two days ago. "Looks like rain. C'mon, get in."

"Alright, Alex-from-the-ditch, I accept."

"Oh, that's my name now?"

"I think it suits you."

"It's got a certain ring."

"I mean it as a compliment. You saved me. And you keep saving me." I could easily find my own ride. But something about her put me in a playful mood. She was fun. Effortless. She unleashed me, my sense of humor. It was the best kind of saving, a type of rescue no one had offered me before.

Alex opened the passenger door, tossed papers from the front seat to the back seat and wiped away crumbs with the palm of her hand. She ran around to the driver's door while I eased myself inside, hoisting the boot off the curb with both hands.

The car was still cluttered with unopened mail but this time smelled vaguely of something…sour. Days old curry? I cracked open the window.

"Guess who came by Brash Barista yesterday?" she said.

"Mick Jagger?"

She grinned and whacked my arm with the back of her hand. "I wish. No. Toni Harp. The mayor. She comes in a lot. Usually gets a spinach croissant and an Americano. Guess what? She just hired me to do some freelance work on the city's website."

"That's great. What kind of work? Adding cameras so she can keep an eye on the Alders?"

"Ha. Just cleaning it up, making it more user friendly. She invited me to a party at her house a few weeks ago. I was introduced to the entire Board of Alders. Based on the characters I met, she probably should consider cameras. I have ideas for the home page. I want to make it clean, modern. Add pictures that really capture the essence of the city."

"Like Grove Street Cemetery?"

"Great idea."

I admired Alex's profile. Each feature came with an angle.

"Turn right, then a quick left on Cedar. There it is, The Anlyan Center." As the Mercedes hummed into the parking lot, I opened my wallet and gave Alex $10.00.

"Thanks for the ride. My ankle will need one less ice pack today."

"See. I come in pretty handy," Alex said, shoving the cash into the front pocket of her jeans. "Do you want me to pick you up

Monday, too? My schedule is flexible. What time do you leave for work?"

Did I want to accept a regular ride? The introverted, overworked side of me did not. The other side, the part of me that found itself wanting to spend more time with Alex, did. Drops of rain speckled the windshield. Colder, wetter weather was in the forecast.

"It varies. Usually around 7:30."

"Ok, I'll be at your house at 7:30. How long are you barred from driving on that ankle?"

"Four weeks."

"Four weeks it is. Deal."

"Are you sure? Four weeks is a long time."

"Time flies when I'm with you."

"Then I'll see you Monday."

"What's your phone number? In case I'm running late." I rattled off my number and she shot me a text with hers.

I walked toward my hallway, replaying Alex's comment. Time flies when I'm with you. Light filled my ribcage and bounced around in it. Then an image of Gen muscled its way into my mind. It chased away the sun and left an iceberg of guilt and confusion. Why though? Hadn't we broken-up? Yes and no.

Students formed a line outside my office. I was one of few researchers to have scheduled office hours. Based on my own experiences in medical school, I wanted to provide students with a non-competitive environment in which to ask questions. Most of them were in line to ask about assigned reading or to complain about the feedback I gave them on lab reports.

I was a stickler about lab. The work had to be meticulous with precise data recordings and rigid adherence to procedural protocol, I constantly told them, like a parent nagging a child to clean their room. "Students without obsessive tendencies will not make effective researchers unless they deliberately hone their attention to detail. Lab skills determined whether students became practicing physicians or researchers or both," I said.

To my surprise, Hety, my research assistant and one of the most reserved, professional, and disciplined students in her cohort, appeared in the line.

"Hety, please come in."

She burst into tears the second I closed the door and handed me her last lab. It bled red words in my handwriting.

"I'll never be accepted into the research rotation with all of these mistakes."

"Not true. You're a competitive student with a sophisticated understanding of cell function. And well respected in the department."

We deconstructed her minor lab errors.

"Oh, I get it." The muscles around her eyes relaxed. "Thanks for walking me through it."

"How's your dissertation coming?"

"Bane of my existence. But I'm on track."

"You've got it. Keep working. It's just a big paper."

She can't see how bright she is, I thought, as she left my office. We worked together well and I hated the idea of being without her next year.

I'd met her parents a few times and could feel their efforts to control Hety. They came across as a pleasant but intense twosome offering a prickly combination of money mixed with a detectable intolerance of chicanery...or levity. They bought her everything they wanted her to have, not necessarily things she would choose, including a new Porsche Cayenne. She confessed to me that she had her eye on something sportier.

I admired the conscientious way she interacted with the world. She was a model student. Driven. Competent. Humble. Too humble?

Rumor had it, Hety wasn't a drinker, but all the best parties were held at her house which was owned by her parents. She seemed to have mixed feelings about the parties. She didn't advertise. People invited themselves, I was told. She acquiesced. "No more volleyball. I've got to get that window fixed before my parents find out about it," I overheard her say to Ling after class last week.

Next, Jonathan filed in and sat down across from me. "I read the *Journal of Immunology* article you recommended, about how cancer deceives immune cells so it can multiply. I don't understand the role of Regulatory T cells."

"They're all about providing the perfect degree of threat detection without destroying healthy cells. They do it by releasing proteins called cytokines. Cytokines are chemical messengers that bind with cell receptors to change a cell's behavior. The crazy thing is, cancer cells can actually *manipulate* T-regs into changing, even deactivating killer T cells. Once killer T cells are deactivated, they can't see cancer, allowing it to hide from the immune system."

I drew the cells and their interactions, twice forgetting what I was about to say.

"We'll go over it ad nauseum in class. You'll be bored with T-regs by the end of the week."

"I hope so."

I stood at the door and waved in the next in line.

The last student left my office. I closed the door and exhaled. My foot hurt. I still had so much work to do. I downed a handful of Motrin and gobbled a peanut butter sandwich. I spent the rest of the day, late into evening at the immunobiology labs with several other research groups, including Gen's.

She found me at a computer, staring at a page full of graphs.

"Hey, when you get a chance, would you mind giving us a second opinion on our methodology? We're starting a new study," she said.

"You just want me for my obsessive-compulsive disorder."

"Yes, I love you for your mind."

"I'll be right over."

"You're the best."

We worked on long rows of white counters with white cabinets and wore white lab coats. Bright patches of purple, green and blue latex gloves were the only sources of color in the room.

Boasting cutting edge technology, the lab contained Bio-Plex II Luminex machines capable of analyzing over forty cytokines in one sample and the magnet vacuum manifolds and shakers needed for assays. We labeled cells, collected large bodies of digital data and ran functional analyses. Photon laser scanners, test tubes, powerful microscopes, slides, and equipment for testing white blood cells clattered and whirred.

We also had a human and a mouse lab. Studies using mice led to important immunologic discoveries over the past fifty years including how T cells identify cancer antigens. Due to inbreeding in mouse strains and the resulting lack of genetic variation, however, immunology research was moving more toward the use of humans. New technology made it ethically possible.

By 9:00 p.m., unable to articulate a coherent thought, my toes, yellowish blue, I rubbed tired eyes.

"Who's going to McClanahan's?" said Gen, hanging up her lab coat and goggles in the closet by the door.

"I'm in," said everyone in ear shot.

"I'm out," I said, squirming out of my lab coat. I hung it up next to Gen's.

"C'mon, Sy. Join us. I haven't seen you in forever."

"One beer." Truth was, I missed her, too.

7

We crowded into the elevator. In pairs and threesomes, we lumbered like hooligans the two blocks to McClanahan's Public House.

The bar reeked of mildew and hops and the floors, chronically sticky. Students and faculty from the microbiology and immunology departments regularly migrated up the long, narrow flight of rickety stairs to the back room where the ceilings were low and crowded with dark wooden beams.

McClanahan's was also popular with the campus in-crowd due to their range of music and frequent live shows. From our loft, we were able to hear the band downstairs and still have a conversation. On nights without bands, we monopolized the juke box.

Years ago, Gen brought up a lamp and plugged it into a dangling wall outlet. Boudoir fuchsia with fringe, the lamp looked out of place against the dark medieval décor. But it gave our corner a pinkish ambiance. Students generally sat at high top tables along the walls while professors held court on a long, seamless central table with seat benches.

Haunted by the usual characters, the table buzzed with conversation. I sat next to my medical school roommate, longtime friend and research partner, Dr. Roberto Sanchez and his husband, Bob Philips.

"How's the adoption process going?" I asked.

"Not well. We get our hopes up only to be disappointed. Last month we met a woman who liked us. The process seemed to be moving along. Two days ago, we got a call from the social worker. She decided to keep the baby," said Roberto, glancing at Bob who shook his head, forehead creased with stress.

"Horrible."

"It's happened twice, now," said Roberto.

"Brutal."

"It is."

"Hang in there. I'm rooting for you."

I admired Roberto. Not only was he an excellent research scientist, he could build and fix anything. On the regular, I traded them dinner for maintenance and construction projects on my apartment.

Despite his brilliance, Dr. Bradly Brommer, also at the table, was most known for his arrogance. Speaking loud and at great length, about himself and his accomplishments, Bradley interrupted anyone who cut in on his monologue.

Bradley's eyes glazed over, roved the room, or looked at his phone on the rare occasions that anyone else had the floor. He relished gossip, interpersonal triangulation, and was at the center of most departmental conflicts.

During his self-aggrandizing speeches, I pictured him as a baby bird, head back and mouth open wide, begging to be fed.

He was in my research group. Worse, he was on my tenure committee. He enjoyed seeing people fail. I had the sense that he believed I was at Yale only because of my father's legacy, not because of my own merit. I sat as far away from Bradly as possible, on the opposite end of the table. He reminded me of my mother.

After a few pitchers of Smithwick's, we all relaxed. The Itchy Rashes, a local grunge band, played downstairs, belting out Sex Pistols and Ramones covers.

Gen and I eventually found ourselves next to each other, debating the subtleties of researching carbohydrates versus proteins and the strengths and weaknesses of enlisting the innate vs. the adaptive immune systems. She wasn't much for small talk. Neither was I.

We sat close to each other on the end of the crowded bench, our thighs welded together. Her leg was warm next to mine and I felt her breath on my face when she spoke.

A brown peanut husk wedged itself between her front teeth and she had a fleck of sleep in her eye. It didn't matter. She was beautiful. I listed words that might capture her particular type of beauty. Elegant? Athenian? Botanistic? Lichenesq?

"You're not listening," she said, with a sharp bang of her knee into my thigh.

"I heard you."

"Okay, what did I say?"

"You said that a group in London reviewed your findings favorably and encouraged focusing on how natural killer cells secrete

inflammatory cytokines that ignite the adaptive immune system."
I hoped I caught all of the details.

"Close enough. You're lucky. I'm heading out. Want a ride?"

"Absolutely." I didn't disguise my enthusiasm in accepting her
offer.

We walked the cold blocks to her car through intermittent yellow orbs cast by streetlights without saying much. What was she thinking? Our arms brushed against each other. I wanted to hold her hand. I didn't.

Beep. Her 2010 green Subaru Legacy revealed its leatherette interior. The frigid seats refused to surrender to our weight until cajoled by an impotent heater, one block from my home.

"I see you still haven't splurged for a new car," I said, trying to start a conversation.

"Why would I? This car runs great. It has less than 60 thousand miles on it. I plan to drive it into the ground."

"I'm not sure it goes with your outfit." I stroked the lapel of her black leather bomber jacket. My speech was different. I joked. I teased, like Alex. Conversations with Gen were serious. My hand slid down her sleeve and landed on top of her hand. My fingers curled around hers. "Come upstairs for whisky and baklava?"

"You have dessert?" She crinkled her nose at me. "So not like you."

"I don't, actually. It's a good idea, though. I bet they would pair nicely."

"Whatever you say, Johnnie Walker. I'm too tired," she yawned. "I have to be back at the lab early tomorrow. Maybe tomorrow night?"

"Works for me."

We kissed.

I stood on the pavement, watching her drive away. Brake lights flashed as she rounded the corner. Exhaustion obscured my thoughts and a deep achiness crept into my joints. I hobbled inside, yearning for the smell of Genevieve's skin and the softness of her flesh against mine. We hadn't spent the night together in weeks. Loneliness masqueraded as lust.

We both worked all weekend. Our tentative plans to get together, canceled.

8

Monday morning was rainy and cold. I waited for Alex on the porch under a black umbrella, holding up one booted foot like the hoof of a resting horse. Office hours started at 8:00. At 7:58, annoyed, I gave up on Alex. I opened the Lyft app just as she appeared at the curb.

"Sorry, I'm late," she said, rushing around the car to open the passenger door. "I had to put air in the tire. It's leaking. I didn't notice until I was leaving to pick you up."

"That's okay." I swung into the front seat. She slammed the door shut and ran back around to the driver's side.

"You look handsome today. Nice jacket. Is that Gortex?" she said, rubbing the fabric in my sleeve between her thumb and fingers.

I didn't answer. I was too busy noticing that, despite the cold, Alex still wasn't wearing a coat. Until now, I hadn't seen her in anything but jeans and a t-shirt. Today, she was scantily clad in black spandex revealing sculpted biceps, triceps and a six-pack abdomen. Drops of rain glistened on her beefy shoulders.

I looked away, not wanting to leer. It didn't matter. Alex's sensuality was in full view. She could make a snowmobile suit look sexy. It wasn't her shape so much as the way she inhabited her body. Confident, comfortable, with no sign of neuroses.

"I'm headed to CrossFit. Total gym rat." She slid the car into drive.

The morning conversations with Alex became a highlight of my day, a break from the grind. I gave up my rigid preoccupation with timeliness despite donating money toward new tires. For less money and more efficiency, I could have called Lyft, but I didn't. I enjoyed being with Alex.

Our conversations flowed. Our interests in books and music overlapped. It felt like I'd known her for years. But it was the way she made me feel that drew me toward her. Vitalized. *Liked*.

She told me she was raised in a fatherless, impoverished home by a depressed mother and kindly but not particularly observant grandmother. Her biological father did not send money to defray the costs of raising Alex, a fact about which she harbored a detectable rage. Her mother had many suitors and worked varying hours, often overnight, leaving Alex unattended.

With an unusual candor, I disclosed that my mother's alcohol use resulted in the loss of her business, her marriage and, to some extent, her children. I complained about my impending application for tenure and its funding requirements.

"Not only do I have to publish, but I have to secure ten million dollars in funding by fall semester to get tenure."

"So much pressure. Ten million? How?"

"Grants. My career depends on them."

"If anyone can do it, you can."

By the third week, my ankle nearly able to drive itself, I lingered inside her unhygienic, tags expired vehicle, not wanting to end the conversation.

"Do you remember Stradlater in *The Catcher in the Rye*?" she said.

"Yep. Big phony."

"And unscrupulous, I think was the word Holden used. Attractive, popular, arrogant. Shiny exterior but his razor blade told a whole different story. It was jammed with hair and grime. A wolf in sheep's clothing."

"A cancer cell disguised as a normal cell."

"You know, you're the only person I can talk to like this."

"Likewise."

I needed to get going. I was already late. But I didn't move. Alex told stories with her gestures, her whole face. Mesmerized, I stayed and listened.

"My mom complained that I was always reading, just not the work assigned for school. I'm self-taught. Learned graphic design on YouTube and by reading Ben Frain books. I just have the knack."

I peeled myself out of her car and greeted everyone on the elevator with a "good morning," rather than the usual grunt.

9

But during the final week of our commuting arrangement, Alex hardly spoke. She slammed on the brakes at red lights and cursed at other drivers under her breath.

"What's up? You're not your usual cheerful self."

"My boss. Such an *idiot*. Has no clue how to run a business. Cut my marketing and website hours. Wants me to spend more time serving customers. There's no way I'll make rent. Not to mention school loans." Her eyes, usually playful, were dull and angry.

"Oh, no. I'm sorry."

"I don't know what I'm going to do."

I quietly climbed out of the car and closed the door.

All day, I worried about Alex. She had nothing and no one.

That night, I lay awake. How could I help? She needed work until her website business picked up. Maybe I could help her get a job on campus. The library. Or the gym? But those positions were reserved for students.

I could hire Alex. I could use some help around the house and with errands. Maybe she would be willing to do some jobs around

Mother's house too, like her grocery shopping? It would both free up my time and help Alex. I fell asleep the next instant.

Chipper and up early, I showered and made coffee. I collected thumb drives, articles and lab reports, placed them in my beat-up satchel, slung it over my shoulder and waited in the window.

Alex arrived at 7:35. I bounded down the stairs without the boot and in minimal pain. The following day was the official end of our arrangement. I would wrap it up that day with a big tip and a reasonable work offer. Alex smiled from the driver's seat while I landed, uncharacteristically agile, onto the passenger's seat.

"How are you this morning?" I said.

"Just not going to worry about it."

She seemed fine. Problem solved? I questioned the value of my idea. I lost the nerve. She probably wouldn't want to run errands and clean for me anyway. It was a stupid idea.

We pulled up to my building. I opened the door.

"Goodbye, Alex. Thanks for carting me around for the last few weeks. I enjoyed getting to know you. It was a pleasure, really." Awkward, I handed her the tip money stashed in my pocket.

"Are you sure the streets of New Haven are safe with you back at the helm?"

I made a circle with my right foot. "Ankle's good."

"Call if you need anything."

"You too." I closed the car door and headed toward my building. Alex made a U-turn in the parking lot.

I flagged her down, ran around to the passenger side and crawled back inside. "Hey, any chance you'd be interested in doing some work for me? Maybe ten to fifteen hours per week. I'll pay better than minimum wage. It would be flexible so you could freelance and still work at The Brash Barista."

"What kind of work?"

"Housekeeping, errands, maybe yard work, grocery shopping."

She hesitated. "No. I don't know. I'm not much of a housekeeper, just ask my roommate. But I am an amazing cook. I could cook for you."

It wasn't the reaction I expected. "I especially need help with errands and cleaning. But maybe some cooking once in a while. For both my mother and I."

She furrowed her brow and looked up at the ceiling.

I waited.

Eyes wide, she turned to face me. "I'll do it."

We hashed out the details, exchanged email addresses and made a plan for her to start next Friday, a day I could finagle working from home.

"You're a good egg, Brust."

"I'm hoping it'll be a win-win. And you're not so bad yourself."

I climbed out of Alex's car, job offer and tip accepted, feeling generous and helpful. The contentment of having done a good deed lasted all day.

But behind the positive feelings, questions lurked. Why did Alex hesitate?

And the bigger question: what made her change her mind? I pushed away the thoughts and got busy at the lab.

10

I walked home from work that night with barely a limp. Chimney smoke wafted through the crisp, night air. I inhaled the changing season, the harbingers of dormancy, nature's impending deep sleep.

I thawed frozen leftover chili in the microwave, sliced a tall stack of cheddar cheese, poured a pile of Saltines, and wrote Alex's to-do list at the table between bites.

"I should have hired someone sooner," I said out loud while compiling the list. Pain shot through my ankle as I carried dishes to the sink, further validating the decision.

Around 1:00 a.m., I pulled sheets up to my chin and fell asleep. I dreamt I was in a shadowy Alpine Forest beside an angry river scrambling to get away from Frankenstein's monster. I tripped over tree roots that were covered in leaves and fell flat on my stomach. The creature loomed over me.

I startled awake, my heart pounding, and listened to the darkness. I jumped out of bed, hurried down the hall and wiggled the door knob. Locked. I crawled back under the covers. I couldn't sleep.

Red numbers on the clock read 2:41 a.m. Still awake an hour later, I reached for my phone, charging on the nightstand, and searched Carl Jung's interpretation of monsters in dreams: the shadow or dark side of the psyche. I typed in the meaning of river: the unconscious. Then the meaning of forest: a journey into the mind.

Whatever that meant. I wasn't going anywhere, much less on a journey into the mind. I didn't even have time to go to the dry cleaners. I plopped the phone back down on the nightstand.

The hours clicked by. At 5:00 a.m., I threw off the covers, pulled on socks and sweats and walked directly into my office.

I read an *Immunology* article suggesting that the longer cancer cells go undetected by the immune system, the better they are able to acclimate to the microenvironment and hoodwink immune cells.

Vaguely punctual on Friday, Alex appeared at the curb. I watched for her car from the window like when I was chauffeured to work. This time, Alex parked and walked to the door carrying a shopping bag.

I ran down the stairs, opened the double doors to my building and invited her inside.

"Brought some of my favorite environmentally friendly cleaning supplies. Hope you're good with that."

I peered inside the bag. "Same brand I use."

"Of course. We're practically the same person."

We climbed the flights to my apartment.

"Awesome building. I've been dying to see the inside of this place since we met. Beautiful oak." She traced the grain on the banister.

"It was originally a single-family home, built in 1866 by Henry Austin, as you already know. Over time, it's been modified, carved into apartments."

"I studied Austin in a design class at Southern Connecticut State. I consider myself a bit of an architect of web design. I think about the structure of the page, its balance, supporting walls."

At the top of the stairs, I opened the door to my apartment.

"Whoa, twelve-foot ceilings. Your windows are huge." We stepped into the living room, extending the entire length of the front of the house.

I toured Alex through the space, describing the work I hoped she might be willing to do.

"I consider this to be my sister's room, Alice, for when she visits. And this is mine, across the hall."

At the end of the hall, I opened a door that led to a steep, narrow stairwell. We ducked and thumped upstairs into the large, dusty space with dormer windows.

"It could probably be turned into another room or a studio apartment but I use it for storage."

"You have a lot of bikes."

"I used to race cyclocross. Can't remember if I told you. So, I've collected a few over the years. Got a couple road and mountain bikes, too."

"Cyclocross look the same as road bikes."

"They do but cyclocross are lighter, a little more upright, more comfortable than road bikes, actually."

"I like the green one, the Cannondale. Never ridden cyclocross. Let's take it for a spin."

"Now?"

"Just around the block."

"But you don't have a helmet."

"I'll be fine. Let's go."

I unscrewed the valves and pumped air into four tires, grinning to myself. I liked her sense of adventure.

We bumped out of the attic and down the stairs of my building carrying bikes. Metal dug into my shoulder. Once outside, I lowered her seat and buckled her into one of my helmets. Too big. It sat on her head crooked. My hands brushed against her neck and chin as I adjusted the straps.

"The bike's probably too big for you."

"It'll be fine." She threw her leg over the frame and tore off into the street. I hopped on mine and pedaled up next to her.

"Race you to that fire hydrant," she said.

I zoomed past her and kept my lead for four blocks to the hydrant. I pulled over and watched her speed toward me.

"You're fast. Especially since you can barely reach the pedals. Or the brakes," I said.

"Brake schmake. This bike is smooth. Still can't tell the differ-ence between it and a road bike, though."

We sped back to my building and returned bikes to the attic.

"Aren't you invigorated?" she said.

That was exactly how I felt.

"Your apartment is a lot like you, tall and handsome. Dignified. I bet you don't ever plan to move."

Did she just say handsome? I walked a little straighter. I thought about asking her to dinner. I didn't. I couldn't.

Gen. I wasn't ready. I had to talk to Gen first. It felt wrong to be with someone else without first letting her know. She deserved the respect.

"I've thought about buying a house, but I like it here. And I don't have to worry about mowing the lawn and shoveling snow. I get enough of that at my mother's house."

"Great rug," she said, pointing to the blue, plum and rust col-ored centerpiece.

"Family heirloom, given to me by my father. He inherited it from his father. It's delicate. I'd prefer you didn't vacuum it. Just sweep it off and spot clean it with some stuff I have labeled in the laundry room. Once in a while, I haul it outside, throw it over the porch rails and beat it out."

"I'll handle it with *utmost* care. You're picky, aren't you, Profes-sor?"

"You're just realizing that now? Are you still in?"

"I've known it from the second we met. Even before we met. You can tell a lot about a person just by watching them. Might have been the sport coat or the white button down that tipped me off. Could have been all the tissues you pulled out of your pocket. One after another after another. Definitely still in," said Alex, with a nod that dislodged wavy strands from behind her ears.

"Check this out," I said and pulled open the two sets of French doors in my living room, both leading to Juliet balconies. "My friend Roberto helped me build custom screens. Keeps the bugs out. Each of the bedrooms has one, too. For an upstairs apartment, the place stays fairly cool in the summer."

Alex fumbled with the lock. She slid the screen open and stepped onto the small balcony overlooking the front yard. "This is official-ly my favorite part of the house."

"I have one more room to show you." I veered toward my office, just off the living room.

"More French doors. Oh, and artifacts."

"I'm especially fond of this one." I held up a twelve-inch clay fig-ure of a large-breasted, fleshy woman with no feet. "It's a statue of the Woman of Willendorf, also known as the Venus of Willendorf. The original is only about 4 inches tall. Dates back to somewhere around 26,000 BCE. I've been to Willendorf, Austria, where the original was found."

"It's beautiful."

"You don't have to clean the office, except for maybe vacuuming the floors. It's organized. I have a system. Don't move anything in here, even slightly."

"Okay, crazy. I'm just glad I don't have to dust in here. That thing must be worth a fortune."

"The Venus? No. Just a replica. Invaluable to me, though, because I visited the excavation site while on a bicycling trip with my father. I don't see him much."

We finished the tour, the explanations, and Alex went to work. I closed the door to my office to score labs. I wasn't used to someone being in my home, cleaning, while I was otherwise occupied. Beyond research assistants, I wasn't used to people working for me at all. If you want something done, do it yourself, my father always said.

After a few hours of solid productivity, I left the apartment to buy food in the form of tacos, chips and guacamole. My non-date version of dinner. When I returned, the apartment was clean and tidy. I stood at the door and removed my shoes.

"The place looks great. Smells good."

"Glacier. I bought you a couple of my favorite soy candles. One's in the bathroom. The other is in your room."

Alex tossed supplies back into her bag.

"Could I interest you in a taco? A beer? Or some water? I have tea, too." I headed toward the dining room, bags of food in hand.

"Do I look like someone who would say no to tacos and a beer? You owe me two beers, considering the layers of dust I just took off your books and CDs." She followed me into the kitchen.

I opened the refrigerator and grabbed two bottles of East Rock Dunkel. I pried off the tops with a church key and handed one to Alex. "Cheers to the end of a hard day's work."

After dinner, deep into my third and Alex's fourth beer, she meandered over to the shelves of albums and CDs, pulled Aretha

Franklin's *Aretha Now* and Tom Petty's *Wildflowers,* and handed them to me.

"Great choices," I said.

"Play Aretha first."

I loaded the discs. Alex dumped dominoes, appearing out of nowhere, with a clatter onto the dining room table. I turned up the volume on *Think.*

"Do you play?" She shouted.

"As a kid. Don't you just match the numbers?" I yelled back.

"You're in big trouble, my friend."

"Where'd you learn?" I asked, while she walked me through the basics of double sixes.

"On St. Martin. I worked as a bartender on the island a few of years ago. The locals taught me. They play fast and loud, slamming the tiles on the table, like this. You can hear a game from across the street. They wouldn't let *you* in the door. Too slow," Alex smirked. "It's how I landed the Mercedes. My ex bought it, to lure me back to the states. Long story."

I lost the first three games.

"C'mon professor. It's just multiples of 5."

With every beer she downed, my odds improved.

"Domino. That's what you get for the smack talk," I said.

"It's my strategy. Lull you into a sense of complacency."

Alex left, winning four of six games. I stood alone at the door as her footsteps retreated down the stairs. How long had it been since I had just hung out with someone? Roberto? Maybe, but we were usually in the middle of a construction project. Gen? Definitely not. We were either skiing, hiking or talking about cancer. She wasn't one to chill, playing games and listening to music. She'd think it a waste of time.

I felt light. Almost *happy*.

11

I cleared the remains of our meal from the table, picked up the phone, and called Mother.

"Where have you been? I've been waiting for you all day."

"Sorry."

"My car doesn't start."

The requisite shame and self-loathing welled in my chest. I planned to visit Mother after Alex finished cleaning but tacos, beer and dominoes interrupted my routine. Unless socked in at the lab, I spent Fridays running her errands and occasionally preparing an evening meal for us to eat together.

"Might just be a dead battery. Hey, I think I just hired us an assistant," I said, eager to change her criticism into words of approval.

"What?"

"I'll fill you in later." Why try? She wouldn't even remember the conversation.

I didn't mention Alex the next morning at Mother's house. I bought her three brimming bags of groceries, mostly food that didn't require much preparation: Nuts, raw carrots, hummus and pita chips, eggs, bread, cheese and frozen dinners. She could cook. She just didn't. I put them away and made us green onion and feta omelets for brunch. Hungover and irritable, she wasn't much for chit chat.

After loading the dishwasher, I changed and washed Mother's sheets, vacuumed the floors and refreshed Stanley's litter box. My theory about her car was correct. Dead battery. I drove it to Sears and waited for a new one to be installed. "You have to drive now and then or the new battery will die too."

She barely muttered a "thank you" when I left.

I spent the rest of the weekend at the lab.

The week flew by. Before I knew it, Alex was back to clean the apartment. From my window, I saw that the top was down on Alex's car and that she was struggling to remove a huge plant from the front seat. I rushed down the stairs, held open the door for Alex and the tree.

"What's this?"

"It's a gift. You need some greenery in the mansion. I know just the spot for it too."

"What's the occasion?" I said, as we muscled the leafy beast and its heavy clay pot up the stairs.

"I saw it and thought of you."

She thought about me.

Alex steered us straight for the turret which housed a beige, modern loveseat that faced the window. It seemed an idyllic reading niche, but I never sat in the turret and neither did any of my friends. Alex shoved the loveseat closer to the windows and centered the ficus behind it.

"I thought it would look nice right here."

"Or turn the loveseat so it faces the living room with the plant behind it, so it's closer to the windows?"

"No. Right here. It creates a space," said Alex, as we hoisted the tree into its heavy metal base.

With the ficus acclimating to its new home, I wrote in my office while Alex cleaned the other rooms. I eventually left the apartment to pick up dinner. I ordered extra and drove it straight to Mother's house.

She and Stanley were "sleeping" on the couch. All of the lights were on and the television blared the news. On the oak coffee table, near her head, sat an iced beverage. I picked it up. Whew. A strong one. Pure alcohol. A puddle glistened on the table. She must have spilled.

Her chest rose and fell. She was breathing. Alive. I flipped off the TV and all but one of the lights then sponged up the liquid on the table. The wood, already discolored. I pulled open a drawer, found a coaster, and placed the drink on top of it. Proper. Like I was *taught*.

Rage ripped through my gut and landed in my throat where it congealed and solidified, making it hard to swallow. I grabbed the drink off the coaster, walked it into the kitchen, and poured it down the drain. I yanked open the doors to the liquor cabinet and grabbed the half-empty and the one remaining unopened bottle of vodka. I unscrewed their caps and sent their contents into the plumbing after Mother's cocktail. A chaser.

I stood at the sink, my fists clenched, ready to pick a fight. I banged around in the kitchen hoping to wake her up. She slept on. I calmed myself by scratching and feeding Stanley who had since jumped off the couch and purred at my feet. I left the pizza in the fridge and a note on the table that read, *"Stopped by with pizza. I tried to wake you but you were out cold. It's in the fridge. Simon."*

I didn't mention or apologize for the empty glass and bottles left on display next to the sink.

Carrying two large thin-crust pizzas through the door to my apartment, I basked in its cleanliness. I was less jangled in an orderly room. Alex popped out of my office with a mop.

"Pizza?" I said.

"You read my mind."

I opened the refrigerator and offered her a beer.

"Kolsch please, if you have one."

I chose an IPA for myself.

"You're so trendy," she said.

"And Kolsch isn't at all trendy."

I turned the playlist to shuffle and we settled into the dining room for another evening of fast food, music and dominoes.

"I stopped by my mother's house to bring her a pizza. She was passed out. Her drink spilled and left a water stain on the coffee table. When I was a kid, she would have grounded me for bad manners and lack of respect for her furniture. Such a hypocrite.

So, I dumped her drink and poured a couple of bottles of vodka down the drain. I left them out where she would see them."

"This can't be the first time you've dumped her stash."

"Yep. First time. I've thought about it. Always seemed like a waste of money. She'd just buy more."

"Good for you. I'm guessing you made your point. If it makes you feel any better, my dad walked out on Mom and me on my 5th birthday."

"No."

"Yep. Right in the middle of cake and ice cream. He was mad because she bought vanilla instead of chocolate chip. Domino. Beat you again, sucker." She did a little jig in her chair.

The following week, the post-cleaning ritual unfolded in the same manner. This time, however, after I placed burgers and fries on the table and offered beer, Alex asked, "Got anything stronger?" I opened the liquor cabinet. "Pick your poison."

"Tequila," she said, holding up the bottle. "Let's do shots."

"Shots, as in plural? Experience has taught me that nothing good happens after one."

She helped herself, rummaging through kitchen cabinets in search of salt and the drawers of my refrigerator for limes. She held them both over her head. "Look what I found." I sat at the dining room table in front of uneaten food. Shot glasses were unearthed, limes were cut into wedges and alcohol was poured.

"Cheers." We clinked glasses and licked salt before tossing the contents down our gullets. The tequila went down smoothly. In poor judgment, I agreed to another. With bottle enthusiastically raised, Alex poured herself a third.

"That's it for me." I shook my head, walking toward the kitchen for a tamer alternative, beer. Alex placed the tequila, salt, and limes nearby on the table and kept on pouring until the bottle was empty.

By the end of the evening, she was smashed. Despite switching to beer after two shots, I wasn't exactly sober. Alex's inebriation improved my odds and I won the last three games of dominoes. We stacked tiles and returned them to their case.

"I don't think you should drive. Can I give you a ride? Actually, I'm not in any condition to drive either. I'll get you a ride."

Alex's eyes were bloodshot, unfocused. She could barely hold up her head. "I don't feel good." She zigzagged in the direction of the bathroom.

I ordered a Lyft and watched my phone as Lou in a black Kia approached the neighborhood. Arriving in 3 minutes. When Lou's lights flashed at the curb, eleven minutes later, the apartment was silent. No sign of Alex. I wandered down the hall. The bathroom door was open. The bathroom, empty.

"Alex." No response.

I went down the hall and found her asleep, fully clothed, on top of the bed in Alice's room. "Your car is here," I said, shaking her ankle. I shook it, again, harder. I jiggled the mattress. "Alex, your ride. Alex? Alex?" I canceled the car. Sorry Lou. I winced at the impoliteness.

I opened the closet in my room and collected a t-shirt and pair of shorts that I thought might do. I stacked them on Alice's dresser along with a clean washcloth, hand, and bath towel.

Back in the kitchen, I put plates and shot glasses in the dishwasher, wiped the table then checked on Alex. She was breathing, in and out through her nose, soft and regular, asleep in the same position. An image of Mother, passed out on the couch, popped into my mind.

I shook it off. She was nothing at all like Mother. I covered her with a soft blanket, shut the door to Alice's room and crawled into my bed. I tossed and turned all night.

I woke early. My sheets smelled of clean laundry. The scent reminded me of the guest in Alice's room. I crawled out of bed, slipped into jeans and a sweater, and tiptoed into the kitchen. I boiled water, and poured it over foaming coffee grounds.

I carried my cup into the living room, set it on the side table and opened the *Journal of Immunological Science*. I was about to launch into the Results section of an article when the door to Alice's room opened. Alex's footsteps made their way toward me.

"Good morning. How's your head?" I said, leaning over in my chair so I could see down the hall, so that my greeting was made with eye contact.

Alex was stark naked.

12

I recoiled and sat straight up.

"I'm good," said Alex, yawning. "Slept like a rock. Your sister has an awesome bed."

The door to the bathroom closed. Something wrong with the clothes I offered? Too warm? Too big?

I collected my coffee and the journal and hustled over to the dining room table where I had no direct line of vision to the hallway or to the bathroom.

The door to the bathroom opened. Surely, she was headed back to the guest room and the clothes that were in there. But no. Footsteps left the bathroom and headed straight for the kitchen.

From my un-easy chair at the table, through the open pocket-door to the kitchen, I witnessed a naked Alex pour a cup of coffee, move toward the refrigerator, open it, remove a carton of half and half, add it and a bit of sugar to the cup, locate a spoon, stir. I couldn't help but notice her firm proportions. Oh, no, she was turning toward me. She walked, unabashed, into the dining room.

"Uh, hi? Shorts no good? Could I offer you a robe, perhaps?"

"I prefer to be nude. I find clothing to be confining and oppressive. Don't you? People in this country are so repressed. Unaccepting of their own bodies. It's liberating. You should try it," she said, with what's-the-big-deal eyes. She pulled out a chair and sat down across from me at the table. "I can throw something on if you're uncomfortable."

"Whatever works for you, jaybird. Scrambled eggs?"

"Yes, please," said Alex, the hair above her temple mashed into an unkempt swirl.

I slid my chair away from the table and dashed into the kitchen. Hiding. I opened the refrigerator and gathered eggs, cheese, onions, and jalapenos. I scooped a head of garlic out of the fruit bowl on the counter.

I sliced a neat pile of yellow onions that stung my eyes and tossed them, sizzling, into a sauté pan with olive oil and salt. I cored, seeded and chopped jalapenos, grated cheddar cheese and pressed a plump clove of garlic. When the edges of the onions browned, I added peppers and garlic.

Alex popped into the kitchen. "I prefer egg whites only, if that's ok with you."

I cracked 6 eggs into a bowl, removed the yolks with half an eggshell, splashed milk and a pinch of black pepper on top.

She poured herself another cup of coffee. "Need help? I can slice. I can dice."

"I'm not sure it's safe for you to handle a knife with all of that exposed flesh," I grinned, eyes averted.

Alex hovered in the kitchen, peering out the window above the sink, sipping coffee, while I whisked the eggs.

"Actually, would you mind peeling a couple of oranges?"

Alex walked past me and collected two oranges. Her shoulder brushed against my arm. It affected me the way I suspect she had intended it to, in the way I wasn't ready for it to.

She glided back to the sink, washed the oranges then stood across the room, peeling them at the counter, buttocks exposed.

She was upping the ante. Perhaps she sensed my reticence and was trying to get me to make a move, to cajole our relationship out of the friend zone. I pictured myself walking over to her, kissing her shoulder, pulling her toward me. But I kept on whisking. Gen deserved to know about Alex before I acted on my feelings.

Alex ate breakfast, buck naked, delivered dirty dishes to the sink, and vanished down the hallway. She reappeared, dressed in last night's clothes.

"Thanks for the tequila and the great night's sleep. Killer breakfast. Those jalapenos were a nice touch, by the way. I'm off to the gym then to work, cowboy. I had a really nice time. See you next week." She left my apartment.

The minute the door closed behind her, the room started spinning. Dizzy and flushed, I sat down at the table. Too much alcohol last night? As the spinning subsided, I made my way to the sink, filled a glass with cold water and drank it down in one long glug.

What was *that*? Was I crazy or was that the weirdest experience I'd ever had? It *was* odd for Alex to be naked in my house. Wasn't it? Maybe not. She was unpredictable, a free spirit. Clothes were oppressive to her.

And she was definitely coming on to me.

Later that afternoon as I strolled the frozen food aisle shopping for Mother, an image of Alex's nakedness standing in the sunlight at my kitchen window flashed through my mind. I reached for a box of Stouffer's Lasagna with meat sauce and flung it into my cart.

While parked at Mother's house, lifting a bag of groceries from the hatchback, I had an intrusive thought of Alex's full lips, curled into a devilish smile as she won yet another game of dominoes.

At the lab, a picture of her peeling oranges popped into my head, her backside in full view.

Roberto and I were the only ones in the lab. We were closing up shop for the night, putting away instruments and logging off computers.

"I had an unexpected overnight guest and naturist breakfast this weekend," I said.

"Sounds fun. Figured Gen was far too refined to eat in the nude." He clicked off the microscope.

"Wasn't Gen. Her name's Alex. Says clothes are repressive and confining."

"They are. She's right. Who's Alex?"

"She's starting her own business. Needs the money. Blah. Blah. I hired her to do some work for me and maybe Mother. She stayed for dinner, taught me how to play dominoes."

"You finally hired someone? Hallelujah. Way overdue. Between your mother and work, I've been watching you drive yourself into an early grave for years. Wait, did you say she stayed the night? Did you have sex?"

"No. Alice's room. Passed out. Tequila."

"But you *want* to have sex with her?"

"I'm not opposed to it. I mean, yes. Yes, I would. It's more than sex, though. She's smart. Fun to talk to. I enjoy her company. But..."

"But what? Don't tell me. Gen?"

"Yes, Gen. Of course, Gen."

"God, Simon. Move on, already. Gen's great, love her like a sister, but you'll always be second fiddle to cancer research. She dumped you, remember?"

"The break-up was mutual."

"Right. Right. Whatever you say. One question. Was this Alex person naked the whole time or just at breakfast?"

"Breakfast."

"Why would she, if truly a naturist, wear clothing for an evening game of dominoes and not for breakfast? What's the difference?"

He seemed more baffled by this inconsistency than the overall fact of the nakedness.

"Good point." I changed the subject. "You and Bob doing anything special for Thanksgiving?"

"The usual. Turkey, cranberries, mashed potatoes. Want to join us? Clothing optional."

"Thanks, but I'll pass. Careful what you wish for. It's more disturbing than it sounds," I said, flicking off the lights as we closed the door to the lab.

Alex arrived in a whirlwind, late, on Friday, carrying a full grocery bag and a sack of cleaning supplies. I couldn't make eye contact. I was still confused and a little embarrassed about last week's breakfast and about the images that had since been swirling through my mind. In spite of Roberto's reminder that Gen and I were no longer together, it felt to me like we were.

"I'm cooking tonight," she said, plopping supplies onto the coffee table on the way to the kitchen. "I'm an amazing cook and you're going to love the deliciousness I have planned for you." I joined her in the kitchen and helped unload the bag.

"What's the occasion?"

"You. Because you're awesome and because you work day and night to fight cancer."

"Sick of fast food already?"

"Yep. That crap will kill you. And it's impossible to work off those empty calories."

"What's on the menu?"

"We're having seared scallops with roasted Brussels sprouts and a chard salad with homemade olive oil and balsamic dressing."

"Sounds healthy. And delicious. I'm headed to my office. Let me know if you need anything." I disappeared.

Two hours later, I took a quick break, walking through the living room to the bathroom. A dry mop leaned against the frame of the front door. A stack of unused rags, still in a folded pile on the coffee table where I left them that morning, stood next to Alex's bag of supplies. They hadn't been touched. The place hadn't been cleaned. Water ran in the kitchen. Metal clanked against metal. I kept moving, avoidant, and returned to my office.

Thirty minutes later, "Dinner's almost ready. Prepare to be blown away," said Alex.

Obedient, I left in the middle of writing a grant proposal and found Alex, giddy, in the living room.

"Close your eyes. It's a surprise." She covered my eyes with one palm while the other cradled my elbow, guiding me into the dining room.

"Fancy," I said, when she removed her hand from my eyes. The dining room had been transformed by a white tablecloth and white place settings, both given to me by Gen. They had never been used. Alex must have found them in their original boxes in the pantry. Lit candles on the table and buffet were the only sources of light in the room.

I couldn't remember the last time anyone prepared a meal for me.

Gen and I often cooked together but that wasn't the same as pulling up to a fully made meal with ambiance. It made me feel tended to in a way I didn't realize I wanted or needed.

"This is impressive, Alex."

"Now for the final touch."

She darted over to my music collection and stood, twisting a lock of hair. She chose a few Louis Armstrong CDs, pushed play and turned the volume down low.

I stepped into the kitchen and rummaged through the refrigerator. Behind tall, green bottles of sparkling water, I found a long-lost bottle of Sancerre, also given to me by Gen about a month ago. It would go better with scallops than beer or Cabernet, the only other bottle of wine in the house. I cleared a path, about to extricate the wine when Alex said, "Got any vodka? I make a mean martini."

"Does that mean you're off the tequila?" I glanced over my shoulder at Alex.

"Aw, loosen up, professor."

I left the wine in its place.

Alex procured a martini shaker and two martini glasses from the sideboard and a lemon and a jar of green olives from the fridge. She shook up the ingredients with ice, "slightly dirty with a twist."

She was full of life. Her energy transformed mine.

By the time I finished my first martini and the buzz of alcohol was softening the world, blurring lines, warming flesh, Alex was downing a second. We started dinner with a salad. Alex then seared the scallops while I pulled the sprouts out of the oven. Pungent and crispy. Bright green and brown.

I took a bite of scallop. "This is every bit as delicious as any I've had in restaurants."

"I told you I could cook. Another trick I learned on St. Martin. We used to snorkel for them. They're even better fresh from the sea."

"You snorkel?"

"Every chance I got. I love being in the water. I'd like to get certified in scuba. Couldn't afford it when I was working in the Caribbean."

"I'm certified. It's a great addition to a beach vacation."

"Are you afraid of sharks?"

I shook my head. "You?"

"I'm not afraid of anything. Another martini?" she said, holding up the shaker. She filled her own glass before I had the chance to answer.

"Absolutely."

"You saw Game of Thrones, right? Which actors did you like?"

"Peter Dinklage, without question."

"Ha, figures. Mine too. Did you see him in *The Station Agent?*"

"One of my all-time favorite movies." I couldn't believe my ears. How did she know that movie? "That's not one many people have seen. I liked the way they contrasted stark natural beauty with emotional pain. Patricia Clarkson can do no wrong."

"Agreed. She brings a believable quirkiness to every role."

I cleared the table while Alex whipped up fresh crème and rinsed black berries for dessert. She placed the two simple ingredients in two bowls.

"Let's take this to the living room," she said.

"Want some port?"

"Hell, yes."

She cranked the volume on Louis Armstrong and sat, legs crossed, in the recliner across from me, bowl of berries in her lap. I took a sip of port and settled into the sofa, sated and hazy from alcohol. I savored the vanilla and sour berry.

Instead of lounging in this pleasant state, I felt compelled to clean the kitchen. The second my bowl was empty, I left Alex and my comfortable seat on the couch and went to work. I scooped leftover sprouts into a glass container and began washing the dishes.

"Do you mind if I bring the left-over chard to my mother? She probably hasn't eaten anything green all week," I shouted. I thought Alex was still in the living room.

"Not at all." Alex was in the kitchen. Right behind me. She slid her hands into the pockets of my jeans and pressed her body against mine.

I stiffened and pulled away. Her lips kissed my neck, moving slowly toward my ear. Part of me wanted to sink into it. Another part of me knew it was too soon. I hadn't spoken to Gen. It wasn't fair to her. It wasn't right. Alex nibbled my earlobe.

I caved. I turned around and kissed the lips no longer relegated to my imagination. Firm and soft, Alex's mouth kneaded mine until I was woozy.

13

The kiss still on my mouth, Alex blurted, "C'mon, let's dance. I'll show you some steps. Got any Latin music?"

She slipped a finger inside my waistband and pulled me into the living room. I replaced Louis Armstrong with Buena Vista Social Club.

Spontaneity was unfamiliar to me. My actions were plodding, measured, methodical, like most of us in the Ivy League world of academia and research. She was free. She shook me out of the interpersonal coma I slept inside.

And Alex could dance. Barely able to walk a straight line perhaps, but she could dance. Alex's hands held my hands, touched my hips, my back, and my arms. Our bodies brushed and met, faces close as I was taught Rhumba (quick, quick, slow) and Salsa.

After a couple of hours, dripping with sweat, we opened the doors to both balconies to let the cold air support the lesson.

"Where did you learn to dance?" I stopped, gasping for air.

"I used to date a famous dance instructor. He's been on TV."

"Mercedes guy?"

"That's the one. Am I wearing you out? Poor thing." Alex changed the CD back to Louis Armstrong. "Let's slow it down. How about a waltz?"

Damp with sweat, arms locked in position, rising and falling across the living room, we practiced and practiced until, mid-step, she kissed me.

Alex lazily unbuttoned my shirt. She looked me straight in the eyes as my shirt fell to the floor. I reached for the buttons on her shirt.

"Just you right now. I want to see you." She brushed away my hands.

Her comfort in her own body made me feel less inhibited in mine.

With slow confidence, Alex removed every stitch of my clothing until I was standing naked, on fire, in the middle of the freezing cold living room.

The next morning, I woke curled up next to flesh thinking, in my hypnopompic state, that the body next to mine was Genevieve's. I pulled the body closer. It felt unfamiliar, smelled more musky than woodsy, more loamy than floral. It wasn't Gen. Rustling under the sheets, Alex rolled over, scooted next to me, and put her head on my chest.

"Hi. Did you get any sleep?"

"Yes, but I think I pulled a muscle doing the Salsa."

"You nailed those moves, by the way. Who knew a science geek could dance?"

"Definitely not me." After a minute, I said, "You're smart. And sexy. No, I think sensual is a more accurate description. You just have a way. Self-assured."

"And you have handsome calves. They're shapely, like Henry the VIII's. I also like your nose. It's a little big, yes, but doesn't dominate your face." She traced my crooked nose and my eyebrows, one at a time, with an index finger. "I'm falling for you, Simon Brust."

Suddenly I was wide awake. As she stroked an eyebrow, joy welled out of lonely recesses and I let myself experience the contentment for a moment. "I think I'm falling for you, too."

We lounged in bed all morning, drowsing between wakefulness and sleep until, "I'm dying to meet this infamous mother of yours. Get up. Let's bring her the leftovers."

Two naked butts sauntered down the hall, toward the kitchen. Together, we made strong coffee and toast with avocado, eating breakfast in the nude.

Sticking unpleasantly to my chair and chilled by the cold left over from last night's open doors, I slipped back to my room and dressed in sweatpants and a sweatshirt, officially ending my naturist experiment. Still naked, Alex lounged in the living room.

I phoned Mother, asking if it was a good time for me to drop by and introduce her to the person I hired to assist with odd jobs.

"Oh, I didn't know you hired someone."

"I mentioned it a few weeks ago."

"No, you didn't. I wouldn't have forgotten that news. But you're welcome to come over any time."

On the way to Mother's house on the opposite side of campus, we listened to the radio. Alex's hand rested on my thigh.

If Alex and Mother resonate, it could benefit us all. Alex needed money and Mother needed more attention. Between residents and grant applications, next semester was shaping up to be even more demanding. Alex's quick wit and sense of humor might be entertaining to a woman who otherwise spent her days watching the news and slowly drinking herself into a stupor. Maybe Alex could get her outdoors.

Mother lived in a neighborhood constructed in the 1920s and 1930s, boasting grown trees and pedestrian-friendly sidewalks. The bungalow-style houses on her block were newer than the mansions in my neighborhood but still part of the historic district.

Surprisingly sober, she met us at the door showered, dressed and coiffed. It appeared that she had spruced the place up for our arrival. Past the puffy redness around her eyes, I caught a glimpse of her former appeal.

"Hello Simon," she said, embracing me. She smelled like apples. A new perfume? She usually wafted a mixture of dryer sheets, greasy hair and vodka.

"Alex, I'd like you to meet my mother, Laurel."

"Pleased to meet you. Come in." She shook Alex's hand. "So this is where you've been keeping yourself. No wonder I never see you anymore." Her jab at me didn't match her smile. My face fell. Alex seemed unfazed by her comment.

"Pleasure to meet you, Ms. Brust. Pretty shirt. Is that periwinkle? Brings out your eyes. We brought you some greens and roasted brussel sprouts, leftovers from the dinner I made for Simon last night." Alex thrust the bag of food toward my mother. "Your place is beautiful."

"How thoughtful," she said, placing the bag on a coffee table. My mother surveyed Alex. She seemed to approve. I relaxed.

Alex glanced around at the visible portion of the house, gushing about the built-in shelves, the arched doorways, and stained-glass windows.

"And this is Stanley," I said, as he trotted toward us rubbing against each of our calves. Alex scooped up Stanley and stroked him. Stanley howled and wiggled out of her arms, meowing as he scurried away. He hid for the rest of our visit.

"Ready for the grand tour?" Mother walked us through the main floor kitchen, dining room and her bedroom. It had its own bathroom and a small, screened in porch made private by an oasis of trees and shrubs. Beyond the trees, a flat area. "I used to do quite a bit of gardening. It's all gone to weeds."

"She has a knack for roses, too," I said.

"Most of them are dead now. I'm afraid I've neglected them."

She didn't go outside much anymore. I didn't have time to keep up with the gardens, but suspected it would cheer her and distract her from cravings if I did. We climbed the steep staircase to the top floor.

"This is Simon and Oscar's old room."

It was a large, sterile space, housing twin beds and two dressers, void of the posters and knickknacks typical of a teenager's room. No visible signs of me or Oscar were anywhere to be seen. Wall marring decorations weren't allowed. Alice's old room across the hall was similarly blank.

We stayed long enough for the tour and for me to rinse and chop leaves and add walnuts and parmesan to the microwaved sprouts. I placed oil and vinegar on the table next to her salad.

"Lunch is served. We're headed out."

We climbed back into my car. "Your mom's really nice. You made it sound like I was about to meet a fire breathing dragon. She didn't even seem drunk," said Alex, as we pulled away.

"She looked better than usual. Maybe it's a new trend. But I'm thinking it was just a fluke."

"I like her. We'll make soups together. Casseroles. She can freeze them and heat them back up, whenever. I'll buy groceries. Lots of fresh, organic fruit and vegetables. I'll clean her windows. They were filthy, by the way," she said, poking me with an elbow before her hand flopped onto my leg. "In the spring, we'll plant a garden and I'll help her resuscitate the roses."

A wave of gratitude and relief came over me. I scooped up Alex's hand and kissed it. I held it there, against my lips and said, "Thank you." Besides Alice, no one had ever offered to help me with anything. Responsibilities all fell to me. At that moment, I realized how badly I needed help with Mother.

"I've got this. Don't worry. You can count on me."

"It means a lot to me."

"I'm worth a million in prizes."

"You're worth a billion. Wait. I know that one. Iggy Pop, *Lust for Life*, released in 1977."

"You know the date?"

"Idiot savant."

"You're such a geek. I love it."

The minute we were back inside my place, Alex collected her things and gave me a long kiss.

"Going to the gym."

"See you Friday?"

"Can't wait."

I spent the next few hours cleaning, since it hadn't been done yesterday. Visions of us swirling, her liveliness, her wit swam through my head as I vacuumed the living room.

Alex *got* me. We meshed. We dissected movies, music, everything, with an intensity and depth I'd never before experienced. She challenged me, opened my mind. She opened me.

But what about Gen?

Smashed with a leaden sadness, I flipped off the vacuum, squeezed my eyes shut and covered them with both hands. My mouth tasted coppery, like blood. I betrayed her. I cheated. I couldn't even control myself long enough to have a conversation with Gen first. I'm such a jerk, I thought. It would change everything between us. I wasn't even sure yet if I wanted it to change. My actions made the decision for me. The reality of losing Gen ruined my weekend.

14

By the time Monday morning arrived, my disposition found its way back to optimistic. I remembered what a colleague told me during my psychiatric clerkship: love is the best anti-depressant. My mood swing provided anecdotal evidence for the hypothesis. I was hopped up on infatuation, high on the feeling of being chosen, desired, and accepted.

Or, I'd been hypnotized, like a macrophage, I thought as I reviewed notes for the day's lecture.

I felt surer of myself than I had in years and it splashed all over my Basic Immunology class. All residue from the concussion, gone. My thoughts, lucid. My mind, keen. I jumped on top of the desk, a trick I stole from a high school English teacher, Mr. Molting.

"You all look so sleepy this morning. Rough weekend?"

They peered up at me over laptops and cappuccinos to go. "Pop quiz," I said. They groaned and rolled their eyes. "Jonathan, draw us a natural killer cell. Ming, draw salicylic acid, Shay, Siglec-9 proteins, Lucas, PD-1." I tossed them each a white board marker.

They finished their drawings and straggled back to their seats, "Good job, everyone. Looks like you did your homework." I leapt to the ground.

"Dr. Genevieve Hale and her group, one of a handful across the globe, are researching carbohydrate antigens on cancer cells. They work with the innate immune system to modify sugars on the surface of cancer cells and sugar-binding proteins on natural killer cells. Who can tell me what Dr. Hale's group is finding? Shay."

"That removing sugars from the surface of cancer cells rouses immune cells so they can identify and attack the cancer."

"Exactly. It's impressive. If you haven't had a chance to get to the lab and see their work, I recommend you do so. If cancer cell proteins bind to receptors on macrophages, then immune cells fall into a state of hypnosis. It seduces the macrophages into complacency, causing them to ignore the cancer cell. Carbohydrate-targeted treatments are waking up macrophages and other cancer-fighting cells of the innate immune system."

No one in the department, except Gen, was interested in researching carbohydrates due to their complexity and elusive positive findings. Grant money was more available to projects with guaranteed findings. She also spent more time writing grant applications than the rest of us. I didn't mention these facts in class.

I secretly incited interest in her work because she needed and deserved the assistance and because I suspected she was on the verge of an important discovery that would further the development of successful cancer-fighting treatments.

"My group is working with white blood cells, referred to as T cells, part of the adaptive immune system. We're studying ways to block the cloaking interactions between the surface protein antigens on cancer cells and proteins on T cells. For example, if proteins on the surface of T cells link with proteins on a cancer cell, the T cell can't function. It's handcuffed, rendered useless in the fight against cancer."

We hashed and rehashed the material in words and in drawings until each student had it down pat, like the adaptive immune system confronted with a familiar flu virus.

After class, I made a beeline for my office to work on a grant proposal with a looming deadline. Gen's office door stood open. Instant nausea. Wasn't she usually in the lab on Mondays? I wasn't ready for the Alex conversation. But it was past due.

I could slide by, undetected? Put it off a little longer? Best to get it over with. I walked straight to her door and peeked inside. She sat at her desk, engrossed in work. Her face brightened when she saw it was me.

I felt horrible. I was such a stereotype.

I didn't go in. I felt shy and hovered in her doorway. "Hi."

She took one look at me. "What's wrong?"

"Nothing's wrong. But there is something. Something I would like to discuss with you when you have time."

"Sounds ominous. How about now? I have a half hour before I'm due at the lab. We're this close to finding a reliable method for removing sialic acids."

"I know. I heard. That's great...I'd rather not talk at work. Free for dinner tonight or tomorrow?"

"Not tonight. I'll be at the lab until late. But later tomorrow, around 8:00?"

"8:00. Bombay Palace?"

"Our usual place. Meet you there."

I arrived early with sweaty palms and a queasy gut. I wanted time to think through my words. From my seat, a doll sized vinyl booth at the window, I watched Gen's Subaru meander rows in the parking lot and pull into a space.

She got out of the car, opened its back door, and grabbed her bag. I watched, stricken with a sadness and fondness that melded into dysphoria. A stabbing headache formed behind my eyes.

She approached the booth. Her smile conveyed happiness to see me but the furrow in her brow suggested trepidation about the reason for our meeting.

She wore a tweed blazer, turtleneck, jeans and wing tips. We hugged each other with our whole selves. I breathed her in. She smelled of wool and verbena flowers. Her shampoo. I knew it well. It was the scent that hung in my bathroom so many times in the past.

She kissed me on the mouth, like a lover, before sitting down across from me. The physical contact, familiar, satisfying.

Her thick mane of silky brown hair was thrown into a haphazard bun held together by what might have been actual chopsticks. As she brushed away unruly strands, I noticed a few previously undetected wiry grays at her temples.

I gazed at the freckled face I knew and loved, at the astute hazel eyes from which nothing could hide, her cheekbones, delicate, narrow nose, pointed chin.

What are you doing? Tell her that you miss her, that you want to get back together. Officially. This minute, I told myself.

Intellectually and physically, Genevieve was the product of generations of natural and social selection from both family lines; brilliant, beautiful and well formed. She was the perfect spawn, genetically honed by the last three hundred years of money and social standing.

Easily distracted by her beauty, most people underestimated her intelligence. I suspected it resulted in a need to prove herself that fed her staggering professional drive. Or maybe she was simply unburdened by financial worry and appearance-related insecurities enough to access her full potential. Considering what I knew of her family and the social pressures they managed and inflicted, I suspected the former.

The second she sat down my mouth said, "I think I might be seeing someone."

She looked confused, then blindsided. Her eyes reddened and welled with tears. Her tears triggered mine. Unexpressed, they got caught on the lump in my throat.

The waiter approached with large, amber tumblers of ice water, interrupting the moment. We both ordered Taj Mahals. I requested chicken tikka masala, hot, and plain naan, as usual. Like always, she ordered dal and aloo gobi, medium hot.

"I thought you seemed jaunty, lately," she said, in what appeared to be an unsuccessful attempt to hide the shock and sadness on her face. "Is it serious?"

"No. I don't know." My chin fell, unable to hold up the weight of my words. "Maybe."

"Then, I guess we're really *over*?"

"I suppose so. I always thought we'd figure it out and get back together."

"Me too."

"Really? You've never told me that."

"*You've* never told *me* that. We're not the most effective communicators when it comes to emotional matters," she said, with a sad smile.

"Let me clarify. You thought we might get back together someday?"

"Yes. But you know how we are together. All the pressure and guilt because there's never enough time for each other. Then, when we are together, it's constant arguing. I'm sure it's just pent-up work and family stress, but we take it out on each other."

"I'm sorry. I know I added to the problems between us. It's too hard, sometimes, between work, my mother and the expectations of your family. And it seems like all we talk about is cancer research. It gets heavy." I lost my appetite. I straightened the napkin on my lap and swallowed. "It feels wrong to be ending things when I still like you so much."

"You're my closest friend. One of my favorite people on earth," she said. True for us both. "We can still be friends, right? I can't lose that part of you." She touched my hand for a second then pulled away.

"Me neither. My day is better when you're nearby."

Changing the subject to something that probably seemed easier, but wasn't at all, she pummeled me with questions in rapid succession.

"Okay, so where did you meet this lucky person? How do you possibly have time to meet someone? Wait. Do I know them? A student? No, you would never cross that line. Give me all the juicy details. On second thought, leave out the juicy parts."

Carrying a large tray, the perfect distraction, the waiter brought our food and beer, serving it all at once. I shoveled spicy masala on top of jasmine rice and contemplated my answers. For the first time in all the years I've known Genevieve, I didn't speak the truth.

I failed to disclose Alex's name or the fact that she worked for me. I definitely did not disclose that Alex had deliciously unearthed previously unexperienced levels of conversation, intellectual stimulation and sexual pleasure.

It wasn't that the relationship with Gen didn't meet those needs. It did. It was more the uncanny *degree* to which Alex's interests and humor matched and validated mine. Angry at myself for omitting information, I felt ashamed by my dishonesty. Just tell her, I thought. But I spoke in vague terms. It wasn't like me. She had to have noticed, but didn't say anything. That wasn't at all like Gen.

"I suppose this puts the kibosh on being friends with benefits." Her tone was light-hearted but the lines around her eyes suggested she knew the answer but hoped it wasn't true.

"It does. I'm apparently one of those modern-day anomalies who can only be with one person at a time. I hate duplicity." In that moment, I was being duplicitous.

We parted ways after dinner with a grief-seared hug. The finality of us, palpable.

Numb, I drove home. I didn't recall the commute. I didn't remember walking up the stairs to my apartment. Recovering from the stupor, I found myself wandering from room to room, collecting the photographic remnants of our relationship and placing them in a box.

Into the box went a framed picture of us taken after scuba diving off her family sailboat near Mallorca. Her damp, scraggly hair flailed in the wind. Her cheeks still wore the impression of her mask. The background of the photo captured the rocky cliffs and the clear water of the Balearic Sea. We had our arms around each other. We looked happy.

I removed from the wall above my dresser an enlarged, black and white, close-up photo of Gen's face, eyes downcast, and freckles visible. We were backpacking in the Alps near Lake Como. I took the picture while Gen was laying out the tent after a long day of hiking. The hair visible in the photo was matted and gritty from sweat and she wore no make-up. The image captured not just her beauty but a vulnerability, a rarely seen softness.

The trip to Lake Como was our first vacation together and the first time we really had each other all to ourselves. I walked from room to room carrying the photo, my face wet from tears. I couldn't place it in the box. I would hang it in the hall.

Wretched were the days that followed the second and final end to Genevieve and Simon, the couple. I executed my academic and scientific duties with a grim, absentmindedness. Intermittently nauseous and headachy, I avoided Gen and everyone in the department.

Most troubling to me was the fact that, prior to our Indian dinner and my Alex escapades, I had been unaware that Gen imagined we might reunite sometime in the future.

15

Significantly later than the appointed time of the weekly house cleaning, Alex assuaged my angst, bearing gifts of chocolate, a book, *100 Love Sonnets* by Pablo Neruda, a blue ceramic soup pot, a CD of *The White Stripes*, and my very own set of double sixes dominoes.

With her hands on my hips, Alex walked me backwards to the couch, sat me down, curled up beside me, fed me chocolate, and read from the book:

I love you without knowing how, or when, or from where.
I love you straightforwardly, without complexities or pride;
So I love you because I know no other way than this:
Where I does not exist, nor you,
so close that your hand on my chest is my hand,
so close that your eyes close as I fall asleep.

We spent the afternoon in bed.

Famished, we eventually dressed and ventured out into the cold for an Italian dinner at Adriana's Restaurant. "Look at that couple. And that one. And that one. Bored with each other. Emotionally disconnected. They aren't talking or even looking at each other. That's what makes us such a great couple. We never run out of things to talk about," she said.

Alex stayed the night. An impending storm was predicted to dump up to two to three feet of blowing snow overnight and into the next day. We turned out the lights and watched as fat flakes fell from voluptuous, low-slung clouds.

The storm began without sound.

By the time we went to bed, the wind had arrived, banging against windows and walls like an angry drunk, locked out of the house during a fight.

We spent the next day puttering around inside, fire burning in the fireplace, while a blizzard whipped the city, whirling, grey and white.

In sweats and flannel, I slowed down and relaxed. I wasn't expected to be anywhere. For once, it was acceptable to be gone from the university, to be away from Mother and I let myself enjoy the unscheduled time. I called to make sure that she and Stanley were warm and had enough provisions to see them through the storm.

We cooked ham and cheddar omelets with buckwheat pancakes, Alex's recipe, and ate on the couch by the fire. Empty plates remained stacked on the coffee table. I let them sit there like that, unwashed. Taking my cue from Alex, I opened a novel and started reading. Not a journal article. I couldn't remember the last time

I'd read for pleasure. We lazed on the couch, her legs flopped over mine.

My father's name flashed on the screen of my phone. Why was he calling? I ran into my office, closed the door, and answered.

"I understand you're in the middle of quite a storm," he said.

"It's a doozy. How'd you know?"

"Made international news. I got a notification from my radar app. Are you safely tucked in? Your mother okay?"

Ask her yourself, I thought. "I've spoken with her twice this morning. We're both fine. You?" In that second, I decided that I no longer wanted to protect him. I no longer wished to be the vessel for the hurt he caused Mother, to be the go-between. "You know, she always asks about you. Always asks me if you have plans to travel to the US."

"I'm doing well," he said, not responding to the comment about Mother. He didn't even take a breath to consider my words. Disregarded again. "I read the article on MHC class 1 tumor proteins that your group recently published in *The Journal of Immunotherapy and Research*."

I braced myself. "What did you think?" I stood in the window, shivering from the draft. Snow fell. My neighbor swept a mound of it off the top of his car.

"I think the article makes a well-supported case for proteins on the surface of macrophages and how they bind to the surface of cancer cells to prevent the macrophage from destroying the cancer cell. But I don't think your article fully takes into consideration the extent to which cancer cells can evade the immune system.

The concept has potential but you are far from using the data to facilitate the development of actual immunotherapies."

"You think the argument is weak? I think it captures good progress made on a potentially transformative intervention." He was the weak one.

"Keep working on it. But, I'm not sure that article will land you a big pile of grant money." Straight for the jugular. He knew what I was up against with my tenure application.

"Thanks for the feedback. What are you up to?" I changed the subject.

"We're still running clinical trials on glyphosate, Roundup weed killer, and its link to lymphoma."

"I'm sure that's keeping you busy."

"It is. Well, I should let you go. Can't wait to see you. Looking forward to our hike on the Matterhorn. Just bought a waterproof cover for my backpack. Say hello to Gen from me."

"Me too. I will," I said, with a lump in my throat. It argued with the rage in my chest. He didn't usually say that he couldn't wait to see me.

Was that fatherly warmth, perhaps love, transmitting through the line? When I was a kid, I admired him. I wanted to be just like him. But as an adult, I was disgusted with him for avoiding Mother, for leaving us to tend to the ongoing mess of his departure, for being so far away.

He'd be crushed to learn that Gen and I were no longer together. He said she was a "star" and read everything she published. He would not understand my attraction to Alex.

I sat at my desk and reread the recently published article on LILRB1 proteins on the surface of macrophages, the culmination of one year's worth of unending nights at the lab. He was right.

Was he demonstrating some twisted version of support, rather than antagonism, during our conversation? Maybe his feedback stemmed from the belief that I was capable of more, not that he thought I was a failure. A had a twinge of longing to be with him. He didn't know me. I didn't know him, either.

Alex cranked up the music. Pots clanged across the apartment. Visions of a naked Alex cooking up something delicious in the kitchen propelled me straight out of the office. Fully dressed, she chopped a pile of celery next to my new soup pot, warming a pool of salted olive oil.

"Nothing like a blizzard to put me in the mood for minestrone." She radiated heat while a wicked storm blew outside. "Chop some carrots, please, you handsome lug. Who was that on the phone?"

"My father."

"You don't mention him much. How's he doing?"

"Good. I guess. He read my latest publication. Didn't think the argument was strong enough." I pushed a pile of chopped carrots to one side of the cutting board making room to slice an onion.

"That can't be easy to hear. What's wrong with your argument?" Alex rinsed a leaf of kale at the sink and patted it dry with a paper towel.

"Basically, he didn't think it took fully into account how well cancer cells hide from the immune system, how hard it can be for them to be seen. Thing is, he's right."

"Sneaky little buggers, eh?" Alex dumped a can of cannellini beans into a sieve. "Remind me to buy you some raw beans. I'll show you how to cook them. Less mushy than canned. What are you going to do about the article?"

"Talk to my research group. Do another study. Write another article." I peeled potatoes over the garbage can.

"Win the Nobel Prize in Medicine. The world-renowned Dr. Simon Brust. Buy us a villa on the Italian Riviera." She took the peeler from my hand, placed it on the counter and wrapped her arms around me. "We'll get a boat. Host parties attended by the world's most fascinating people." She pulled me toward her and kissed me into a hypnotic fog.

We made out in the kitchen, while the soup simmered. She turned off the stove and led me by the hand down the hall, into the bedroom.

We eventually meandered back to the kitchen. I splashed olive oil on rustic bread, sprinkled it with shredded Asiago cheese, and then popped it into the oven to bake. "Should be toasted by the time the soup is ready." She made margaritas on the rocks, with salt.

After dinner and several rounds of dominoes, we were relaxing on the sofa when Alex said, sloshing another full cocktail, "Let's go for a walk."

"We just got three feet of snow. Maybe more. The streets haven't even been plowed."

"So?"

"Good point. I like the way you think. Mother would call it tomfoolery, but I'm in," I said, tipsily. I loved her spontaneity, her quest for new experiences. I couldn't predict what would happen when we were together. It was one of the things I appreciated about her most.

I scrounged the attic for a coat, pair of boots, gloves and a hat I thought might fit Alex who arrived without a jacket, as usual. They were all too big, but would do.

"What about my margarita?" She put an arm into a borrowed coat.

"It'll keep in the fridge. Or the freezer." I stomped boots into place around my feet.

"I want to bring it."

"Really? We can't go for a walk without it?"

"No. *We* can't."

I unearthed a flask from the pantry and poured her drink into it through a funnel. She put it in her coat pocket and we ventured out.

The sky was clear. Still. A full moon. Pointed moon shadows mimicked our every step as we penetrated the night. Tree branches, heavy with snow, leaned toward the ground as if listening in on our conversation, as if straining to join us on our walk.

The city was indoors. We were alone on the landscape.

Alex guzzled from the flask. She offered me a swig. I took a drink and gave it back.

We slogged for blocks. The snow was knee deep, up to our thighs in some places.

Alex scooped up a handful of snow and hurled it at my chest. It disintegrated in the air, leaving a trail of dust where it landed on my coat. I collected a wad and plopped it on Alex's hat. She gasped. It must have melted and slithered down her neck.

I scrambled away. She chased in my path, caught up, and pushed me. I went down, buried in a drift. I reached a gloved hand toward the grinning troublemaker. She grabbed hold, lifted me halfway off the ground, and then let go. I dropped back into the snow.

Laughing, I reached again. Almost up, Alex not only released my hand but gave it a good shove. I fell, careening back into the quicksand. I landed badly, wincing from the shooting pain that jabbed at the site of my ditch-ankle-injury.

I attempted to lift myself out of the drift using every muscle in my abdomen and thighs, struggling to find leverage in the deep, slippery fluff. Each effort failed, only burying me deeper.

I finally found my footing when Alex, with a running start, body slammed me back into the white.

My ankle screamed. I struggled to a stand.

Again. She whammed into me, full force.

"Knock it off. What the hell was that?"

I was pissed. I pulled myself off the ground, testing my ankle's weight baring capacity, flinching from pain. I brushed snow off coat and legs.

"Oh, come on. I was just messing around." She blasted my face with a handful of snow.

I flicked water and ice out of my eyes. A knot formed in my stomach. Anger squeezed my chest. Alex walked way ahead of me, all the way back home while I limped across patches of ice and stumbled through drifts of snow.

Bone cold, inside at last, I pulled off my right boot. The ankle was swollen and in searing pain. How could she just walk off and leave me like that?

"I think you should go," I said.

"Don't be mad." She was already dressed in dry clothing, listening to music on the sofa, sipping a fresh cocktail. "Do you want me to make you one?"

"I would like to be alone."

"Oh, God. Are you serious? What's your problem? You're making a big deal out of nothing."

It wasn't nothing. "Get. Out," I said, through clenched teeth.

In slow motion, Alex gathered a few of her belongings. She slammed the door on her way out.

16

My heart raced. I needed to pace. I couldn't. The ankle hurt too much. I tried to read. I couldn't concentrate. I went to bed and stared at the ceiling. What just happened?

I replayed every detail of the last two days. Why did she shove me like that? Was she angry with me? Because I told her not to bring the drink? That couldn't be the reason. Or was it? It seemed like such a small reason. But it was the only even mildly tense interaction I could remember. I must have done something to make her act like that.

The shoves felt mean.

I couldn't recall Alex's mood as anything but cheerful. Pleasant. Maybe she was just goofing around. She didn't shove me *that* hard. She didn't *intend* to hurt my ankle. Maybe I *was* overreacting. Those thoughts chased away the rage and delivered a much needed sense of relief.

Why was I so angry? I shouldn't have been angry. I had no justifiable reason. In fact, it was cruel of *me* to make *her* leave, drunk, in this weather. The roads were terrible. What if she had an accident? The whole mess was my fault. I shouldn't have made the comment about taking the drink on our walk. Who cared if she brought one? It was none of my business. It was not my place to say.

After a couple of hours of fitful sleep, I startled awake. A sharp pain stabbed my chest. My heart. I sat up straight, unable to catch a breath. My hands were shaking. The urge to vomit swirled through my stomach. Saliva filled my mouth. Beads of sweat erupted across my brow. I was going to die. Cardiac arrest.

Call an ambulance. Or someone. Gen? Roberto?

The floor tilted. I stumbled as I dressed in the still wet clothing, found in a heap on the floor. Breathing shallow, rapid breaths, I used the wall to brace myself as I limped down the hall to the bathroom. I stopped by the kitchen and took small sips from a glass of water. Don't pass out. Must not pass out, I told myself. Gelatinous legs threatened to drop me to the ground as the room spiraled. With trembling hands, I slipped on boots and coat, fumbled for keys and wallet. About to launch myself to the emergency room, the chest pain subsided.

Strange.

I sat down at the table, coat zipped for the outdoors, and forced myself to focus. I searched my memory for facts gleaned from my cardiac rotation. With a heart attack, the pain gets worse, not better. Was the chest pain accompanied by a sensation of pressure? No. Did the pain radiate to arm or jaw? No. Had I been exerting myself prior to the onset? No. I had been asleep. If the pain dissipates after a few minutes, it probably wasn't a heart attack.

I exhaled, hard. But then, what *was* it? Something was heinously wrong with me. I was still shaking, legs still wobbly. Maybe I should still go to the emergency room.

I collected my thoughts again and took the approach that had been instilled in me during the long, arduous years of medical training. I created a list of differential diagnoses. After a few minutes, I identified the probable etiology of my symptoms: Panic Attack.

Ridiculous.

I'd never had a panic attack. I'd been through medical school, rigorous written and oral exams, job interviews, public speaking engagements, article submissions, grant applications, the destruction of my family unit, the departure of my father to another country and the trepidation of walking into a house possibly containing an unruly or dead drunken mother, and I'd never before had a panic attack. Sure, I'd experienced anxiety and went through a brief period of excessive handwashing. But nothing like that.

I removed coat and boots, traded wet clothes for dry, pressed an enormous mug of black coffee and retreated to my office, ankle iced and elevated, in a vain effort to distract myself with the mounds of work left undone by two days of hedonism. I opened articles and tried to read. I opened manuscripts and tried to write.

But I was distracted by a thought: what if I have another one? When would it get me? In the middle of class? In the middle of an international presentation?

I did what I had always done when faced with a dilemma, I called Roberto, who answered on the first ring, despite the early hour.

"Sorry to bother you."

"I'm up."

"I think I had a heart attack. Or a panic attack. I had some kind of attack."

I explained my symptoms, in detail, to a sympathetic ear and medical mind.

"Sounds like a panic attack. But you should probably see a cardiologist, maybe get an EKG, to rule out a medical cause. What's going on? What triggered it?"

I didn't want to get into it, but it was Roberto, one of the few people in the world I trusted, so out it came, "I had a big, ugly fight last night with someone I've been dating. Sent her home in the aftermath of a blizzard."

"The naturist?"

"That's the one."

"Do you want to talk about it?"

"I wouldn't know where to begin. I haven't even sorted it out for myself yet."

"I'm sure I don't need to tell you this but, the recommended treatment for panic disorder is medication and psychotherapy."

I considered his words. "Neither of those appeal to me. I've only had one. Doesn't meet the criteria for a disorder."

"Simon, I've watched you try to have relationships. You're not very good at it. You've got baggage. I think you should consider therapy, at least. I have a few names, people I highly recommend. I've seen one or two of them myself."

"Even if you're right, how am I going to find the time for therapy? I don't have it. And I don't need anyone judging me."

"It's not like that."

"I know. I'll be judging myself."

"You'll do that, regardless."

"Let me think about it."

"I hope you do. Call me if you change your mind."

"I may have baggage but it doesn't affect my relationships."

"Uh, okay...Denial."

"You're a really bad friend. I'm hanging up now."

That morning and the following days were some of the most wretched of my life. I was confused, mopey, brimming with righteous anger. I conjured excuses in the form of retrieving clothing, books, music left in my home and called Alex. No answer. I didn't leave a message. She didn't return the call.

I contemplated texting something hateful, *Get your crap out of my house, I don't ever want to see you again.* I considered texting something benign, *Did you make it home OK?* Then, something romantic, *I miss you.* I didn't. My stomach felt like an achy clot of fury and remorse.

I slipped behind in my work. I couldn't concentrate. I wandered between obligations, fulfilling none. I couldn't function.

I skipped out on lab and canceled a class. With a runny nose and a fever of 102, I had forced myself to teach, in the past. I'd never before considered canceling to be an option. I avoided everyone and everything. I didn't even bother to ask Hety to cover for me.

I spent wasted hours in my office, staring at the wall, forgetting to pick up Mother's Glucotrol. "Simon, what's the matter with you? I need my medication." Good question, Mother. What was the matter with me? I couldn't eat or sleep. I barely showered. I didn't tend to my ankle. It was healing fine without me.

I experienced terrifying intermittent chest pain which I monitored and scanned for with the paranoiac hypervigilance of a combat veteran, afraid it might be the start of another panic attack.

I wondered, over and over, if my anger regarding Alex's behavior was justified. But I *did* detect hostility in Alex's shoves. Didn't I? No. Alex wouldn't act like that. Would she? Why would she? It didn't make sense.

With pangs of regret, I concluded that I had overreacted and chased away the one person I managed to find in the world who might just be the best match for me.

I called Roberto.

"I figured you'd call."

"You were right."

"What's going on? Haven't seen you at the lab. Everyone's been asking about you. I was about to send the police over for a health and welfare check."

"Not doing so well."

"Want to meet for a beer? Dinner? On me."

"I couldn't do that to you. I can't even stand my own company. I suppose you better give me those names."

Within five minutes, Roberto sent four names via email. I proceeded to call each of them in the order they were listed. Two hours later, I'd scheduled an appointment for the next day with a Dr. Claire Snellen. Of course, the only slot she had available collided with class time. See, I didn't have time. Forget therapy. Instead, I canceled another class so I could make the session. Hety agreed to cover lab for me.

I chose Dr. Snellen over the others mostly because of her name. Snellen eye charts have been around since the 1800s and, until recently, were used to test visual acuity. To me, her first and last name together meant clear vision and I certainly needed some clarity.

I also liked how she sounded on the phone; smart, direct, friendly but not sappy sweet. She seemed to know her way around the symptoms I was reporting and asked the types of questions that got to the bottom of things. I appreciated that about her. And found it a little unnerving.

The next day, I pulled into the underground parking lot of a twelve-story glossy building downtown. The gatekeeper told me her office was on the fourth floor. A sickly pit formed in my gut as I rode up in the elevator. I entered the waiting room and pushed the button, as directed by a sign, to let her know that I had arrived, early, as requested.

The waiting room was small and windowless with twitchy, fluorescent lighting. Children's toys cluttered the floor of a far corner. Along the wall, a cart on wheels offered coffee or tea. Wicker baskets overflowed with sweeteners, natural and chemical, raw and granulated, nondairy creamers and shakers of nutmeg and chocolate. I contemplated a cup of coffee but declined, deciding I was too jittery. My empty hands already felt too full to juggle one more thing.

I completed stacks of HIPPA compliance paperwork, also indicated by a sign, and answered a variety of self-assessments pertaining to my mood, symptoms of anxiety, use of substances, suicide and homicide risk, family mental health history and history of traumatic events.

I answered with dubious transparency because I had mixed feelings about how much I wanted to get into right off the bat. I definitely did not divulge much about my alcoholic mother. I minimized the fact that I hadn't really eaten in 5 days, barely slept, was riddled with guilt and terrified of having another panic attack.

At 9:02, the door to her office opened and she stepped into the waiting room to meet me. Poised, shortish, roundish, softish, she looked to be 40 something, with shoulder-length, straight black hair and all eyes. Wearing jeans with high heels, cream blouse, and a red blazer, she shook my hand, firm, confident, no-nonsense. She looked directly at me. I was sure she could see right through me, had already detected all my flaws and secrets.

Her office was corporate, slick, with grey carpet and grey walls. Boasting a view of the city, her large, rectangular windows were the kind that didn't open. Just the look of them made me nervous. What if I needed air?

She created a comfortable space out of the sterile room with warm tones in modern rugs, furniture, floor lamps, and left off the overhead lights. I sank down into the leather sofa. My guard went up.

For fifty minutes, as part of the initial assessment, I answered questions about my family history and the lone panic attack. I didn't disclose that Alex pushed me down in the snow, over and over again. Not exactly the kind of thing people liked to admit to anyone, much less themselves. I did tell her that my panic attack occurred the morning after an argument and possible, who knew, termination of the relationship.

"I'm hoping you can tell me why I had the panic attack. I can't afford another one. I'm up for tenure. I teach. I give long presentations to scientists from all around the world. I can't be having panic attacks. It'll ruin my career."

"I don't know what caused it." She looked up at me from her notepad.

I leaned back and scratched my head. "Then why am I here?" I said, half joking, half not joking.

She put her pen down. "You're the only one who knows what caused it."

"But I *don't* know."

"I can help you figure it out."

I gazed out the window. "It must have something to do with the fight with Alex. But it's not the first time I've had an argument or broken up with someone."

"Good point. Then there's more to it. What is your gut trying to show you?"

"Nothing. Can't see a thing. I killed all communication with my gut a long time ago."

She chuckled. "That's a big part of your problem. Beyond the genetic component, anxiety is caused by the avoidance of emotion."

Her laugh disarmed me. I settled into the couch. I took in my surroundings. She had a lot of books. Abstract paintings hung from the walls. They reminded me of Rorschach inkblots.

"I thought anxiety was irrational fear."

"An irrational fear of emotion. You're very in your head."

"Like a good scientist."

"I appreciate your need for objectivity. But emotions are a warning system. They're trying to help you. But you've shut them down by engaging your psychological defenses. We need our defenses, to a point. Yours are in the way now. They've made it so you can no longer see what your emotions are trying to show you."

"Like cancer, hiding, so the immune system can't see it, can't confront it and deal with it."

"Exactly. Except I don't think emotions are toxic. They can feel pretty bad, though."

"I'm aware of feeling angry and hurt. What more is there? What am I avoiding?"

"It must be something important or your body wouldn't be reacting so strongly."

I left the session. I'd missed a class and still didn't know what caused the panic attack or how to prevent it from happening again.

But I made another appointment. For the rest of the day, I felt unburdened, less anxious, more focused.

I drove home and parked the car, satisfied, content, almost back to my old self. A dark figure perched near the door. I strode across the lawn. With each step, the mass morphed into distinguishable features.

Alex. She sat on my veranda, leaning against the house in a navy pea coat, blond strands splayed starkly across the dark blue. The orbit of her eye and the angle of a cheek bone were illuminated in the porch light. The rest of her face, in shadow.

I climbed the porch steps and stood without speaking. Next to her sat a grocery sack and a sauce pan with red splotches on the lid. Inside the bag, I spied a package of penne pasta, a head of lettuce, a baguette, and two bottles of wine. She grinned up at me.

"Hi handsome. Pasta with homemade marinara?"

I glanced at the unlit street and kicked a stone off the porch. I wanted our fight to go away too but it didn't seem like it could. Or should. Shouldn't we be talking about more than dinner? Why was she here? Why at that moment? I figured we were over. I shook my head.

"How's your ankle?"

"Fine. Good. Back to normal."

"You know I was just messing with you."

"Didn't feel like it." Was that a tear on her cheek? In the dim light, I couldn't be sure.

"I didn't mean for it to come off that way. Don't be mad at me."

"I am mad. You kept shoving then just walked off. Without any regard for me or my ankle."

"I worried about it all week."

"How would I have known?"

"You're right. I should have called. But I wanted to wait until you were less pissed. Can we just go inside and talk?"

I sat down on the porch next to her and leaned back against the house.

"Or we could talk out here." She smiled.

I didn't know what to say so I said nothing. Her smile filled me with hope before I could quash it. Hope for what? It was a hope I shouldn't, didn't, want to be feeling. I pushed it away.

After several minutes of silence, I said, "Why did you keep shoving? What was that?"

"I was just goofing around."

"You weren't the slightest bit angry with me? Was it because I told you not to bring the drink?"

"Maybe. A little. I don't appreciate people telling me what to do."

"I have no business telling you what to do. But you know I struggle with my mother's drinking. It bothered me that you wanted to bring the drink on our walk. Especially since you were already buzzed. It felt like you weren't considering my perspective or me at all. And you didn't even ask about my ankle."

She stared straight ahead. I glanced at the side of her face. She seemed to be processing my words. The hope resurfaced.

"I shouldn't have brought the drink. It was insensitive. You drink. We drink together. I didn't think it was a big deal. I'm sorry. I didn't mean to offend you or hurt your ankle."

"I drink. We drink together. And I don't mind it, up to a certain point. Beyond that, it starts to remind me of her."

"I get it."

"And I won't boss you around."

"That would be wise."

The tension that had been straining my shoulders and neck for days let go their vice grip. I forgave Alex that instant, stood up, reached for her hand and helped her off the porch.

We went upstairs, boiled pasta, heated sauce, ate and rehashed for hours. No music. Just us. We found our way back to each other in the middle of the night.

Our reparation was grittier than the ones I remembered with Gen. It went deeper, into our childhoods. More layered. But then, the fights I had with Gen were simpler.

The next morning, Alex rolled over and curled up against my back. Her nose tickled my neck. Her lips found my ear.

"I hated being away from you. I never want to do it again."

I closed my eyes and lay there, in her warmth. In her words.

"I hated it too."

She traced my ear with her finger tip. I drifted back to sleep.

"Simon?"

"Yes?"

"Let's live together."

I did not tend to make decisions on the quick, especially decisions of that magnitude. But when I compared the bliss of that morning with the loneliness of the previous week, "When can you move in?" I said.

17

By the end of the next weekend, Alex's belongings were moved out of Camille Benoit's rented room and into my apartment. Moving day was the blizzard's antithesis: slushy streets and brown clumps of exposed grass.

I followed Alex's car in my own to make more space for boxes, creeping into intersections, edging my way forward, unable to see around plowed stacks of dirty snow into a neighborhood developed in the 1980's.

Camille lived in a nondescript house with a nondescript yard in a similarly nondescript neighborhood.

"It's nice to finally meet you, Simon. I've heard so many good things. Come in. Make yourself at home. Coffee anyone?"

I didn't answer. I couldn't. The only information I could register was Camille's body art.

Red, yellow, and orange tattooed flames swirled and licked up her chest, back, arms and shoulders. She appeared as if she were being consumed by fire.

Petite and slender but hardly diminutive, Camille's flaming arms were pure sinew and her neck was thick with muscle, like the neck of a competitive swimmer. She had short jet-black hair and intelligent eyes, the color of fertile soil.

Despite the chill, she wore the tiniest black tank top, rightfully exposing as much as possible of her magnificent tattoo. How much more of her body was covered in flame, I wondered.

In stark contrast to the exterior, the inside of Camille's home was anything but plain. Large and small marble abstracts mixed with nude sculptures congested her living space. From wood and metal, I learned, she also built her own dining table. Rows of drawings, mostly nudes, covered an entire wall.

"I sculpt from them." She pointed to the drawings. "I started out forging metal but stumbled into sculpting marble about five years ago. Since then, I've been taking every class I can get my hands on. It's more my thing. I spent six months in Volterra Italy, training on alabaster with Giorgio Finazzo. Profound experience. Completely changed directions after that."

I wandered the space in awe. After a long look, I held up a small nude, a leaning torso emerging from the stone, one slender hip exposed. The positioning of the arms and the facial expression captured a pained, straining effort to pull itself out of its entrapment.

"Tell me about this one," I said.

Alex and Camille looked at each other. "It's Alex," said Camille. They both burst out laughing. "Most of the nudes are from sketches I made of her. That's how we met. Alex was a model for the studio where I rent space. Sculptures of her have been purchased by collectors all over the world.”

“I had no idea. Alex, you never mentioned it.”

“I figured you’d judge.”

“Why? I think it’s cool.”

“Here’s the actual sketch for that piece. These eight rows are all sketches of Alex,” said Camille. “When things went to shit with her ex and she needed a place to stay, we bartered modeling for cheap rent.”

“Yes, Camille is amazing. Helped me get the job at the Barista, too. But posing for that drawing was torture. I leaned like that for hours. Charlie horses in my feet and calves.”

“Right. I could barely pin you down long enough to finish the sketch. Most of it was done by memory because my model was MIA. That’s the last sculpture I made with Alex as the model. She totally bailed on me. We have a few new models at the studio, but I don’t find them as interesting to draw or sculpt. At least they show up.”

“Modeling *sounds* glamorous. Turns out, it’s a complete bore,” said Alex.

I scrutinized the sculpture. Carved into the bottom, the completion date, 9/5/16, finished just a few weeks before I met Alex. I had to own it, and not just because Alex was the model.

It depicted the human struggle to climb out of destructive patterns. Or it simply portrayed the toil of someone trying to pull themselves out of quicksand. In either case, it moved me and I wanted it.

"Explains why Alex is so comfortable being naked. How much would you charge for it? Is it even for sale?"

Four thousand dollars and five hours later, I owned a sculpture and had a live-in lover.

We collected and boxed Alex's belongings, strewn across every room in Camille's house. I boxed Arcteryx waterproof rain gear unearthed in the guest bedroom, designer boots, shoes, and jeans found in Camille's closet, a top-of-the-line MacBook Pro and Canon color printer in the office.

"Camille gave me a loan to help pay for those when I started my business," Alex said, as I set off to scrounge the original boxes from the garage.

"You have impeccable taste," I said, a few minutes later, holding up Alex's Klipsch Forte III speakers. "They put mine to shame. Do you mind if we hook them up when we get home?"

"I do have impeccable taste. And I chose you." Alex blew me a kiss.

"Only the best for Alex," said Camille.

Born and raised in Quebec City, Canada, Camille was ten when her father landed a graphic design job in New York City. At eighteen, she moved to New Haven, lured by the Creative Arts Workshop. She had a French accent.

"My father's from Geneva. He's living there now."

"So you speak French?"

"Enough to order food and get directions."

"What else could you possibly need it for?"

"Wish I was fluent. Makes travel more interesting, provides insight into the culture that you can't get otherwise. My father didn't have time to teach us and the classes I took in college didn't stick."

"I'm around if you ever want to practice."

Sun setting, barely able to see out of mirrors and windows, we clambered into our jam-packed vehicles. The bubble wrapped sculpture of Alex rested safely on the floor of the passenger seat.

Backlit, Camille's frame appeared larger and her features, lost in shadow. She was a big person, despite her small stature. I accelerated into the street in the direction of home.

We climbed up and down the apartment stairs with box after box. My ankle didn't complain. When the last one was inside, we unwrapped the sculpture.

"How about here? Or here." We tried it on the hearth, on a table near the door, on the buffet table in the dining room. I decided to keep it on a bookshelf in my office so that I could empathize with it while I worked.

"Could use an art light. I bet Roberto could wire one up. Hey, let's hook up your speakers. They'll blow mine out of town."

"Then let's make dinner. I'm starving."

Music blared out of the new speakers while we chopped yellow, red and jalapeno peppers, onions, and squash for steak fajitas, our first meal as cohabitators.

"You have the best knives. How do you keep them so sharp?" She pulled one out of the butcher block on the counter.

"Good old German engineering and a sharpener." Questions I wanted to ask, words I wanted to say, but didn't know how, ran circles in my mind. "I enjoyed meeting Camille. She's talented."

"Developing quite a name for herself in the art world."

I crushed garlic into the sauté pan. "This is none of my business. And you don't have to answer. But were you two ever romantically involved?"

"Never. Just friends." She slid sliced red and yellow peppers into the pan.

"Did you ever have sex?"

"Just friends."

It took me a minute to find the words. "As boring as it sounds, I'm a total serial monogamist. I was hoping we could be exclusive from now on. Just me and you. What are your thoughts on that?"

Alex stopped stirring vegetables and looked at me. "As far as I'm concerned, it's always been just me and you. I'd marry you tomorrow. But aren't you the one still pining for your ex, Genevieve?"

"That chapter of my life is over. For good." My stomach twisted from the truth of it. Gen and I would never again be anything but friends. Emotionally, she was a lot like my father.

"Then we're on the same page. I think we're a perfect match. Perfect complements to each other. Yin and yang. You help me focus, give me structure and I free you from your gilded Ivy League cage. I picture us buying matching hearing aids together when we're old, complaining about the price. I've been around. I'm old enough to know. You're the only one for me."

"Hearing aids are expensive." I walked to where she was frying steak. "I think we're a perfect match, too."

"Hey, we should celebrate us living together. Let's take a trip or something. Don't you have time off between semesters?"

"I do. And Alice stays over the holidays to give me a hand with Mother. I usually end up working in the lab or holing up in my office writing an article or a grant."

"That's what you do with your breaks? Lame." She thumped me on the forehead.

"What do you want to do? Ski in Vermont? Snow shoe in New Hampshire?"

"I'm already sick of winter. Let's go somewhere warm, like Florida or Arizona. What about Tucson? I want you all to myself somewhere sunny, wearing nothing but shorts and flip flops, far away from labs and cancer research. Maybe you could ditch your phone and that damn computer."

"Wherever you want. You do the planning. I don't have time. I might be able to free up a few days after Christmas."

"Let's ring in the New Year far away from here," said Alex with her arms around me, landing a fat kiss. "I'll take care of every-thing."

Joy beamed through the fissures of my overworked, overstressed, preoccupied-with-grants-and-my-alcoholic-Mother psyche.

After dinner, as Alex unpacked boxes, I created tidy spaces in drawers and closets. She filled the emptiness with disheveled piles of shirts, sweaters, socks, and underwear. I liked seeing Alex's clothes next to mine. Why had I been so dead set against cohabitation in all of my previous relationships?

Oh, yes, there was Ruby, my tumbleweed of a medical school girlfriend, the most serious relationship I'd had until Gen. She had an untamed mane of auburn curls and blew into my life as ferociously and as passionately as she left it.

My childhood of unending parental conflict combined with the Ruby experience left its mark in the form of a general wariness about relationships and especially, cohabitation. I built a wall around my living space.

Convinced we were in love, we moved in together after dating for only three weeks, my second and her first year. We had been living together for about thirteen months when she slept with my lab partner. Devastated, I sent her packing, leaving myself with the rent, utility bills and a year's lease.

Roberto sat behind me in anatomy class at the time. He endured my Ruby lamentations for months. He had just started dating Bob and I, in turn, endured hearing him gush about their relationship. Before long, he became my new lab partner, roommate and friend.

I was doing it again. Moving in with someone I had just met. My heart rate picked up speed. My ears went hot. Oh no. Chest pain. I couldn't catch my breath. The room swirled. I sat on the bed and clutched my chest as lungs strained for air.

18

I kept my appointment with Dr. Snellen. She was warmer than I remembered but still a blank slate with frightening, penetrating eyes.

I pushed myself to be more open. I had to get rid of the panic attacks, for good.

"Alex moved in. We're living together now." I searched her expression for judgment. Nothing.

"How's it going?"

"Really well. My anxiety spiked afterwards, though. Had another panic attack. Got any tips for what to do when I'm in the middle of one of those? They're horrible. I seriously feel like I'm about to die."

"Yes. Breathe. Hyperventilation prevents your brain from getting the oxygen it needs to function properly. Your body kicks in and tries to get you to pass out so you'll breathe correctly again. Long, slow exhales will stop the hyperventilation and, with practice, cut the panic attack short. Especially if you catch it early. How are you doing with pin-pointing the cause?"

"I'm trying to figure it out. Maybe the decision to live together was a little impulsive."

"Impulsive?"

"I don't usually move this fast. I tend to perseverate for weeks, ruminating about every possible outcome. But why? It's an exhausting waste of time. We're solid. It's nice to just be together, to be able to see her every day."

"It feels right despite being counter to your usual decision-making process."

"It was Alex's idea but I was in complete agreement. Strange, since I vowed to never cohabitate again."

"Strong position to take."

"I lived with someone in medical school, Ruby. We talked about marriage. But she ended up cheating on me. I'm probably afraid it'll happen again. Maybe that's the emotion I'm avoiding. Fear. That I made the wrong decision. That I can't make good decisions when it comes to relationships. That I'll be crushed again." It made sense. My shoulders relaxed. "Is that the cause of the panic attacks?"

"I think you're getting close. You'll know when you've gotten to the root of it. Your panic attacks are trying to show you something that you don't want to see."

"Why don't I want to see it?"

"Fear. Fear of the pain that seeing might cause. Fear that you won't be able to handle the feelings that come up."

"So, what do I do?"

"Face your fear. The treatment for anxiety is to let yourself experience feelings and stop avoiding them. To quit shutting them down. The more you feel, the less afraid of feeling you'll become."

"Sounds like a prescription for disaster," I said.

I didn't schedule another appointment.

In the week that followed, I came home to music and an often buck-naked Alex in our kitchen, cooking something delicious. After dinner, we turned up the music and danced. My Salsa skills were developing superbly.

At the end of the evening, we'd lay awake in bed, twisted up in each other. I'd read a journal article or make notes for the latest grant application. She'd open her laptop, flip through color palettes, shapes and symbols, fonts, for the web page she was designing. We'd ask for each other's opinion, share the minutia of each other's lives.

It was my favorite time of the day, resting next to Alex's soft skin and sharp intellect. It had become a sort of haven for me, a place where I could finally let go of the weight I carried. Our bed was a nest. A home inside a home.

But I wasn't comfortable with my lover cleaning the house and doing my odd jobs. In bed one night we hashed it out, at length and in detail, agreeing to transfer all paid duties to my mother's house for the sake of our relationship. Alex still needed the money and I still needed help with Mother.

We agreed to share household chores as would any couple occupying the same living space. I gave Alex a credit card, "For Mother's expenses. You can put our vacation on it too."

In the first couple weeks of working for Mother, Alex twice shoveled snow, taught her how to play dominoes, cajoled her out of the house for an afternoon of shopping, encouraged her to try on and purchase two new outfits, cleaned windows and dusted the shelves, stocked the kitchen with vegetables, repaired the leaky dishwasher with a new hose, installed a motion detector light for the porch, and donated unwanted bric-a-brac.

They cooked and dined together and, instead of news blaring all day, incorporated music into the ambient sound. Alex taught Mother to tango and Mother offered pointers on the jitterbug.

They also drank too much alcohol together.

On these occasions, Alex stayed the night at Mother's house in the room of my youth. I found the whole situation unsettling. It threw off my sleep and I had a harder time focusing the next day.

Late one evening, we were in bed reading. Alex had spent the previous night at Mother's house, too drunk to drive home. I pretended to read while I struggled to put together words that might express my thoughts and feelings about her drinking with Mother. Nonjudgmental, non-controlling words. Words that wouldn't be insulting or make her feel unappreciated. I couldn't find them. I gave up and turned the page.

But I still couldn't read. "I missed you last night."

"I missed you too." She scooched closer and plopped a leg on top of mine.

"I was hoping you might encourage sobriety." There, I said it. It was out.

"She's very persuasive. And she makes a mean gin and tonic."

"Just don't introduce her to your dirty martinis."

"Too late."

"I'm serious. I don't expect you to police her alcohol consumption. No one can. It's not your problem. You can't fix her. But maybe just don't offer or participate with so much enthusiasm."

"Hazard of the job, I'm afraid." She slapped my thigh. "Just kidding. I hear you. No more cocktails with your mother."

While I suspected Mother appreciated the company, she didn't express satisfaction or gratitude and, unfortunately, continued to complain that she didn't see me often enough. Consequently, my visits with her were almost as frequent as they were before Alex.

Under pressure to spend time with Mother, finish our research and get another grant written before the semester came to a close, the one hope getting me through the grind was the prospect of seeing Alex at the end of the day.

After another late night at work, I pulled up to the curb and put the Rover in park. I glanced up at my apartment. Light streamed through the windows. Alex illuminated my home.

With an energy absent from all other daily activities, I leapt up the stairs. Wafts of caramelizing onion with garlic in a red wine sauce met me at the door. Except for a couple lounge cookies, I hadn't eaten since the sausage sandwich at breakfast. Alex greeted me with a big grin. The frustrations of the day slid off my back like a heavy coat in spring.

"You're finally home. I've been dying to tell you; our vacation is booked. Guess where?"

"The Poconos?"

"What? No. Burr. Pack your swimming suit, sport. We're going to Tahiti! I found a great deal on an over the water bungalow in Moorea. Yes, they were a little more than a regular hotel room but we'll have our own porch right over the water. And the airfare was less than you would think. I put it all on the credit card you gave me."

I scratched my bald spot. "Tahiti is on the other side of the world. I was thinking we'd road trip to New Hampshire. Maybe fly to Sedona. Stateside. What are the dates? You've already booked it?"

"You are small minded for someone so smart. It's *Tahiti*. Look at these pictures." Alex shoved color photos of palm trees and white sand beaches into my hand. "It's just nine days. Look at the color of that water. I'll get certified in scuba. We can dive. South Pacific. You and me."

Alex danced around the kitchen with pictures of our vacation in her hand.

Her ebullience penetrated my tired skin. I stopped worrying about the expenses, the time it would take away from work, looming deadlines, grants, tenure, or Mother's reaction. Nothing. All I could see was Alex.

She stirred an adventurous side to my personality, part of myself that I liked. A part of myself I hadn't allowed.

I took the photos out of her hands, set them down on the counter and pulled her close.

"Then I guess we're going to Tahiti. Thanks for doing all of the leg work."

I called my sister, Alice, from my office at work the next day with reports of our plans nestled uncomfortably next to the request that she tend to Mother and Stanley while we were away.

"No problem. I was planning to stay through New Year's anyway. A couple more days won't matter. Real estate is slow this time of year. How'd you talk Gen into getting out of town?"

"I'm not going with Gen. We broke up."

"Again?"

"For real this time."

"Oh, Wow. I'm sorry. Are you okay?"

"I'm fine. We're still friends."

"I always thought you two were the perfect couple. Perfectly melded. Geeky Ken and Science Barbie."

"We do meld but mostly over academics and cancer research, which is something. It...just...isn't enough."

"Let me guess, you're going on a beach vacation with Roberto and Bob."

"No. I met someone. We hit it off. Brace yourself. She moved in."

"Who are you? *My* brother let someone move in with him? Hopefully, this one doesn't come with snarls and the mange like that red-headed carnival ride you almost married in medical school. I thought we Brusts were too damaged by the flaws of our parents to have a real relationship. Wait. I can still stay at your place though, right?"

"The hair is blond, a little messy. No mange. Her name is Alex. She's really great, I think you'll like her. And you'll have a room at my house as long as you keep taking shifts with Mother once in a while."

"Done. I'm bringing someone I want you to meet, too."

"I'm sure this one is as terrible as the rest."

She had a pattern of fleeing from reasonable romantic interests after about three months, around the time infatuation ended and deeper feelings began to germinate. She'd hone in on a flaw, magnify it, decide she couldn't possibly tolerate it, and abruptly end the relationship. The poor saps never knew what they were in for.

For the next two weeks, I left home before 7:00 a.m. and didn't return until somewhere between 10:00 and 11:00 p.m. I pushed myself to finish grading and collecting data for our journal article. I wanted the manuscript to be exactly right. It was the last chance to publish before my application for tenure was due in the fall.

But it wasn't so much the grading or the manuscript and their deadlines that troubled me.

It was the big grant proposal. Due on May 1st. If I wasn't awarded a total of ten million in grants this academic year, I wouldn't make tenure. Regardless of the publications, I would lose my job.

19

Late one night, I opened the door to my apartment. It was dark and empty and I was edgy and irritable. Buzz. I checked my phone. A text from Alex. "Hi handsome, staying at your mom's. She's trashed. Worried she might fall." The note came with two heart emojis and a selfie of Alex blowing me a kiss.

I went straight to bed, missing Alex. As if strung out on caffeine, I lay awake and constructed a relentless schedule that might allow me to finish exams, grading and at least a rough draft of the manuscript before I left the country, the day after Christmas.

Partial success. Final exams ended in a whirl and grades were submitted on time. The manuscript, however, was still not ready to send for peer review. I had articles to incorporate, data to analyze, and sections to write in collaboration with my group. They were all busy too, distracted by the holidays and related family obligations. Defeated, I accepted that I'd be taking work with me to Tahiti.

Dread. Dread had always been the word that best described my personal anticipatory experience of the holidays. The same sentiment applied to birthdays, dinner parties and weddings. All family gatherings, large or small, were precipitated by a certain amount of nausea and clammy hands. My entire body revulsed at the thought of them.

Consequently, I'd developed and perfected avoidance patterns that successfully took me almost to the hour of the event. My career choice supported these efforts especially with regards to Christmas because research didn't end when the semester did.

The aversion to family gatherings stemmed from an inevitable uptick in Mother's criticism and the increased likelihood of an emotional explosion. Despite years of data confirming that anything that happened in our family during the holidays would be disappointing at least and combative at most, I still looked forward to spending time with Alex and Alice.

Oscar would be absent. He quit attending family functions when he was still in high school, manufacturing ways to be otherwise occupied.

In our family, parties came with walking on eggshells, unchecked anger, broken stemware, late arrivals, and histrionic departures. We tried to avert the inevitable. We hid the alcohol, served only sparkling non-alcoholic, met in public places. Calamity found its way to our picnic, regardless. We underestimated the ingenuity and tenacity of addiction.

Through the years of chaos, though, we did learn two ways to garner some control. One, if we held the feast at Mother's house, we could flee if the situation warranted. Two, if we plied her with food, early in the day, we could slow the rate of alcohol entering her blood stream, thus delaying the drunken shenanigans until later, even after it was time to go home. The latter intervention wasn't as easy as it sounded as she often, very purposely, didn't eat so as not to kill her buzz. Concealed in the spirit of Christmas, we brought her favorite foods hoping they would tempt her to eat.

With Christianity mixing with father's Swiss heritage, the Brusts celebrated Christmas like most North Americans, with a few idiosyncrasies. Devoutly Catholic, in her own mind, Mother occasionally still attended St. Patrick's Cathedral where, as children, we lined the pews, impeccably dressed.

Father refused to attend mass. He didn't encourage or support religious education. It was yet another source of conflict between them, another simmering cold war, with us in the middle.

Abstractly, as an adult, I could appreciate the solace, and golden rules offered by religious rituals and tradition. As a teen, however, it was difficult for me to consolidate the church's teachings when they so contrasted with my mother's behavior, particularly the lies, the verbal abuse and the fact that it wouldn't be unusual if she spiked her coffee with Bailey's prior to service.

"Advent starts the fourth Sunday before Christmas. It's a time of waiting, of introspection," she'd say. I hoped my mother would use the spirit of Advent to see that she had a problem. She didn't.

In spite of everything, when I reflected on the Christmases of yore, it was the light I remembered most. Or it was the lighting of the light. Rituals around the lighting of candles and the lighting of the fireplace were a positive experience in a home otherwise fraught with tension.

On Christmas Eve, at dark, we gathered around the table while Mother lit one pink and three purple candles from the Advent wreath. "They symbolize expectation, hope, joy and purity," she said. The white candle, representing the light of God, was lit on Christmas morning, after mass.

According to Catholic tradition, they were to be lit one week at a time, in synchronicity with the Advent calendar, but strict adherence was lost on the Brusts. We were the epitome of how traditions became watered down and forgotten over time.

After the lighting of the Advent candles, my father, bringing customs from his Swiss heritage, would light a fire in the fireplace. His tall, lanky frame hunched over the hearth on one knee while he meticulously swept it clean. He'd stack a triangle of logs while telling the story of Yule, the winter solstice festival in Europe, a tradition practiced since the Middle Ages.

In scholarly Dr. Brust fashion, he'd say, "In medieval times, fireplaces were so large you could stand inside them and the Yule log was an entire tree trunk. Carefully chosen, branches sawed off, delivered to homes in a parade, the Yule log was decorated with holly and pine cones and doused with wine and salt to purify the air and to welcome spring. The ashes were kept and used for medicinal purposes or sprinkled around to guard against evil.

The largest end of the log went into the fireplace first. The rest stuck out into the room. It was lit with remnants of last year's tree by someone whose hands had to be clean," he pontificated. "Over time, as fireplaces shrunk in size, people modified the tradition by baking cakes decorated to represent the Yule log."

We slept with wooden sticks under our beds and kept the fire going all twelve days of Christmas. When the story was told and the fireplace ready, he ceremoniously washed his hands, procured a burnt stick, claiming it was from last year's fire, and set the pyre ablaze. It was my favorite time, the calm before the storm.

Traditions changed after Father left the country. Now, I lit the fire at dark on December 24th and in the morning of the 25th. The Advent wreath, missing a purple candle, stayed packed in a box in the closet under the stairs.

Due to The Drunken Mother, we modified the holiday schedule to include an early dinner on Christmas Eve and Christmas brunch, both at her house. Over time, we also shifted gift giving from the evening of the 24th to the morning of the 25th for the same reason.

Christmas Eve morning, I woke up alone again, freezing cold in my bed. I burrowed under the covers. Alex had spent another night at Mother's house. According to the clock, she'd probably already left there for a shift at the Brash Barista. *Staying here tonight. Laurel had one too many martinis. Going to the gym at 6:00, then work until 3:00 tomorrow. I'll be at your mom's as soon as I'm done,* she said, in yesterday's text. Only one too many?

I had left a balcony door ajar the previous night. The cool air helped keep me awake while I worked on the manuscript. I'd forgotten to close it before stumbling off to bed.

Under bare feet, the floor was another assault on my flesh. I scurried to the closet in search of slippers. In the way back, I scrounged a wooly pair and sunk into them. I shuffled into the living room, assessed the clouds, closed the balcony door and locked it. Snow possible.

I had two hours to write before I was scheduled to be at Mother's to prepare for dinner. I found my largest French press, ground beans and boiled water. Mug of coffee in hand, I headed for my office and picked up where I left off, closer to completing a rough draft before we left for Tahiti.

As lead author with a deadline looming, it was a terrible time for me to be gone for nine days. I rubbed knots in my neck and shoulders. Couldn't we skip Christmas?

After two hours of writing, nearly finished with the literature review, I fumbled through the closet again, this time in search of my cranberry V-neck cashmere sweater, a gift from Mother circa 2013. I wore it exactly once per year. There it was, creased, moth-eaten, in dire need of dry cleaning or at least a hot iron. I pulled it on over a blue and white striped button down.

On the way to Mother's house, I stopped at a crowded grocery store and an even busier Dutch bakery where I picked up special orders, made at each over one month earlier, including fresh crab legs, live lobsters, and a Yule log cake.

Around 10:00, I pulled up to Mother's house with plans to cook and distract her from her cocktail. The cake had been crushed in transit, dislodging holly berries and pinecones, leaving a thick layer of chocolate frosting on the box.

Mother surfaced, lucid, showered, out of her robe and into a clean green sweater and a black skirt. Positive signs.

"Merry Christmas, Simon," she said, embracing me in a loose hug. Mild metabolized alcohol odor. "I'll take care of the cake."

"Hi, mom. You take the cake."

I unpacked groceries onto a filthy countertop. The knives I needed were dirty, sitting under water in a sink piled high with unwashed dishes. Crumbs crackled under foot as I shifted, back and forth, from counter to fridge. Why was this place such a mess? Alex said she would tidy up. Why didn't Mother clean? She's expecting guests. I blamed last night's martinis.

As usual, my day was a pressure cooker of demands. I scrubbed the bathrooms, vacuumed, mopped the floors, and took out the trash while Mother washed the dishes and placed the Yule log on a cake platter, deftly restoring its exterior. The physical labor improved my mood. I wanted to build the fire.

I hunched over the fireplace on one knee and swept the hearth. I made a pyre with bunched up newspaper and small sticks surrounded by medium sticks surrounded by three logs.

The wood felt rough and dry in my hands. I could see my cranberry clad self, building the Christmas fire. The image morphed into a memory of my father lighting old newspaper while my siblings and I watched. That kid again, I smelled the fire before it was lit.

I wished he were there, building the fire in the tradition he established for the family.

Behind me, Mother, more sensed than heard, hovered out of sight then vanished. I lit the fire without witness. Blackened paper ignited sticks. Red balls of heat bored into the wood like ticks.

I watched the family tradition burn and, again, perceived Mother's presence. Her footsteps retreated. Ice clinked against glass. A typical Christmas Eve at the Brusts had begun.

I joined her in the kitchen. She poured vodka over ice, added tonic and a slice of squeezed lime. The tang of citrus tickled my nose.

"Will you taste the cheeses I bought and slice them for the appetizer tray?" I said, eager to encourage food down her gullet before the alcohol hit her bloodstream.

She ate one little bite, not even a full slice, from each of the four packages of gruyere, manchego, brie, and gouda.

"The gruyere would be better with a few more years on it. What do you have against plain old cheddar?" She gulped down half of her cocktail then sliced the manchego and gouda, arranging them in attractive rows on a platter next to the brie. "Some fig jam would be nice with the brie. Did you remember to buy fig jam?"

"No, Mother. I did not buy fig jam."

I took another swing at it. "Let me know what you think of the crab salad. More salt?" She loved crab salad. It was her favorite. I dug my knife deep into the freshly made mixture, heaped it on top of five Table Water crackers, placed them on a plate next to a bunch of grapes and a couple of slices of cheese and delivered the food to her uninterested hands. She nibbled on a solitary cracker.

"Maybe a little more salt. And pepper. More cilantro. And the crab chunks, better when they're smaller." She returned the uneaten half of cracker to her plate. She set the plate on the counter next to her drink, wrapped her liver-spotted hands around her cocktail and took off with it toward the living room. "Let me know if I can help," she said, and left the kitchen. She had no intention of helping. She had other plans.

I ran through a list of other handy high protein foods with which to line her stomach. All of my ideas required preparation. I opened her fridge. Nothing. I opened her pantry. Behind boxes of dry spaghetti and a pair of Grey Poupon mustard jars, sat my solution. Mixed nuts.

I ripped off the protective seal, chucked a couple of cashews into my mouth, poured a large portion on the plate next to the uneaten crab salad and the grapes and delivered it to where she sat under a blanket, staring at the fire. A tear wobbled at her jowl. It dropped, disappearing into the fabric of her sweater.

"Please eat. Dinner isn't until after 3:00." I set the plate down on the end table next to her empty cocktail. "Would you mind cleaning lettuce for the salad?" I said, changing strategies from feeding to distraction.

"Maybe in a few minutes. I'm enjoying the fire. Do you remember when your father used to light it?"

"I miss him too. Are you okay?" I asked. Dangerous question.

"I'm fine. Could you make me a drink?"

"Of course," I said, delighted by the opportunity to enlist my final sobriety strategy: dilution.

I poured the weakest vodka tonic she'd probably ever had and squeezed the juice of two whole limes into it, hoping to conceal the dearth of alcohol. I carried it, and over time, three more, as requested, directly to her waiting hands.

Promptly at 3:00, my sister arrived with her latest love interest. Besides trips to the restroom, answering the door was the only reason Mother had left her chair in the last few hours. She did not clean the lettuce. She did not set the table.

In shocked disbelief, I watched as my mother zigzagged to the door. She was wasted. How could she be that drunk? I glanced over at the chair she had just vacated and spied a bottle neck peeking out from under her blanket.

She had a pint hidden under the cushion of her chair. So, while I was in the kitchen, believing I just saved Christmas, she was in the living room dressing up the drinks I persisted in delivering. I thought I found a way around her but she, of course, found a way around me.

"Happy holidays. Mom, Simon, I'd like you to meet Sam Mitchell." Burly, bearded, Sam wore green and brown plaid flannel with khaki carpenter pants. He had thick, sandy brown hair and sincere eyes.

"Merry Christmas. Nice to meet you." We took turns shaking Sam's hand.

"Great haircut, Alice. Makes you look like Debbie Harry," I said as we hugged. Her straw-colored hair, usually worn to her shoulders, was dyed platinum and cut into a short, edgy bob with bangs, magnifying her elfin features.

"*When I met you in the restaurant, you could tell I was no debutant,*" she sang, in perfect tune, flipping her new doo from one side to the other.

"Dreaming. 1979," I said.

"Alice, must you be so loud?" Mother covered her ears.

"See Sam. I told you. Simon has this bizarre memory for songs and the dates they were released. And my mother prefers it if I don't speak."

My fingers tightened around Alice's peanut butter cookies and sweet potatoes.

"Your hair is too short. And what is that color, Alice, rat's nest? Sam, don't you prefer her natural color?" Mother said, her words, thick.

Sam didn't answer. From the slurring sting in her speech, I was certain, Mother was smashed.

"Simon and Sam both like it," whimpered Alice.

Poor Alice. The hurt in her voice filled me with hatred. I brought her contributions into the kitchen, threw crackers, crab salad and assorted olives and grapes on a platter and delivered appetizers to the living room where everyone collected around the fire.

20

I fueled the fire and returned to the kitchen. I stirred Mother's dressing, basted the duck, filled a pot with water to boil the lobster and turned the soups down low. I tried to collect myself, but the muscles in my jaws wouldn't unclench.

It was 3:30. Where was Alex? I could have used some of her enthusiasm right about then. I stared out the window. I paced around the kitchen, eager to put everything on the table and start dinner before Mother slipped into the agitated state of inebriation where calamity was most likely to ensue. It was coming. She had been drinking on an empty stomach for hours.

Outside, nothing but the opaque, homely greys and browns of winter.

Mother laughed, too loud, and asked Sam, "Where do you work?"

Buckle up, Sam, I thought.

"I'm a software engineer. I work for CyberCoders."

"You should start your own business," she said and launched a slurring monologue on corporate tax law.

Shattering the grey, a red Mercedes zoomed up to the curb. Alex collected a bouquet of roses in one hand and a bottle of champagne in the other, slammed the door closed and glided toward the house, without a coat, sleek, meticulously dressed, in a black turtle neck, black velvet pants and tall, black boots. Her hair swirled in the wind, covering her face as she burst through the door.

"Happy Holidays! Hi everyone, I'm Alex." She tossed her hair back into place. "Smells amazing in here." In an instant, the atmosphere in the house changed from tense to festive.

I scooped her up off the floor and held her, my cheek against her temple. "I'm so glad you're here."

I set her down, gathered champagne and flowers from her hands, and introduced her to Sam and Alice who lurked, timidly, near the door. From her chair in the living room, next to the vodka, Mother waved.

The afternoon slipped past twilight and disappeared into evening. I closed the drapes and dimmed the lights. My hostility evaporated. Alex had that effect on me. I popped open Alex's champagne and poured a round.

"Dinner is served," I said, relieved to put it on the table, eager to see food in Mother's mouth and approval on her face. The sooner we ate, the quicker we'd get out of there. Maybe I'd even have time to work on my manuscript before bed.

"Where should we sit?" said Sam.

"Anywhere you like."

Sam pulled out a chair at the end of the table.

"Don't sit there," said Mother, out from under the blanket, off her chair, moving faster than she had in years. "I like to be near the kitchen."

There it was. The surly. Her frontal lobes were going offline.

Sam chose another seat and we all sat down.

"A votre santé," said my mother, in the tradition of my father, holding up her glass.

"A votre santé."

"Yum. You made my favorite lemon tarragon dressing, Mom," said Alice, collecting greens, toasted almonds and shaved parmesan between a salad fork and spoon. "Alex, Simon tells me you design websites."

"I do. Did one for Hard Rain Brewing. It's been a big hit. I can show it to you later. The Hollow Shells, a popular local techno band, is hiring me to build theirs, too. They raved about what I did for Hard Rain," said Alex.

"Which software system do you use?" said Sam.

"Usually WordPress. I've taken a few design classes. Mostly self-taught. It comes easily for me."

"That's kind of how I am with writing code. It's intuitive."

"Can't teach intuition." I discreetly hurried platters and bowls of food around the table. "So, Alice, how did you meet Sam?"

Sam ground pepper onto his salad. "I introduced myself at the grocery store where we both shop on Sunday mornings. Early. Before anyone else is up. I'd noticed her a few times. She has this stiff, angry walk. Like she's about to punch someone. Like she was just cut off on the interstate, or robbed. She and her cart tend to hog the organic produce section."

"I can see why you wanted to meet her," I said, passing Alex the salad.

"You've got to really check the fruit and vegetables. They always try to slip mold and bruises past you. Cover them with stickers," said Alice.

"And she's pretty adorable," said Sam, stroking the back of Alice's neck, a truth to which we all nodded, except Mother, who didn't seem to be listening. "I could tell she could handle herself - protect me in a fight if things got ugly in the meat section. Scrappy. I found the nerve to introduce myself when she went tearing off with a cart that had a bad wheel. It was thumping down the aisle, sent her swerving to the left. So I brought her a different cart and returned the broken one."

"Isn't that sweet? Who does that?" said Alice. "I flirted, told him he could cut in front of me in the line at check out. He said he'd rather I bought him breakfast. I did. Breakfast turned into lunch, lunch rolled into dinner…We've been hanging out ever since."

Alex stabbed at her salad, dislodging a crouton. It flipped onto the table then bounced to the floor. "I've got to get this dressing recipe, Laurel. It's got a nice zing," she said, bending to pick it up. She set it down on her plate. "That's way more romantic than the way *we* met. I watched your brother trip, fall into a puddle, smack his head on concrete and pass out in a construction zone."

"Oh, that is sexy. I can completely see why you wanted to date him," said Alice.

Alex puckered her lips and scrunched her eyes into an angry face that admittedly looked a lot like mine. "You should have seen him. He was out of it. And so mad. Clothes covered in mud."

We all laughed, even Mother.

"Alex talked me into seeking medical attention, waited for me to be treated, then drove me home. Who does *that*?" I said.

Mother passed the dinner rolls to Alex. "So where did you get off to last night? I woke up, around 2:00. Your car was gone. I thought maybe you couldn't sleep and went home. But in the morning, surprise. You were here."

"My car was there. I was here. Dead asleep. You must have been dreaming," said Alex. She looked squarely at Mother, chin out, shoulders back. She flipped hair behind an ear in one swift movement, maintaining eye contact.

"I wasn't dreaming." Mother's tone was menacing. "And it's not the first time I've noticed you gone in the middle of the night only to reappear by morning." Her hand bumped her knife. It flopped off her plate and landed on the table.

I sat up, straight. Mother's teeth gnashed, elongating into daggers. All I could see were the sloppiness of her movements, the redness and swelling of the soft flesh around her eyes.

"Oh, yeah, maybe I did run to the grocery. Couldn't sleep. You were out of coffee," said Alex, returning to her food.

I changed the subject. My reaction to her mood state, involuntary, biological, like the salivating of Pavlov's dog.

"Anyone ready for soup? I have minestrone, Alex's recipe, and French onion," I said, shoving my chair away from the table and my half-eaten salad. I loaded soup into bowls, talking as fast as I could to chase the hostility out of the air and fill it with something, anything else.

"Alex and I are off to Moorea, Tahiti. Day after Christmas. We plan to do some scuba diving. Alex is taking lessons. Hoping to see manta rays. I've never seen them. Lots of leopard and sting rays, never mantas."

"Alice mentioned you were headed to the South Pacific. Lucky dogs. You must be really looking forward to it," said Sam calmly, colluding with my efforts to shift the conversation and restore civility to Christmas.

"It'll be nice to escape winter. If only for a week," I said.

"It's our first vacation together," said Alex.

Mother glowered.

"The true test of a relationship," I said, rambling, mid ladle, "a week in close quarters. Before you get too jealous, I'm on a deadline, as usual." I delivered Mother's soup first, as ordered. "I'll have to work while we're there. I figure I can write on the plane and while Alex takes diving lessons." I filled and delivered bowls until everyone had one.

"What are you working on?" asked Sam.

"Ways to help T cells, and other immune cells, uncloak disguised cancer cells so that the immune system can fight the cancer," I said, sitting back down at the table with my soup.

"Wow. That's got to be making an impact. Alice told me that you and your father do similar work."

"Yes, sort of, he studies cancer from a genetic perspective. It's a different branch of research."

"Did your father influence your career path?"

"I would say so…definitely. I grew up hearing his lectures, spent a lot of time in his office and in the lab at Yale, where I am now."

"That's incredible. What an opportunity."

"I know. I always assumed I'd go to medical school. It wasn't a question." I glanced at Mother. The talk of our father didn't bode well.

Her arthritic fingers coiled around the knife on the table. She lifted it, high, and dropped it onto her plate with a clatter. She pushed away the soup. Her powdered skin, dry and papery, only highlighted the rage fomenting in her bloodshot eyes.

"Your father would be ashamed of you if he found out that you're flitting off on vacation when you have work to do. You're neglecting your work and neglecting your mother. You leave me in the hands of your plaything who disappears in the middle of the night, doing who knows what, and now, your distracted sister. I'm obviously just a burden to you. It's a good thing your father left the country. *He would be so disappointed in you both.*"

She was angry about my vacation. She liked it best when I was home. Nearby. My mother preferred my brother and me over Alice. She always did and it was obvious to everyone, especially to Alice.

Alice's neck went crimson, blotchy. "Oh, now I'm distracted? How did I get dragged into this? Some moms would say, thanks Alice, for taking a week off work to spend time with me during the holidays while your brother is away." She chugged what was left of her champagne, poured a glass of red wine from an open bottle on the table and downed it.

"How dare you speak to your mother like that?" Her hands curled into claws on either side of her plate.

"Like what?" Alice egged her on, insolence in her jaw line. She poured another glass of wine.

"With disrespect." Spit sailed out of Mother's mouth, landing somewhere near the salad.

My gaze floated inconspicuously over to Alice's. We both got up from our chairs and cleared the table, fast. Sam and Alex watched, confused, hungry. Sam took the cue, stood up, grabbed his dishes and placed them near the sink. Alex grabbed another dinner roll, slathered it in a thick layer of butter, and took a bite.

Despite the duck, yams and dressing warming in the oven, live lobsters wiggling under wet newspaper in the fridge, the Yule log and cookies festively arranged on platters, Christmas Eve dinner was over. We were leaving.

Mother reached for the bottle of wine, poured herself a glass, took a swig, and glared at me, disdain in her eyes. I picked up the pace.

Within minutes of Mother's outburst, we were putting on coats at the door. She was still at the table, topping off another glass of wine. I doused the fire. She would forget or be too drunk to tend to it later.

"Sit down and eat, you selfish brats," she slurred, slamming her fist against the table. "You've ruined dinner. You should be ashamed of yourselves. How *dare* you treat your mother this way."

We tumbled out the door, each carrying various containers of hot food and cold sweets, separated into three cars, and drove away, leaving Mother alone in the company of her favorite companion.

Reunited again at my apartment, no one said a word. I microwaved yams and dressing and scooped them into serving dishes while Alice carved the duck. We each grabbed a portion of this and that and settled down to eat in the living room.

After twenty minutes of broody silence, Sam said, "Does she always act like that?"

"Not always. She saves it up for holidays, birthdays, and company," said Alice. "She likes to let it build until I bring someone over for the first time."

"She's pretty much trashed like that every night. Or every night I stay over," said Alex. "But I've never seen her that mean."

"You're not her disappointment of a daughter."

"You can't take her personally. She's drunk. She blames everyone for everything so she doesn't have to take responsibility for her behavior. That would mean having to quit drinking. Truth is, she prefers alcohol over us," I said.

"Let's watch a movie. *Rebel without a Cause* anyone?" said Alex.

"Go for it. I'll take care of the dishes." I hid in the kitchen. I should have been writing but I couldn't focus. I applied my nervous energy to scrubbing dishes, countertops and the insides of my refrigerator.

I was organizing kitchen cabinets when the movie ended. Alex and Sam trickled off to bed.

Alice appeared in the kitchen in her pajamas. "I'm not tired yet. Come hang out with me." She heated water for tea. On her face, the glum residue of dinner.

"In a second." I straightened the last cabinet, added another bowl to the Goodwill pile, grabbed a beer and joined Alice who had returned to the living room.

I sat across from her, in the recliner, and put my feet up.

"God, she's vicious," said Alice.

"I'm amazed we can function."

"Are we functional? I can't seem to maintain a relationship. Maybe you're solid. Me? Totally screwed up."

"If your own mother doesn't love you, who will?"

"That's why I don't trust people. I fear they'll hate me as much as my mother does," said Alice. She took a sip from her mug. "Trust. Relationships. Who needs them? And, what's with dad? Leaving us alone with that woman? He hit the road and didn't look back. Bye, Bye, kids. You're on your own. Anyway, it was great to meet Alex. Stone cold hottie, that one. Freaking Amazonian goddess. Seems madly in love with you, too."

"Thanks. It's going well between us. But why do you say she's *madly* in love? Frankly, I'm surprised someone like her would be interested in a boring guy like me."

"Probably just wants you for your apartment."

"It is my most appealing feature. Let's face it. Attractive, I am not," I said, pointing to my proboscis.

"What are you talking about? You're handsome. A total catch. Honest. Hardworking. Soon to be a tenured professor at Yale."

"That's if I get tenure. And you're biased. Anyway, I like Sam. He picked right up on my failed attempt to deflect Mother. Smart. Kind. A good guy."

"I'll probably find some way to destroy it, then, for sure. I'm still in shock that you and Gen really broke up. Does dad know? He'll be furious. Probably disown you. He loves Gen way more than he loves either of us."

"I haven't had the nerve to tell him. I plan to, maybe this spring when we hike the Matterhorn." I stared into my beer and picked at the label flooded with memories of Gen at the lab, Gen skiing, Gen sitting across from me at dinner. "Gen is an incredible person."

The room went silent. Alice blinked and waited for me to continue.

"I understand why he's so fond of Gen. I am too, but you've seen us, we're not great as a couple. We compete with each other. Argue a lot." I took a drink and set the bottle down on the table. How could I describe it? "With Alex, it's so easy to talk about anything. *Other* things. Our relationship is more intellectually stimulating than what I had going with Gen, if you can believe it. She makes me feel things I've not experienced with anyone else. She accepts me. She's supportive."

"Acceptance? Support? Never heard of it." She shrugged. "Wouldn't recognize it if it were stuck to my shoe. Anyway, I get your attraction to Alex. You're not crazy. As much as I love Gen, and I do, you can't steer her away from talk of cancer and its carbohydrates. She's intense. Tightly wound. A little scary."

"Not to me, but I get what you mean. You're not alone in your opinion."

"Alex, on the other hand...charming, creative. Effervescent. She's a cool breeze, a slice of key lime pie, a dip in the ocean. But..." Her mouth held a question.

"But what? Al?"

"Hmm...trying to put my finger on it." She set down the mug and crossed her arms. "Tonight, while you were in the kitchen and we were watching the movie, Alex went on and on and on about how great you two are together. She even cried. Like, full on bawling boohoo tears. I didn't get it. They seemed...odd. Too much. But I never cry. I'm dead inside. So, probably not the best judge."

"Huh. I've never noticed anything like that. A sappy drunk?"

"Maybe. And what's with mom saying Alex left her house in the middle of the night?"

"Not sure. She reeked of metabolized alcohol this morning. So, I'm guessing she was pretty drunk last night. It's hard for me to believe anything she says."

"Ignore me. Alex is great. I'm glad you found that kind of connection. It's special. Rare bird." She stood up and grabbed her mug. "Goodnight, Simon, I'm going to bed so I can be fresh for another round of insults in the morning."

"Let's not go tomorrow. Let's stay here. Eat leftovers. You can watch movies. I'll get some work done. You know she won't even remember what she said. She'll deny it and try to make us think we're the problem for having the audacity to suggest that she'd ever act that way."

"Her denial blows my mind. Good thinking, Simon. Yes, let's skip it. Then she'll really come after me next week when you're gone. No way. If we don't go, I'll have a far worse hell to pay."

21

Christmas morning in my apartment was subdued. Alice, wordless and mopey. In an attempt to liven it up, I played old Rosemary Clooney tunes. Showered, dressed, fluffed, we all eventually straggled into the living room, cups of coffee in hand. *Come On-A My House* played in the background.

I drank the last of my coffee, went to the kitchen for a refill and retreated to my office to work on the Results section of the manuscript. Mother's accusation about Alex leaving during the night kept interrupting my concentration. I refocused on the article. It wasn't a good time to have that conversation. Too many people in the house, holiday brunch looming. I'd address it later.

I stayed out of sight. Alice said nothing, didn't stir, when morning turned into noon, the time we were expected to arrive at Mother's. Thirty minutes later, dragging our feet, we put on coats and left the apartment together.

"Alex, you drive. I want a ride in the Mercedes." Alice sprung to life, taking the steps two at a time.

"Me too," said Sam. "It's a sweet ride."

"Thanks. But it's a mess. Let's take Simon's car. The Rover is spotless, of course, and has more room."

"She's not kidding. We could get hepatitis from the inside of Alex's car. Might need a round of antibiotics," I said. Alex slugged me in the arm.

"I don't care. I'm wearing gloves. I won't touch anything. Alex, take us for a ride in your fabulous car," said Alice, jumping up and down like a three-year-old, mid tantrum.

"Ok, but not a single complaint out of you people."

"Mum's the word," said Alice, triumphant, piling into the back seat. We all brushed articles of clothing, papers, and boxes of old takeout wrappers onto the floor. The heft of some suggested they might still contain food.

"Hey Alex, why do you have a bunch of other people's mail in your back seat?" said Sam, holding up an envelope.

"I said no complaining."

"Mr. Gary Ellicott might be missing out on this special offer from Capital One."

"It's from dog sitting. I used to pick up people's mail when they were away. It's just junk mail. Needs to be recycled. Leave it alone."

We spent the ride to Mother's critiquing, out loud, the comfort of the car's leather seats, though sticky, which no one mentioned, and the 1980's quality of its radio speakers.

Mother's smile, her crisp cotton blouse, clear eyes and the scent of baking ham greeted us at the door when we arrived. Awkward and tense, we reentered the scene of last night's debacle.

The place looked nothing like we had left it. The dishes, done. Quiches, cooling. Hash browns, frying. Table, set. Beneath the scent of porcine, I caught a whiff of Pine-Sol. Last night's cruelty had been scrubbed clean by the elbow-greased guilt of morning. We were all tentative toward Mother, except Alex, who was interacting normally, unfazed, acting like nothing happened yesterday.

Mother's attempts to repair the damage with a cheerful demeanor, a clean house and food took a little of the edge off. I scanned the house for a wedge of lime, a glass, a bottle, an odor, but discerned no visible or olfactory evidence that she had been drinking that morning. I didn't light the fire. I wasn't in the mood. No one mentioned that it wasn't lit.

I popped into the kitchen and opened the fridge, planning to make another salad. The lobster had vanished. She must have disposed of them. Should have taken them with us and cooked them last night. I found a head of broccoli and sniffed it. Fresh enough.

Stretching and yawning, Stanley's tail flicked my leg. I scratched him behind the ears. He sat at my feet and watched while I sautéed the broccoli with garlic into a bright green. Mother made a pot of coffee on the adjacent counter. Everyone else collected in the living room.

"When is your flight?" she said.

"Tomorrow morning."

I couldn't look her in the eye. The small talk, her way of trying to make amends, wasn't working for me. I was still angry. I bit back the words that formed in my mouth and answered her questions without a hint of the rancor that sat in my chest.

It was an early afternoon light that streaked through the open curtains, glinting off Mother's delicately flowered place settings. Nonetheless, I felt a sickly sense of déjà vu when we sat at the table in the same chairs we occupied on Christmas Eve.

"Where do you work, Sam?" said Mother.

"I work for CyberCoders. I'm a software engineer," he said, as if he hadn't already answered the question.

"So, Laurel, how are you feeling today? You really tied one on last night. Got a little crazy at the end there," said Alex with a grin.

Sam looked down at his food. Alice froze in her chair. I flashed Alex a look and nudged her leg with my foot under the table.

"You said Simon and Alice were disappointments." Alex dished herself a slice of quiche.

Mother looked around with a helpless expression, a mask of innocence concealing pride. "I said nothing of the sort."

"Alex, how do you get a website to take credit card payments?" said Sam in his brilliance.

Distracted, Alex did not pursue the previous point and launched a soliloquy about how to create links with financial institutions. We finished the meal in peace.

For dessert, the Yule log. The creamy filling had leached into the cake. Sunken and melty, pine cones and holly leaves slipped down the sides exposing patches of unfrosted sponge.

"I kind of prefer it this way," I said.

After Sam saved brunch, we made our way into the living room to open gifts. Perhaps it was the effect of an edible meal prepared by repentant hands or that time dissipated the emotional hangover from last night, but I finally felt compelled to build a fire. The smell of burning wood, its warmth and flicker, calmed everyone.

In the past, Christmas at the Brusts involved a spectacular array of presents. It was how my parents showed love, I assumed. As we children aged and my father disappeared, the gift-giving portion, like the rest, shrunk into a simpler affair.

My anger toward Mother evolved into sadness. "Here, open this one first," I said, handing her a package.

She tore at the brown wrapping, decorated with cardinals.

"It's beautiful, Simon. Thank you," she said, unfolding from the box a full-length silk robe in watercolor combinations of blue, green and yellow. I remembered her tendency to overheat in polyester.

Stanley, who had been watching from his perch near the window, leapt to the floor, walked back and forth on the wrapping paper and rolled around in the box.

"Promise me you'll throw away that hideous maroon thing you've been wearing for the last 10 years. It's weaving itself into a pantsuit," I said, the first direct words I'd spoken to her all day.

"It's going straight into the trash," she chuckled.

I couldn't remember the last time I heard her laugh. It resonated through her entire body, shifting the way she carried herself. From a distance, I could tell when my mother was in good humor by her posture.

My sadness turned into compassion. I felt my sister soften from across the room.

Alice opened my present, a battery-operated drill and an array of drill bits, a gift to match her independence.

"Thank you?" She held up the drill. "Am I planning to remodel my kitchen?"

"You'll grow to appreciate it," I said.

I gave Sam *Blues Explosion, Orange,* and told the story of how I once had the good fortune to see them, live, at a poorly advertised, minimally attended show in a dive bar on the outside of town.

I was gifted an ice blue cashmere sweater and navy tie by Mother, bicycle lights from Alice and bicycling socks from Sam.

When the gift giving was over, Mother left the room, wearing the new robe over her clothing. The clank of the icemaker as it dropped cubes into a glass, the snap and hiss of a can opening, the pop of ice, emanated from the kitchen. Vodka tonic. I could identify her choice in beverages from another room.

Cued by kitchen sounds, I said to Alice, "I suppose we should head out." She nodded in agreement. She must have heard it too.

"Anyone for a game of hearts? Rummy? Scrabble?" Mother reappeared from the kitchen with her cocktail.

"Let's plan on games for tomorrow. You'll be even more tired of me by the end of the week if I hang around any longer today," said Alice.

"One game."

"We still have to pack." I scooped wrapping paper off the floor, compressed it into a ball and put boxes in a pile while everyone else found their coats.

She held the door open. We spilled into the cold, our breath vaporizing as we left my mother in the solitude of her dysfunction.

Back at my apartment, Alex, Alice and Sam watched movies, ate popcorn and drank wine. I holed up in my office, remaining there past midnight, unsatisfied with my progress.

When I finally came to bed, Alex was awake, reading.

"I thought you'd be asleep."

"I have something for you," said Alex, unearthing a green box with a red bow from beneath the covers.

I opened it. "A dive computer." I turned it on and scrolled the menus. "Compact. Clear display. Gas switching capabilities. It's great, thank you. Can't wait to try it. But, Alex, it's so expensive."

"You deserve the best of everything."

"I have something for you, too. Hold on." I ran down the hall and climbed the stairs to the attic where I hid Alex's gift behind the row of bicycles. It was in a large rectangular box wrapped in the same paper I used for Mother's robe.

Alex ripped off the wrapping and flung open the box.

"A wet suit. A shorty." Alex leapt out of bed, naked, and pulled it on. Snug. It fit.

"Wow. Looks amazing on you. I think you should wear it all the time."

She seduced me with one touch. Afterwards, she fell asleep while I laid awake ruminating about the manuscript, the grant, about leaving Alice alone with Mother. But mostly, I wondered about Alex's alleged disappearance.

The next morning, I hit the snooze button twice. I couldn't open my eyes. I forced myself out of bed and finished packing. It didn't take long. Alex, on the other hand, wasn't at all ready and collected items for our trip from every corner of the apartment.

At the door, I said, "Do you have your passport?"

"Shit." She ran down the hall to our bedroom.

We arrived at the airport with barely enough time to check our bags and find our gate. We fell in line for boarding. My stomach growled. Christmas quiche, my last meal, had been eaten a long time ago.

With one long flight to California and a second interminable flight across the Pacific Ocean, I considered bringing up Mother's comment to Alex. Not enough privacy. I decided to work on the manuscript instead. The right time would present itself.

Alex ordered a Bloody Mary and struck up a conversation with the person next to her in the aisle seat, a middle-aged man in a blue pinstriped suit. "You look very professional this morning," she said, heckling him. He told her about the business meeting he had in San Francisco.

I opened my laptop.

During our second flight, we had a new aisle-mate, a willowy woman with designer leather and an assortment of dangly bangles. Beyond a few short exchanges with the person in the seat directly behind her, possibly her spouse, she made it clear she did not wish to talk.

Somewhere over the Pacific, Alex fell asleep against my arm. I kissed her forehead and yawned. I needed a nap, too.

I closed my laptop and crammed the inadequate airline pillow into the crook of my neck. Was this a new pillow or had it been used by someone else? Did they wash it between customers? I was about to fall into an ergonomically disastrous sleep when pain erupted in my chest.

I couldn't breathe. Saliva burst from the corners of my mouth. I grabbed the rectangular motion sickness bag out of the seat back and held it in my clammy hands. An itchy heat crept across my scalp. In my ears, a high-pitched buzzing drowned out the engine roar. My vision narrowed into pin holes. I opened the bag. I was going to die on a plane.

I reached overhead and pushed the button. Alex stirred. Still asleep, her head rolled to the other side, away from me.

A flight attendant appeared in the aisle.

"Can I help you?"

"How far are we from the nearest airport?"

"Three hours. Honolulu. Do you need something?"

Yes, any minute now, CPR and a defibrillator, I thought. "No. Thank you. Just wondering."

"Are you alright, sir?" he said.

The chest pain diminished. I exhaled, long and slow, the trick I learned from Dr. Snellen.

"I'm fine."

"Are you sure?"

"Pretty sure." I forced a smile.

"Would you like some water?"

"Yes, please."

He walked away.

Alex's head lolled toward me. Her eyes opened.

"Are you okay?"

"Did you leave Mother's house in the middle of the night?"

"What? No. I was at her house the whole time." She stretched her arms over her head. "You can't believe anything that comes out of her mouth. She's a crazy drunk." She sat up straighter. "Maybe I did leave, to put gas in my car. I don't remember."

"You said you went to buy coffee. You said she was out of coffee."

"Yeah, probably that too. What does it matter?" She frowned at me, her eyes more blue than green in the bleak, artificial light of the plane.

"I guess I'm disappointed that you left Mother's house but didn't come home."

"Maybe I didn't want to leave her alone for very long," Alex snapped. "She was pretty drunk. She needed coffee and I needed gas. Jeez. Get off me." Alex crossed her arms and looked away, her lips an angry line.

"Okay," I whispered. Why was she so defensive? I pressed on, my voice low. "She's always drunk. It doesn't make sense to me that you would leave her house in the middle of the night and not just come home after you picked up coffee or gassed up your car. Her house isn't far from mine."

She reeled to face me. "So, let me get this straight. I'm just supposed to appear when it's convenient for you? I thought you wanted me to look after your mother. Now you're complaining because I'm not at home. There's just no pleasing you. You're always working, anyway. You barely notice if I'm home or not," she said, drawing a look from the woman sitting next to her and the same flight attendant who had checked on me earlier.

He appeared at our row with a cup and raised eyebrows. I reached for it and said an embarrassed thank you.

I sipped the ice water, cool against my throat. He disappeared back down the aisle.

"You please me in every way. I just wish you slept at home more often. I like crawling in bed and sleeping next to you even when I work late. It's the one thing I look forward to all day."

"Do you know what? You're a selfish, paranoid ingrate." Alex clamped on noise cancellation headphones. Shut out, I re-opened my laptop and returned to the manuscript.

We didn't speak for the rest of the flight. Alex slept. I had a stomach ache. I was a paranoid ingrate. I asked too much of Alex. I spent the next several hours regretting my words, regretting this trip. I should have been at home, working. I should have been keeping an eye on Mother and not inconveniencing Alice. I shouldn't have questioned Alex. I created a wedge between us.

22

After nearly twenty hours of travel, we landed on the teeny airstrip at the tiny airport at Papeete, Tahiti, Faa'a International Airport. The doors opened. Humidity pervaded the plane.

Greasy, with a film of secondhand air from the plane mixing with the balm of the tropics, we boarded the ferry for a thirty-minute cruise to Moorea. A faintly dead fish smell mixing with ocean brine burned the back of my nostrils.

The triangular peaks of our island destination, green with foliage, diminished my fatigue. We took in the surroundings from the front of the boat.

I put my arms around Alex, her body unyielding, she was still not talking to me. The wind whipped a fuzzy halo into her hair. Corkscrew curls twisted her long strands.

We made it to the hotel at dusk, checked in, and flumped across the water on a long wooden dock, trailing porter and luggage to our bungalow, the last in a row. Alex walked straight through the cabin, slid open and closed the patio door and vanished onto the deck while the porter explained bungalow quirks and amenities.

She summersaulted naked into the bay before the hotel's employee was out the door. Scrounging through my bag for a bathing suit, I followed, carefully, with a feet-first plunge.

I crawl-stroked into the lagoon, swimming further and further into deeper water, away from Alex and the dock. I kept going, slicing through the inky blackness until I was out of breath, until the light on our porch was a speck in the darkness. I stopped to rest, treading water, and admired the stars. I wanted to stay there like that. And I did, until I remembered that underwater predators hunt just after dark. I side-stroked the distance to where Alex floated on her back, buoyed by the salt water. "I'm going in," I said.

I crawled up the ladder, grabbed a striped towel from a chaise lounge and wrapped it around my waist. I opened the patio door, dropped my shorts and headed directly into a warm shower. In a few minutes, the shower door opened. Alex stepped inside.

"I didn't want to leave your mom alone for too long." She reached for a bar of soap, and lathered up my back. "I assumed you would prefer it if I stayed with your mom than come home."

"You're right. You did the right thing by going back to her house." I turned to face her, wiped water out of my eyes. "I appreciate the way you look after her. I don't tell you enough how thankful I am to have your help, to have you."

We took turns bathing each other. I shampooed and conditioned Alex's hair. We reconciled with the usual enthusiasm.

Scrubbed, famished, reunited, we clambered across the dock, holding hands, to dine al fresco at the hotel's restaurant. Alex carried a gift bag in her other hand.

"What's in the bag?"

"Surprise, for you."

"You already gave me a present."

"This one is for finishing your manuscript."

"I haven't finished it yet."

"You will soon. And it'll be published in time for your tenure application."

We sat at a table near the water, separated from the beach by a broad swath of grass. Courted by waves and candlelight, we chose lobster with salad and a bottle of champagne.

Alex handed me the bag across the table. "Open it."

I peered inside.

"A bathing suit." I held it over my empty plate. "And it's blue."

"Your favorite color. Putting on a wet bathing suit is the worst. Best to have a couple extra."

"So thoughtful. Thank you."

"There's something else."

I pulled out a CD.

"I made it. All songs that make me think of you," she said.

I scrolled the music list written in Alex's loopy scrawl. "*I'll Be Your Mirror* by the Velvet Underground. Great song. *If Not for You,* by Bob Dylan."

"Winter would have no spring."

"Couldn't hear the robin sing."

"He's such a great writer. Totally deserved that Nobel Prize for literature."

"Couldn't agree more. Maybe the new CD will keep me warm when you're at Mother's."

"I thought we were done talking about that." Alex re-filled our flutes. "Here's to moving on."

Our food arrived. I was a bleary mixture of tipsy from the champagne and punchy from lack of sleep.

"Did you know Melville's been to Moorea? Came on a whaling ship. Doing research for *Moby Dick*. I read that he stayed here for months," said Alex.

"Seems like a place a person could get a good night's rest."

"And you wanted to go to the Poconos."

We skipped dessert and went straight back across the planks. She jumped on my back. "Giddy up."

Alex fell asleep in an instant. I lay awake, unnerved by the water to and froing beneath us, sloshing and slapping against wooden beams and metal. That and the manuscript, its January 5th deadline, and its implications. I flung myself out of bed and fumbled in the dark to find the lock on the patio door. I stepped outside, surrounded by water on three sides. Insects flocked to the porch light as I dialed Roberto.

"You're the only person I know who doesn't sleep on vacation," he said. We clarified references and rehashed aspects of the results. "I'm concerned we won't be able to get through peer review in time for the fall publication."

"Me too. Terrible time to trip off to the islands." Mother was right.

"Don't feel bad. It wasn't just you. The holidays put us all behind."

But I did feel bad. I was principal researcher and in charge of the entire project. If we didn't meet deadline, it was on me.

For the rest of the night, I worked on the manuscript from my laptop at a small table in the dim light of a lamp. At 7:00, I shook Alex awake.

"Let's get breakfast before the dive shop opens."

Alex sprung out of bed and opened all of the hut's curtains, windows, and patio door, inviting the thick sea air and bright morning light.

"This *is* paradise," she said.

I watched her movements and the joy on her face. She was paradise.

After a breakfast of eggs, sausage and toast, we searched the palm-strewn hotel grounds for the dive shop. We found it on the other side of the property, on the marina. As our web search indicated, they offered a PADI Open Water course that started at 8:00.

"Sure, we've got room in today's class. No worries. Let's get you started," said Joe, the dive master, gathering papers and clipping them to a board.

He was unhurried, a hipster, wearing battered flip flops, a worn Blue Divers t-shirt, and a permanent tan. The coppery hairs on his arms glittered in the sunlight. He was unflappable and it slowed me down. Everything would be fine.

"I forgot my wetsuit. Will I need it today?" said Alex, nimbly weaving one side of her hair into a braid that began behind her ear. She pulled one of two bands off her wrist, looped it around the end of the braid, leaving a blond paintbrush at the tip and worked the other side.

"Yep, we're going in the pool. You can borrow one of ours."

"I'll go get it," I said.

I strolled back to the bungalow. She stayed behind and registered. By the time I returned, she and several others were already watching an introductory film. "Thanks," she whispered.

I imagined Alex moving between the classroom and the pool while I jockeyed back and forth between the air-conditioned bungalow and the jungle heat of the patio, scrambling, with intermittent contact with Roberto, to collaborate on the manuscript before night fell on the east coast. I FaceTimed Alice and Mother.

"Why are you calling us? You're supposed to be on vacation," Alice said. "We're doing great. Get off the machine. Hang ten. Hurl yourself off a rope swing."

She had a point and I needed a break. I wandered across the resort grounds to the dive shop to see if Alex was free for lunch. They were in the middle of learning how to attach the buoyancy control device and regulator to the tank. We waved to each other. I hung around and watched.

They jumped in the pool, about to breathe underwater for the first time. I stood out of the way, under the shade of a palm tree. Exciting moment. Alex was the first one under, completely unafraid.

I would have lunch alone. Sweat blooming through my shirt in the midday heat, I made my way to the same open-air restaurant where we ate dinner and breakfast. Seated with a view of the lagoon, I had lunch with the water.

I finished all but a few soggy fries and crossed the lawn toward the beach. I plunged bare feet into the granulated sugar of white sand and headed toward a stack of paddle boards. I found a paddle right for my height and pulled the board into the water.

Cool water splashed up and around my calves, I placed one knee, then the next, onto the board, straightened my torso and paddled out. After a few minutes, I garnered the nerve to stand.

I paddled toward the coral reef, where the turquoise of the shallows ended and the lapis blue of the deep began. Farther than it looked. A bullying wind threatened to blow me back to shore. I paddled harder.

From my height, I could see the sea floor. A yellow and white stripped fish darted away. A wall of transparent minnows changed direction. A red starfish. A turtle.

I paddled and paddled, stroke after stroke. My arms were sore and my legs, a little shaky. A bead of sweat dripped off the tip of my nose. I dropped to my knees, took off my shirt and lay down on the board, face up. I welcomed the sun. I opened my chest to the sky.

I fell asleep.

A rogue wave slopped over the board, drenching my arm and shirt. It woke me up. I quivered into a stand, turned my craft toward the beach and crossed the lagoon with the wind at my back.

I returned to my laptop for a few more hours of work. Around 5:30, I glanced out the window. Where was Alex? The lesson was scheduled to end at 4:30. Maybe they ran late. At 5:45, a text from Alex. *Hope you got a bunch of work done. I'm with my class at The Pier bar on the marina. Come over.*

23

She went without me? I left the bungalow. I walked past shops on the marina, painted in green, blue and yellow pastels. People milled the sidewalks. Fishing boats and yachts came and went in the bay.

At the end of the far pier in an open-air shack, I spied Alex's braids. She stood on a bar stool with her body in motion like she was surfing. People around her were laughing. Everyone's eyes were on Alex, the entertainer, the center of attention. They were macrophages and she had them hypnotized.

Alex waved when she saw me. "Simon! Everyone, you've got to meet Simon. He's a scientist at Yale."

I recognized several of the people from Alex's class. Most of them were crowded around her. Others sat at the bar. Alex introduced me to Henry and Harriet, a father and daughter duo from the UK, who were "calm no matter what," and Mack and Esther, "trouble-makers," a mid-50s couple from New Zealand. She informed me that Parker and Emory, two graduate students from Cal Tech, here on winter break, were "the only ones who can read the dive tables."

I was also introduced to the people in seats at the bar who just happened to be having a drink when the dive class descended, "sarcastic" Sal, "I'll kick your ass" Holly, and "your secret's safe with me" Carlos. Keb did not yet have a moniker.

"They keep calling me Gidget. Gidget goes Tahitian," said Alex.

"That's because she does pushups during breaks," said Mack.

"Doesn't surprise me," I said.

I sat down next to Alex. We all had the local beer, Hinano, and got acquainted. Joe and Vainue, the dive masters, eventually said goodbye, reminding everyone, "Don't drink too much, we're going down ten feet tomorrow."

At Joe's words, most of the class members trickled away.

"One more," said Alex.

We had another beer with Sal and Holly.

On the way home, we lingered in shop windows.

"Black pearls. Let's go in," said Alex.

We learned all about Polynesian pearls. After admiring several, unearthed from locked cases behind glass, Alex scooped up one with a green sheen strung onto a fawn-colored leather band and fastened it to her ankle. Against her tanning skin, the pearl and its tether had an earthy quality. Like Alex. I bought it.

The next morning after breakfast, Alex headed to dive class while I stayed in the bungalow and worked. I felt oppressed and agitated. Pressure built inside of me.

It was the grant.

When I finished the manuscript, I could finally focus my attention on the big grant proposal, the last remaining obstacle between me, tenure and my future at Yale.

At 1:00, I collected dive gear, including my new computer, and met the class on the beach. Oxygen tanks formed a line in the sand behind classmates listening to Joe's instructions.

It was a big day. Students would practice skills in ten feet of water on the floor of the bay, their first time in water outside of the pool and the last section of class before being certified as Open Water divers.

Emory rubbed his palms together, shifted his weight from foot to foot. Alex flashed me a grin as white as her bikini. I would participate in the skills test. It was a refresher for me. I also wanted to support Alex and to give us an opportunity to work together as dive buddies.

After what seemed an eternity, the group assembled their gear. Standing, the weight of tanks on backs, regulators in mouths, masks askew, fins in hand, looking like creatures from the black lagoon, we slogged into the water.

We practiced hand signals, buddy breathing and clearing and removing masks on the floor of the bay. Alex passed all skills on the first try.

That afternoon, still covered in ocean salt, the class met at The Pier to await certification paperwork and celebrate completion of the course.

One of Alex' classmates, Henry, was an epidemiologist. He and I got lost in medical conversations. His daughter, Harriet, had an obvious crush on Parker. When I was wrapped up in conversation with Henry, Alex, Harriet, Parker and Emory played Frisbee and volleyball on the beach.

Esther and Mack owned a vineyard on the South Island of New Zealand, Te Waipounamu. "Come visit us. Anytime. You can stay in the guesthouse."

Holly and Sal weren't in the dive class. They were regulars at the bar and befriended our group. Sailors and part-time ex-patriates, they lived between Moorea and San Diego.

At 8:00 a.m. the next day, we collected on the dock in the marina next to a boat marked Blue Divers as instructed. The bay was flat and the day not yet hot.

"Ready for a real dive, off an actual boat?" said Alex.

"Finally," said Parker, rubbing sleep out of his eyes. They must have jumped out of bed and walked straight to the dock.

Emory nodded but apprehension flitted across his face.

"You don't look so gung-ho, Emory," Alex chuckled, squinting from the glare of the sun off the water. She put a hand over her eyes to block the light.

"Sea sickness. Took Dramamine this morning. And I'm having trouble getting down. I keep floating back to the surface."

"Sounds like you need more weight," said Alex.

Joe and Vainue came down the dock with tanks piled on their shoulders. After a head count, we cruised out of the bay.

"Alex, I like your ankle bracelet. Where'd you get it?" said Esther.

"Thanks. It's from the shop on the marina, the yellow one," said Alex, pointing to the boutique. "The clerk told me that Tahitian black pearls really don't come from Tahiti. And they're not really black. They're grown not far from here, though, in a different group of French Polynesian islands, the Tuamotu and Gambier islands."

"Might have to buzz by," said Esther.

"See what you've started, Alex," said Mack.

Alex winked at Esther.

I quietly listened to the whole conversation. Everyone's eyes were on Alex. She was the glue. The social coordinator. The instigator. The one person everyone had in common.

The boat anchored outside of the bay, just beyond where I had paddled the other day. Our first dive off the boat went to 60 feet and its primary purpose was to practice descending, ascending and the three-minute safety stop at 15 to 20 feet at the end of the dive. The group fumbled with their equipment.

Sweltering in my gear, I said, "Joe, do you mind if I splash?"

Joe checked to make sure my oxygen was flowing, "Whenever you're ready." I rolled backwards off the boat and bobbed on the surface for what seemed like forever, until one after the other newly certified divers dropped into the sea.

We formed an unruly circle on the surface of the water, cleared masks and placed regulators in mouths. Together we descended into a silent, neon world.

In the days remaining, we did two daily dives off the boat. Every morning I set the alarm for 4:00 a.m. so I could work on the manuscript before the boat departed at 8:00. I was nearly finished with my portion. The research group expected a copy by New Year's Day.

I spent the first couple dives chasing Alex. "You can see more if you go slowly," I said when we were back on the boat. But she darted off to dive with Joe or Vainue, whoever was leading the dive. "They know all the best hiding places," she said.

On New Year's Eve, we swam into an area of low visibility, dark and dense with particles in the water. Alex and I fell behind, alone and weightless in the silence.

Through the blue, movement. Something big. A manta. Then another. Then a squadron, gentle, soaring overhead. Several had distended bellies. Pregnant females? Alex's fin brushed against mine. She squeezed my hand. We hung there, suspended together, until they flew away.

Back on the boat, she whispered, "that was spectacular" and shifted to sit closer to me. She hooked an arm inside mine.

"It really was." I kissed her salty temple.

Afterwards, we met at the bar, telling tales of sharks, manta rays and future plans. We were flying home in the morning.

Joe and Vainui came by and ordered beers. "Cheers to a blissed out 2017 everyone. You're all invited to a New Year's Eve bonfire on the beach at sundown," said Joe.

"We'll be there," said Alex. I nodded in agreement but knew I wouldn't stay long. I'd edit the manuscript one last time before I sent it to the group.

We dined at the hotel restaurant at three tables, pushed together. Alex, drinking a cosmopolitan, sat at the other end between Parker and Emory. She must have said something funny because they were looking at her and laughing. She placed a hand on Parker's thigh and leaned into him.

After dinner, we trickled to the beach where Joe had already lit a fire and set up a circle of chairs. Henry and I sat down and struck up a conversation about the overuse of antibiotics.

I kicked off my shoes. Heat and sand on bare toes. Alex, Parker, Emory and Harriet tripped off to throw the Frisbee in the waning light. After an hour, I walked across the sand toward Alex.

"I'm turning in. Want to take another look at the manuscript before I release it. Then I plan to pack and get some sleep. We're scheduled for the 6:00 ferry in the morning."

"Good luck." She threw me the Frisbee. I caught it. "I'm staying a little longer."

"Have fun." I threw it back.

I collected my shoes, said my Happy New Years and goodbyes to everyone at the fire. We exchanged email addresses and phone numbers and promised to reunite for another dive trip, maybe Fiji next year.

Back at the bungalow, I re-read the manuscript. Our results showed promise for a new form of immunotherapy. The data suggested that as cancer cells evolve, they stop making a certain protein released by wounded cells, hypothesized to send danger signals to immune cells. When the protein disappears, the immune system isn't warned about the cancer cells and can't see them which allows the cancer to metastasize. According to our data, when the protein was injected back into cancer cells, the immune system reactivated and attacked cancer cells.

I made a few last-minute edits and sent the manuscript off to my research group who would review it, add their portions and forward it for peer review. Good riddance. Now it was just Mother, teaching and reams of data collection between me and the grant proposal.

With the manuscript off my back, I organized and wiped dry the dive gear and camera and placed them on towels splayed across the floor. I collected wet suits, fins and boots. I pulled shirts and pants off hangers, shorts and socks out of drawers and folded them into stacks on the bed. One by one, they all went back into the luggage.

I crawled into bed, ambivalent about returning home. Part of me could have used another couple of days on the island to relax with Alex without the manuscript hanging over my head. The rest of me, the parts unnerved by the grant proposal, eagerly awaited tomorrow's departure.

In bed, I tried to read but couldn't concentrate. I closed the journal, set it on top of my luggage and peered out the window. No Alex. I dozed in fits.

At 3:12 a.m., I slid my hand across cotton sheets into a void usually occupied by Alex. Empty. Cold. I sat up in bed. In the darkness, I made out the shape of my bags near the door, zipped and ready to go.

24

An abrupt, stabbing pain squeezed my chest. I couldn't catch a breath. Beads of sweat blistered across my forehead. The room spun. I was going to throw up. I was going to die alone on an island in the South Pacific. I flipped on the bedside lamp.

My hands trembled. I picked up the receiver of the hotel phone, put it against my ear and reached for the button that would summon the front desk and an ambulance. The plastic was cool against my skin. I dropped the phone back into its cradle, remembering. Panic attack. Again. Damn it.

I swore I would schedule an appointment with Dr. Snellen the second we got home.

I ripped off the sheets, hopped into a pair of shorts and stared out the window, willing Alex to walk down the planks. I sent her a text. *Where are you?* I called and left a voicemail asking the same question but added, *I'm worried about you. Please call.* No response. Where *was* she? The chest pain subsided but my hands shook and my mind raced.

At 4:00, I threw on a sweatshirt and left the bungalow headed straight for the beach. I rubbed the tension in my jaw.

Either Alex was dead, body tied to a block of cement at the bottom of the ocean or, she abandoned me to get drunk on our last night of vacation with a bunch of people we don't really know and probably won't ever see again. My guts cramped.

Beer bottles, plastic cups and haphazardly arranged chairs littered the empty beach. The cold, charred remains of the bonfire revealed only that they had been gone for a while. I stood in the sand next to the firepit. I called and texted Alex two more times. No answer.

I cased the hotel grounds, listening for laughter, a conversation, while repeatedly calling Alex. Silence. I stopped by reception.

"The party that was on the beach earlier. Do you know where they went?" I said to a neatly manicured man in a white shirt with a green, leaf print.

"Security asked them to shut it down around 10:30. Noise complaints. I don't know where they went."

My heart pounded. I scouted the pool area and sat down on a chair. I needed a plan. I scrolled my contacts, found Henry's number and called. No answer. I hung up. Probably asleep. I dialed him again and left a message. *Henry, Simon. Sorry to bother you. Wondering if you've seen Alex in the last couple of hours. Call me when you get this message, please.*

I waited. Nothing. Then I called Mack.

"Hello?" he answered. I held my breath.

Words gushed out of me. "Mack, I'm sorry to bother you at this hour, but Alex isn't at the hotel. I can't get ahold of her. Wondering if you've seen her?" I hoped I didn't sound as alarmed as I felt.

"Simon, hi, yeah, she was still at Holly and Sal's when we left there, about an hour ago. Wild party. She was doing a line of cocaine with Harriet and Parker, last I saw. Traded her phone for it. Probably explains why you can't reach her. Anyway, that's when we decided it was time to go."

"Don't blame you. Thanks, I'll try Sal." Sold her phone for cocaine? Did it occur to her to call me first?

I consulted my list of contacts again and found Sal's number. I called. No answer. I texted. Nothing.

The night air carried a humid chill. A shiver went up my spine. Mosquitos bit at my ankles. I headed toward the bungalow. Maybe I should call Mack back, get Sal's address. Find a way over there.

Inside the room, holding my phone, I paced. And waited. And paced. And waited.

I tried Sal again. This time, he picked up.

"Sal? Simon."

Loud music and voices in the background made it difficult to decipher his words. I pressed the phone to my ear.

"Ho, Simon, get over here. You're missing out." He sounded drunk. "We're playing some seriously competitive hearts. You should see Emory. Totally passed out. Oh, no, someone grab that bong out of Emory's hands before it spills all over the floor."

"Is Alex there?"

"Yeah, she's around here, somewhere."

"Could I talk to her?"

I overheard a muffled conversation in the background. "It's Simon, looking for Alex."

"She was just here a minute ago," said someone. Maybe Holly. I couldn't be sure.

"They went skinny dipping," said Keb. "Tried to talk us all into it."

"Who went?"

"Harriet, Alex and Parker."

"Harriet's right here. Harriet. Seen Alex?"

"Yeah, we swam out to the boat. I got cold and came back in. Alex and Parker were climbing aboard the yacht when I last saw them."

More muffled sounds then Sal said to me, "I guess Alex went for a swim. I'll have her call you as soon as she comes in."

"Our flight leaves at 8:45."

"I'll remind her as soon as I see her."

"Should I come by and pick her up?"

"You're welcome to. But I can give her a ride. We drove her here."

"Just in case, can I get your address?"

He gave me his address. "It's twenty minutes by car from the hotel. Ten minutes by boat," he said. I hung up the phone. I was no longer worried. Just. Very. Angry. She's out partying with no regard for me. I was going home, with or without her.

It was nearly 5:00 a.m. We had to make the 6:00 a.m. ferry to Bora Bora, the only one before our flight.

I forced myself to function. Robotic, going through the motions, I showered and dressed with an eye on my phone. I packed Alex's belongings and left her passport and boarding pass on top of the luggage near the door.

The phone rang. Henry.

"Just got your message. Don't worry. Alex is fine. She's at Holly and Sal's. Harriet just came home from their house. Woke me up when she came in. Do you want to talk to Harriet?"

"Yes, please."

"Hi Simon," Harriet said. "Alex and Parker were still on the yacht when I left the party."

"I talked to Sal not long ago. He told me he'd give her a ride back to the hotel."

"Oh. Looked to me like Sal and Holly were getting ready for bed when I left."

I hung up with Harriet and called Sal. He didn't answer. I left a message with the flight number and departure time. "*Her passport and luggage are here at the hotel. The airlines won't let me check bags without a body.*" I texted Sal. No response. I called and texted Holly. Nothing.

At 5:45, the cab I ordered before dinner, eons ago, arrived at the lobby of the hotel. I lifted my bag into the trunk and slid into the backseat. My stomach turned.

"Do you mind if we add another stop?" I asked the cab driver.

Beyond the flat numbness of my mind, nausea crept in and the weight of a brewing depression descended, forming knots in my shoulders and tears behind my eyes.

"No problem, sir."

I recited Sal's address from a piece of hotel stationary I kept folded in my pocket. His house was beyond the ferry dock.

We pulled up to Sal's place. Quiet. The front door was open. I went in to find Emory asleep on the couch, the bong intact on the table. I walked through the house and out the back door. No yacht moored at the buoy. Back inside, I knocked and opened doors to bedrooms. No sign of Sal or Holly. Emory was the only one in the house.

A text from Sal's number, *We're on the yacht, heading to the hotel. See you in a few.* Kissy face emoji. *Alex.*

I'm at Sal's trying to find you. Headed to the ferry. Can they take you to the airport?

I climbed back into the cab and tried Sal's number again. No answer. The cab driver paused for instruction, glancing back at me in the rear-view mirror.

If I went back to the hotel, I'd definitely miss the ferry. Would Sal be willing to take us to the airport? Did the airport have a dock? Probably, but I didn't know. What if I went back to the hotel and they'd already gone? My hands trembled. My throat went dry. No, I wasn't missing the flight. I had too much to do back home.

"To the ferry dock, please."

I boarded alone. We pushed off the dock as an orange and yellow sun peeked out of the horizon. I scanned the water for a boat that might contain Alex. Nothing. I tried Sal's number again. No service.

At the airport, I shuffled through the odious requirements of travel, my stomach sick. How could she? I took a seat at the gate. Travelers trickled in. Before long, the gate area was crowded.

Flight attendants began pre-boarding first-class passengers and families with young children. Then, boarding groups 2, 3, 4 and 5. People disappeared into the plane. Still no Alex. So inconsiderate. It wasn't the first time. She went to the bar without me after lessons, too. Didn't invite me to join her until more than an hour later. She didn't even dive with me most of the time. What was she doing skinny dipping with Parker? Naked together on the yacht?

I waited. The last to board, I reluctantly surrendered to the hostile smiles of airline personnel. I climbed over the already napping passenger in the aisle seat of my row and settled in at the window, tucking my satchel into the small space at my feet. Flight attendants closed overhead bins.

I couldn't do it. I couldn't leave without Alex. I had to get off the plane. I grabbed my satchel, disturbed the sleep of my row mate, yet again, and strode toward the exit door at the front of the plane.

A flurry of movement and boisterous laughter exploded from the direction I was headed. Alex. Her tan face and mischievous smirk appeared out of nowhere. She moved rapidly through the aisles, arms raised in victory.

"I made it."

Passengers clapped. A disheveled, bleary-eyed but chipper Alex rushed toward me. She reeked of alcohol; the stench detectable from half the length of the craft.

"Holly and Sal brought me here in their yacht, in the nick of time. They were about to close the gate." She beamed. Alex and I stood in the aisle in a plane full of seated passengers, belted and ready to depart. Our every word overheard and witnessed, as if we were actors in a play.

"I was about to get off the plane and come find you," I said, relieved, for a moment, to see her. Then, my mood shifted, settling into the distinct angles and furrows of anger. "Why didn't you call?"

"I lost my phone."

"Rumor has it you traded it." We both shuffled back into our row, banging into the knees of our disenchanted seat mate.

"Didn't you get the texts? Sal and I both tried to reach you," said Alex, buckling her seat belt.

"I got one text saying you were headed to the hotel. That was only after I looked for you all over the hotel grounds, called half of our friends and took a cab to Sal's." I returned my laptop to its space under the seat. I didn't want explanations and excuses. I wanted an apology, some acknowledgement of what she had just put me through.

"People complained about the noise. It was getting cold and buggy at the beach so we moved the party to Holly and Sal's." She blinked at me. She must have seen the anger in my face. "God. What is your problem? I'm here. On time for departure." She glared and crossed her arms. "You missed a great party, by the way, thank you for asking. They have a roof deck, right on the water. You should be mad at yourself, not at me, for missing out. I met a bunch of fun locals." She lowered her voice, "Someone brought cocaine and, you know how it goes...the night got away."

I shook my head. I didn't speak. I couldn't eat the inflight "breakfast biscuits." Sick to my stomach, I sipped flavorless coffee and peered out the window, miserable, while Alex nodded off in the seat next to me, reeking of last night's consumption. The long return flight over the Pacific, gave me time to think.

25

I thought about the late invitation to the bar after her first lesson, how she left me to dive with Joe and Vainue, last night's disappearance. The selfish disregard.

Boom, the chest pain, the flushing heat, the trembling, the inability to catch a breath. I cradled my head in my hands, elbows propped up on either side of my open laptop. Concentrate on breathing. Long, slow exhales.

That's what, four, now? Why, why, why? They keep coming. And with increased frequency. What if I have one during a lecture, at a conference? I'd be the laughing stock. I'd lose all credibility. I'd lose my job.

What did Snellen say? Anxiety is the avoidance of emotion. What was I avoiding? I was pissed. No avoidance there. I felt betrayed. Right track. Keep going. Shocked she would treat me like that. Like I didn't matter. Like my mother treated me. And my father. The chest pain subsided, the sweat on my brow dried into a grimy crust. The shakiness faded.

By the end of the second flight, Alex had me convinced that my feelings were the product of petty jealousy and the rigid constraints of my pedantic character traits.

"I didn't do anything wrong except have a night out with friends. *I'm* mad at *you* for being so boring, for not joining the party. You should have been with me. It's *your* fault. You always put your work before me. None of this would have happened if you hadn't left, if you'd been at the party."

"You should have called."

"With what?" she shouted. "I didn't think I had to check in with you."

"Did it occur to you to borrow a phone and at least let me know you were safe?"

"And run up charges for them? That's rude."

"You left me alone all night to worry about you, about us missing our plane, with no regard for me. That's rude. And what's with skinny dipping with Parker? How am I supposed to feel about that?"

"You shouldn't feel anything about that. Parker and I are just friends. It's no big deal. You know I eventually show up. I always do. We're almost home. Safe and sound. Scheduled for an on-time arrival."

Maybe I *was* being controlling. I was definitely boring, stuffy, and uptight. Alex made it to the plane on time. Why couldn't I have just gone with the flow? I crumbled into self-loathing. I was a horrible person. Tedious. Unlovable.

Face down, suffocating on mud in the pit of despair, I felt Alex reach across my leg and slide her hand into mine.

"I wouldn't want to go to Tahiti, or anywhere, with anyone but you. It was a complete blast. I had an amazing time. You're my favorite dive buddy. My favorite everything," she said, leaning her head against my shoulder. "I'm sorry I put you through a night of worry. You're right. I should have called. I should have come back to the hotel earlier."

With her words, my shoulders fell, the heaviness in my chest and the sadness behind my eyes disappeared.

"You could have been kidnapped or who knows what."

"You think someone could dare to kidnap me? I can handle myself. I wasn't worried. I knew I would be here on time. Just figured you would know by now. I go with the flow. Things work out. Forgive me?"

By the time we pulled up outside of my apartment, we were reunited. All was forgiven.

Alice and the smell of garlic met us at the door. She had lasagna in the oven and the table set.

"I thought you might be hungry after such a long day," she said, holding open the door while we pulled luggage over the threshold into the apartment.

"Smells good in here. I'm starving." I hugged Alice a great big hello and thank you.

Over pasta and salad, Alex held court, avoiding all mention of our troubles from the previous night, with tales of diving lessons, manta rays, and our new friends.

"I was the best diver in class, right Simon? Barely used any oxygen. I could stay down as long as Simon and it was my first dive trip."

"Simon, was Alex really the best diver?" said Alice. She seemed annoyed.

"Took to it like a fish. Excellent buoyancy control, too. Not easy for a new diver."

"Aww. Thanks." Alex ruffled my hair. "I've got to show you something." She yanked off a short brown boot and a blue sock to reveal the pearl encircling her ankle. "Simon bought it for me."

"Someone must really like you," said Alice, her eyes resting on mine. "My week was far less pleasant. It was constant." She mimicked our mother to perfection, "*You should let your hair grow. You're so pretty when it's long. What would your father say? And, You don't make eggs the way Simon does. You forgot the jalapenos. Simon always adds jalapenos.* I'm glad you're back and I can get the hell out of here. I can't take another minute with that woman. One thing though, she's much less steady on her feet than I remembered from our last visit. She's a fall waiting to happen."

"I've always chalked it up to drunkenness. You think other forces are at work?"

"Not sure. Watch her. See what you think."

After dinner, Alex and Alice both disappeared to bed. I opened the application for the grant proposal that had been harassing me all week, all of last semester. It required far more detail than anticipated. As principal investigator, I had volumes of work to do. And it would take months to complete. I pulled together a few articles that would need to be incorporated, made a file, and then got distracted by more immediate obligations. I organized and prepared my schedule for spring semester.

Alex was up cooking the next morning, long before I registered that she had left the bed. She whipped us up a breakfast of fried eggs, hash browns and whole wheat pancakes. Standing at the door, bellies full of sugar, fat and protein, we waved goodbye to Alice.

For the remaining four days of winter break, Alex and I spent the mornings with Mother and the evenings at home, playing dominoes, watching movies and listening to music. After she went to sleep, I retreated to my office and chipped away at the grant.

"I like it when I have you all to myself," she said one evening as I shoved the tin-foiled pan of Alice's leftover lasagna into the oven. "We have 25 minutes before this is ready. Do you think you can lift me?" She threw an arm over my shoulder and hoisted herself off the ground. I caught her legs and carried her to bed.

Our relationship reset and congealed in those four days. We were back in sync. I bought her a new, top of the line, replacement phone. I felt content, sure of our relationship, sure of myself. I suffered not a single panic attack.

However, I was hounded by the fear of having another and felt a desperate need to stop them from ever happening again. I kept the promise I made to myself and set up an appointment with Dr. Snellen.

In the next session, I came clean about Alex shoving me during the blizzard and about her disappearing on our last night in Tahiti.

"What do you make of it?" said Dr. Snellen.

"I understand where she's coming from. I should have been at that party with her instead of working. But she can be insensitive. She admits it. She's usually great, though. Keeps me from being too serious. I can be very dull. We're such a good match. And our relationship is better than ever. I just need to figure out why I'm having panic attacks."

"They don't come out of nowhere. They're triggered by something. Do you have a sense of what's causing yours?"

"Fights with Alex are a definite trigger. Work pressure. Stress from taking care of Mother. I'm angry with my father. It's a combination of things."

"It's probably not a combination of things. The cause is usually more specific. You said the first one happened after the blizzard. Let's pull it apart, try to tease out the cause. Tell me everything that happened that night. Don't miss a single detail. From the start." She scooched her chair closer to mine.

Tell every detail? I didn't want to. It was embarrassing. My girlfriend pushed me down in the snow and I hurt my ankle. Me, a six-foot former athlete. Sheesh. But I had to get rid of these panic attacks. So I did what she asked. I told her the whole story of our fight. Every minuscule detail. Start to finish.

It was awful. All the feelings that I had at the time reappeared. It was as if it were happening all over again.

"What's coming up?" She leaned toward me, pen in hand.

"Anger. That's the feeling I'm avoiding. Anger."

She scrawled notes on her yellow pad. "Let it come up. Notice where it is in your body. Notice the thoughts and feelings that go with it."

"It's in my chest," I said, as rage roiled inside my ribcage and foamed up my neck. "I'm angry that she would be so cruel."

"Why *would* she be so cruel?"

"I don't know. Because she's mad at me? I did something wrong. The anger just changed into sadness."

"Why are you sad?"

"I'm sad because I failed in some way."

"If you failed, what does that mean about you?"

"That I deserve it."

"And if you deserve it, what does it mean about you?"

"That I didn't try hard enough."

"If you didn't try hard enough, what does it mean about you?"

I searched. "That I'm not enough. That I'm a failure. A worthless person."

"There it is. The distorted, generalized beliefs that underlie and fuel anxiety are some version of *the world is dangerous* or *I'm worthless.*"

"That's what's causing the panic? The belief that I'm worthless?"

"Yes and no. It's more the painful feelings that go with that belief. We spend our lives trying to avoid these feelings. When we avoid them, they can cause anxiety."

"What do I do?"

"Face your fear of not being enough. Of being a failure. Feel the feelings that go with it."

"Why? What good will it do?"

"It will help you see the truth."

We started meeting weekly.

After the session and several days without panic, amid a gratifying relationship with Alex, I returned to the lab and to the classroom with increased confidence and energy.

Spring semester was an explosion of research and academic demands combined with an unending pummeling of questions by my new residents, Drs. Patel, Wang, and Martz. Smothering any prolonged sense of joy or gratification, I also had a five-million-dollar grant to write that would make or break my career.

As part of my unwritten supervisory obligations, I served as social coordinator, introducing the residents to other students and professors. I spent many a late night out at McClanahan's, another duty that stole time from grant writing.

Alex had become a feature at the bar. A gifted conversationalist, she could hold her own with students and professors alike, unfazed by their degrees. I enjoyed watching her engage, the way she made people laugh, her insightful questions and comments.

But as soon as the music started, she was on the dance floor. Even the self-contained and repressed Hety was learning how to Cha-cha.

One February night, Alex and I climbed the stairs to our corner at McClanahan's. It was loud, crammed with students and faculty including Gen and Roberto. A good song was playing on the juke box. "I'll catch up with you later." Alex headed straight for the dance floor. Roberto was immersed in conversation at a high-top table next to one crowded with my residents and several students from my Basic Immunology class. I said my hellos, sat down at the central table, and ordered a beer, bangers and a mound of mashed potatoes.

I was quietly eating my dinner when Roberto plopped down next to me and helped himself to a bite of potato.

"Everyone's talking about you."

"Me? Why? I'm the most tedious person in the room."

"Not according to your residents. I overheard an entire conversation speculating about your love life. Do they think I don't have ears? Patel started it by asking: Who's the dance instructor with all the lean muscle and hair? Then Wang said, her name's Alex, Brust's assistant or something. There's a rumor going around that you and Alex are romantically involved. Oh, and they said that anyone who can get Hety to cut loose must have some Jedi power of mind control. They were trying to figure out how you could have landed someone like Alex."

"How generous of them." But sometimes I wondered the same thing.

Roberto laughed and took a drink of my beer.

"Hey, get your own."

"Wang came to your defense, though. She apparently has a crush on you because you're quote, broody, and because you're willing to spend time explaining things. Patel said Gen scares the bejeezus out of her. That cracked me up. And they all know that you and Gen have a past."

I finished what was left of my beer and said, "Please stop. You're starting to sound like Bradley."

"Are you sure? There's more."

I studied Genevieve, huddled with her research group at the opposite end of the table, for some recognition, some opinion, regarding me and Alex. Nothing. She seemed completely unaware. I figured she'd know that Alex and I were an item the second she saw us together. Strange. Genevieve welcomed Alex as just another regular.

The rumors were out. I had to find the nerve to tell Gen that I was *with* Alex. She should hear it from me, not from the rumor mill. Right then. That night. But I didn't want to make her feel bad or jealous or make interactions with Alex awkward. I didn't have the guts.

"Gossip is the least of my problems."

26

I had less than three months to finish the grant proposal, the last chance to secure tenure and my position at Yale.

From my seat on the bench, I sent my research group, including Roberto, another urgent email: *Please forward your equipment and personnel budgets for the National Foundation for Cancer Research grant no later than February 28th. Best, Simon.* One by one, they looked at their phones then at me. I waved. Bradley flipped me off.

Roberto read my email, took another bite of potato, and said, "Is this why you're so uptight? You'll be fine. And I'll get you my numbers by the end of the week."

The next morning, I went to the lab extra early to collect data. With forty-five minutes left before class, I ran from the lab to my office to write a draft of the introduction for the grant.

I hurried to my desk, sat down and opened the file. Tab after tab of requirements looked down their noses at me. My hands trembled. Chest pain. I couldn't breathe. I stood up and paced. Long, slow exhales. Fifteen minutes later, the panic subsided.

I returned to my desk but couldn't concentrate. I stared at the wall. I rifled through the pile of articles I planned to include as precedence and validation for my grant request. I unclenched my fists and forced myself to write something, anything. My fingers pounded out one measly paragraph. But with the effort, my thoughts coalesced. I was in the middle of transforming the words into coherent sentences when my alarm sounded. It was time to teach. At the rate I was going, I would never finish the grant on time.

After class, I had an hour before I was expected to meet my group at the lab again. I went straight to my office and re-opened the introduction. The same thing happened. Another panic attack.

From then on, every time I sat down to work on the grant, I first had to contend with panic attacks. They delayed me. Consumed me. Controlled me. They undermined my confidence. They stole what little time I had.

In March, the department traditionally threw a big party to celebrate grants awarded during the year. This year's party was important to me because Gen's research group had finally been honored with a whopping twelve-million-dollar grant. And it was my turn to host. I wanted it to be special. So, I planned to have it catered rather than the usual potluck.

The night of the party, Alex and I lit candles, lowered lights, sliced limes, and placed wine and cocktail glasses on the buffet next to silverware, plates and napkins. I checked my watch. The caterers should have arrived twenty minutes ago.

I opened a bottle of champagne, filled two flutes and handed one to Alex.

"Here's to hoping the food arrives," she said.

"I'll toast to that. Where *are* they?"

"Want to do a shot? Might take the edge off."

"That's the last thing I need right now."

Double fisting, she filled a shot glass with tequila and swallowed it before she had even finished the champagne.

The doorbell rang. "Please be the food." I ran down the stairs. The caterers. Behind them, several unfashionably early guests, including Gen. I planned to tell her that Alex and I were together, that night. The first chance I had. I couldn't let it go unspoken any longer.

She wore retro jeans and platform doc Martins and carried a huge box full of wine undoubtedly from her own cellar. Her penchant for opera and her wine collection were two of the few ways where the family money revealed itself.

I pointed at her pants and in my best Jon Spencer cadence said, "*The fabulous, most groovy, Bellbottoms.*" I took the box from her arms.

"Thanks, Sy. Another musical reference?"

"Yep."

"Who is it this time?"

"Jon Spencer Blues Explosion. You've got to hear that song. It's a classic."

"I'll get right on it."

"How did you get this box in and out of your car? It's huge and heavy."

She flexed her muscles at me. I led the parade upstairs.

The minute we all piled through the door, Alex bellowed, "*Bellbottoms. Bellbottoms,*" in the same cadence I used a few minutes ago. "Cool jeans, Gen. You're looking swank tonight."

"Alex knows the song," Gen said.

Milling guests spilled into the apartment in clusters, most going straight for the alcohol, forming obstructions between the table and the incoming food. I welcomed everyone, directed traffic and shouted directions to the caterers.

In the center of it all, Gen unfurled, one after the other, bottles of fine wine from Piedmont, Valpolicella, Loire, and Napa, placing them on the buffet table next to the wine glasses I set out. Interrupting my instructions to the caterer, mid-sentence, she held up a wine bottle.

"Sy, where's the decanter I gave you for your birthday? This Barolo needs to open up."

"I'm not sure," I said.

"Sir, where would you like the appetizers?"

"Coffee table. Maybe a tray or two on the dining table."

"I bet you've never even used it," Gen said.

"I rarely own wine worth decanting?" I returned my focus to the caterer.

"The desserts, sir. Dining table with the main course or would you rather have them on the buffet?"

"Buffet, please."

"Knowing you, it's still in the box in your pantry. Give me a minute, I'll find it," she said. Perceived over the din, through my divided attention, her words revealed a familiarity with my home, my habits. The flirtatious tone in her voice made me wince, fondness tinged with grief.

She blazed into the kitchen, opened the door to my spacious pantry, switched on the light and stepped inside like she owned the place. She must have found it. Probably on the top shelf because she opened the ladder and started climbing.

Alex stepped inside the pantry. She reached up and held the ladder for Gen. A kind gesture, I thought. Big of Alex. I hoped they would get along. The door to the pantry closed.

"Hety, could you help me with the furniture? I ran out of time to make a dance floor," I said, ducking into the living room. We lined chairs up against the wall.

We were in the middle of moving the couch when Gen stormed into the living room, sparks of rage shooting out of her eyes, out of the jerky precision in her movements.

"Gen? Are you okay?" I said, my hands full of sofa, as she blazed past me.

She didn't answer. What happened to her? We set down the couch. "Thanks, Hety. What would I do without you?"

Alex slid into the room with a full glass of wine and a drunken smirk. She paused, leaning against the wall for support then sashayed over to Hety and said, "You've got to try this Barolo."

I searched the room for Gen. She was in the far corner, near my office, with Dr.'s Patel and Wang. I took off in her direction.

"Simon. Hey, Simon," shouted Roberto from the other side of the room, over music and the murmur of conversation. "Can you come here for a minute?" He waved me over to where he was standing next to Bob and Shay.

I spun around and headed toward Roberto.

"Shay's asking about R.A. positions. With Hety graduating next spring, I thought you might have an opening," said Roberto. They were all drinking from cans of Hard Rain IPA.

"I will have an opening. The position should be posted in a few months. You might want to talk to Hety to find out more about the job and what it's like to work for me," I said.

A tap on my shoulder. Dr. Martz.

"Could you play something else? We've heard The Violent Femmes *Good Feeling* twice now. It's a great song, but you can't really dance to it."

"Promise I will. We should make announcements first. Dr. Martz, you know Roberto, I'd like you to meet Bob and Shay."

I silenced the music, returned to my spot next to Roberto, and collected myself. Roberto tapped his wine glass with a pen from his pocket. Ting, ting, ting. The room went quiet. The crowd closed in around us.

"I'd like to start by honoring my dear friend Dr. Genevieve Hale, principal investigator on the largest single grant awarded to the department this year." Gen and I maintained eye contact from across the room and the warmth of our friendship passed between us. But she still seemed miffed by whatever happened earlier. "Gen, could you come up here, please."

She pushed through the crowd and stood next to me.

"For those of you who haven't had the opportunity to spend much time with Dr. Hale, she may seem intimidating. I'm here to tell you, she's even more intimidating when you get to know her." People chuckled. Some nodded in agreement. "She's a power house of knowledge and skill. I'll ask her some obscure fact about an immune system protein and, while she's in the middle of doing five other things...I'm not even sure she's heard my question...and her brain produces a detailed and thoroughly correct answer. She's encyclopedic. We all know it. We all fear it. But we shouldn't. Because behind the might of her intelligence, her meticulous research skills, and the ferocity of her dedication to fighting cancer is a deeply genuine and compassionate person. I'm not surprised and am so pleased to announce that her group's research on the innate immune system has finally been recognized and awarded...*twelve million dollars.*"

Everyone cheered. I clapped the longest.

"Gen's group can all keep their jobs," shouted Bradley. "Might not be the case for ours, Brust. How goes that grant application?"

Gen took the floor. "I'm sure Simon is still waiting on your budget proposal, Bradley."

She announced the grants I had been awarded so far, amounting to a total of five million. She didn't mention the fact that I needed five million more to fulfill my dossier for tenure, to keep my position at Yale.

We took turns with the remaining announcements. When we were finished, most of the crowd disappeared into the kitchen to fill plates and glasses.

I seized the opportunity and pulled Gen aside. "Are you okay? You seem upset."

The anger returned to her face. "I was in the pantry earlier. Then Alex, the one who works for you..."

Patel appeared next to us with a full plate of food. "Congratulations on your grants. I'm completely intimidated by the whole process. Do you have any tips for a newbie?"

Gen glanced at me and turned her attention to Dr. Patel.

I excused myself and headed for the stereo. I scrolled through the playlist for music that might resonate with all ages. I clicked on the blues file.

Hound Dog Taylor growled, "*Yes, I'm wild about you baby, but you just won't treat me right.*" Alex shimmied to the dance floor with a full glass of wine, leading a rowdy pack of students and residents, tipsy or stoned, considering the skunky wafts coming from my bathroom. She seemed normal, wasn't acting strangely. I hoped they didn't spill wine on the Persian. She lured Bob into the fray then went for Roberto's arm, pulling him into the circle. He hated to dance. But he would, for Alex.

When the song was over, she wandered with her empty glass over to Hety, who was sitting alone with a full bottle of wine on the loveseat in the turret, facing the street.

I went back over to where Gen was explaining the ins and outs of grant writing to Dr. Patel. Before long, the other residents caught on to our discussion and had us surrounded. They pummeled us with questions.

When they finally trickled away, Gen and I were alone again.

"What were you about to say before?" I said.

"I don't even know if I want to get into it."

"Just tell me."

"I was in the pantry…"

Lucas appeared. "Hey, do you have any more forks? You're out."

"There should be a big box of them in the pantry," I said. Speaking of the pantry.

"I looked. Didn't find any."

"I'll be right back." I left to scrounge the kitchen for forks. They were in the pantry.

When I returned to the living room Gen was barreling toward the restroom. "Your students have been bogarting the bathroom. They've been smoking pot in there for the last half hour."

By the time she was out of the bathroom, I was deep into a conversation with Roberto.

"We just had another adoption fall through. That's three now. We really thought this baby was ours. An aunt appeared out of nowhere at the last minute and said she wanted to raise him."

I watched as Gen was snagged into a discussion with Bradley.

"How are you holding up?"

"Not well. Bob's a mess. I'm not sure he can take much more of this. Last night, he said he's about ready to give up."

"I don't blame him. What do *you* want?"

"I'd really like to have a baby. I want to know what it's like to raise a person. I think it would be an incredible experience."

"Then keep trying. Don't give up. Something will work out."

Gen and I moved in parallel lines for the rest of the evening. We didn't intersect again until she was at the door putting on her coat.

I excused myself from a conversation with Lucas and met her at the door.

"Leaving, already?"

"Got an early morning."

"Please take what's left of your wine."

"No, you keep it."

"I won't give it the appreciation it deserves."

I grabbed the box she came to the party with and loaded bottles back into it.

"At least keep a couple to get you through the rest of the night."

We left the apartment together. I carried a much lighter box downstairs to her Subaru. She opened the trunk and stood by while I deposited it inside.

I slammed the trunk shut and said, "What happened?"

"I'm not even sure. It was so weird."

"Weird how?"

"Remember, I went to find the decanter?"

"Yes. I saw Alex go in after you. She held the ladder."

"That's not all she did."

"What do you mean?"

"When I stepped up to the next rung, she grabbed my ankle and wouldn't let go. I couldn't move. I couldn't go up. I couldn't go down. Seemed funny at first, I guess. Must have been hilarious to her because she was laughing maniacally. She kept holding on to my ankle. It went on and on for too long. I finally yelled at her to stop. I'm not sure why but something about it really pissed me off."

It definitely wasn't the time to be telling Gen that Alex and I were a couple. "I can see why it pissed you off. But it sounds like she was just joking around. Maybe took it a little too far."

"I don't know."

"Do you want me to talk to her about it?"

"No. I've already addressed it. It's over. In fact, I'd really rather you didn't mention it to her all."

"I'm not sure I can do that."

"See, now I wish I hadn't told you. Please don't say anything to Alex. It's been handled. Go, back to your party."

I went back upstairs, puzzled about the conversation, annoyed with Alex for making Gen uncomfortable. I scouted the room. Alex was on the loveseat talking with Hety. I debated pulling her aside. But I didn't. I respected Gen's wishes.

At approximately 2:00 a.m., the last guests departed. "Thanks for a great party, Dr. Brust," said Lucas. I wandered through the apartment collecting glassware and stuffed a garbage bag with paper plates. I found Alex, asleep, still in the turret and shook her awake.

"Everyone's gone. Let's go to bed."

She sat up and yawned. A furrow appeared on her brow. She wouldn't look at me. "We should probably clear the debris first."

She seemed sullen and went about cleaning the kitchen without the usual chatter.

"What's the matter? You're so quiet," I said as I wiped the counter.

"Nothing. Tired." She wrapped cupcakes and put them in the refrigerator.

"Are you sure? You seem off."

She opened the dishwasher and filled it with silverware and glasses.

"Does Gen even know we're together?"

"I don't think so. I've been meaning to tell her but we haven't had a minute to sit down and talk."

"Don't."

"Don't what?"

"Don't tell her we're together."

"Why?"

"Because it's none of her business."

"She'll find out sooner or later."

"Fine. Let her hear it through the grapevine. I just don't want her to hear it from you."

"Why?"

"I just don't."

"I'm not sure I can do that." Why all the secrets?

"I will consider it a profound betrayal if you tell Gen about us."

27

Two days later, after a long stint at the lab, I dragged myself home late to find Alex in the kitchen in a rage, slamming cabinet doors.

"I've been waiting for you to come home for hours. I made dinner. You have no respect for my time. Why didn't you respond to my messages?"

"I was at the lab. Left the phone in my office. I didn't see your texts until I was getting ready to come home." I stepped toward her. I reached for her. She backed away from me.

"I am so sick of you working late and not letting me know when you'll be home. You were with Gen, weren't you?"

"What? No. She was at the lab, but we weren't *together*."

"If she was at the lab and you were at the lab, then you were together. I know you're still in love with her."

I wilted and leaned against the counter, physically and emotionally drained. "Alex, what's going on?"

"I heard you flirting with each other at the party, *Sy, where's the decanter I bought you*? And you, *She's a genuine person*."

"What are you talking about?" I searched for her eyes but she wouldn't look at me.

"You still want her." Tears rolled down her cheeks.

"Gen and I are just friends. You're the one I want."

"If that were true, you would call me and let me know when you'll be home. You would have more respect for my time." She glowered, crossed her arms. "You'd stop hanging out with Genevieve. She's such a snob. How were you ever with such a shallow trust funder? I want you to stay away from her."

"Okay. I'll be better about calling. I'll let you know how work's going and when I'll be home. But I have to talk to Gen. She's in my life. We work together. We're friends."

"You still have a picture of her in the hall, so don't tell me you're just friends."

"Gen and I are over. I'm going to bed. Coming?"

Alex collected an apple from the fruit bowl and hurled it across the room. It collided with the wall near the ceiling, exploding into raining bits. A browning patch of flesh stuck like spackle. I left the kitchen and retired to our room in a confused fog.

Alone, I lay awake all night, feeling guilty about my relationship with Gen and how it hurt Alex. At 3:00 a.m., I found her in Alice's room and crawled under the covers next to her.

Alex wouldn't speak to me in the morning. We ate breakfast in a silence that made my stomach ache. Firmly, consciously, I formed a resolution to prove my fidelity to Alex. I started by removing the picture of Gen that hung in the hall. I put it in the attic, behind a box of old photographs and replaced it with one of Alex and me on the dive boat in Tahiti.

The gesture seemed to bring Alex out of her funk and brightened the air between us. She was back. We were back. Back in the nest. Back to the routines of our togetherness that nurtured and sustained me through the pressures of writing the grant and the many other demands that so weighed me down.

In the weeks that followed, with the same type of precision I applied to my research, I texted or called Alex with up-to-the-minute details on my progress and expected completion times, never allowing my phone to be anywhere but my front pocket. I tapped the pocket, twice, checking for its presence throughout the day, fearing I might miss a call from Alex or forget to provide information on my location.

I became irritable and curt, a product of my desire to not spend too much time with anyone, worried it would be perceived with suspicion. I quit attending the socials at McClanahan's to avoid making Alex angry. When supervisory duties or other obligations forced me to mingle, I scrupulously veered away from Gen and made sure that none of my behavior toward her, or anyone, could be perceived as flirtatious.

I stopped the sessions with Dr. Snellen. Alex didn't seem to like me going to therapy. It put her in a mood. "What did you talk about?" she'd demand to know.

"Panic attacks."

"Did you say anything about me?"

There was no easy way to answer that question. Yes or no, either one led to a fight.

"Are you joining us for a drink?" said Roberto one evening as we left the lab together.

"Next time. Have a Smithwick's for me." I pushed the down arrow on the elevator.

"You've been keeping yourself scarce lately. Is everything alright?"

My phone buzzed. Alex. "I'm fine. Just a second. Let me answer this text…" I said, worried that any delay in answering would arouse suspicion and Alex's ire.

The elevator doors opened. We stepped inside. "Spending a lot of time on your phone these days. Who is that? Your mom again? What is she switching to bourbon?"

"Still on the vodka."

"At least she's consistent."

"It's Alex. Checking to see when I'll be home."

"Really? Why?"

"Why what?"

"Why is she checking?"

"So we can plan dinner together. Because she cares."

"If she cares, seems like she'd want you to come home when you're finished working and give you the time and space to do that."

"Bob never asks when you'll be home?"

"Not really. He trusts me. He knows that I'll come home when I've done what I need to do."

I zipped up my jacket and fixed my gaze on the numbered lights as we dropped toward the ground floor. He was insulting Alex, criticizing our relationship, and it only served to make me question him, not Alex. He barely knew her. He didn't understand us, our connection. "Lucky you," I said. We left the elevator and went our separate ways. I would never again discuss Alex with Roberto.

I came through the door of my empty apartment that night and went straight to the bathroom to check my throat. I palpated lymph nodes for signs of inflammation. The old fears of salmonella returned with a vengeance.

I took my temperature once a day, twice a day, then four times a day, checking for signs of infection, of fever. Several times a week, students interrupted my washing ritual at the bathroom sink. I'd stop immediately, wipe my hands with paper towels on the way out of the door, and go find an empty bathroom to finish in peace.

I forgot office hours and neglected the residents. I no longer lingered after class to field questions, absenting myself with the excuse, and the reality, of pressing deadlines. My answers to their texts and emails went from reliable to spotty at best. When she asked, I freely allowed Alex to read the emails. I wanted her to be sure I wasn't flirting with any of them.

Worse than the fears about germs, the panic attacks.

They came frequently and with force. Especially when I was working on the grant. But I'd also get dizzy and sweaty in the middle of class, shaky and nauseous in the middle of lab. "Excuse me, I've got to take a call," I'd say. I'd leave the room and, most often, not come back.

Hety ran interference when she could. In her eyes, I saw concern and unasked questions. I didn't offer information. Hety must have mentioned my erratic behavior to Gen because she came looking for me in the lab one April afternoon.

"Simon, got a second?" She stood right next to me. I could smell her shampoo.

The proximity made me anxious. My hands went clammy. How would I explain this to Alex? "Not right now. I'm in the middle of something." I peered into a microscope.

"It'll just take a minute."

"Sorry. Now's not a good time."

"When then?"

Gen was persistent. She would continue to pester me until I met with her.

"Alright, let me finish with this specimen."

I hoped she would walk away and forget about whatever was on her mind. Instead, she watched and waited.

When finished, I said, "What's up?"

She glanced around the room. "Let's go somewhere private."

We took the elevator to the classrooms and chose an empty one with a conference table. Gen closed the door behind us. She sat in the chair next to mine.

"Hety is worried about you. I am too. Don't be mad at her, but she told me that you've been leaving in the middle of lab, sometimes in the middle of class, that students and residents are saying that you're never around. They can't get ahold of you."

"I had a rough week. Or two. I'm fine now."

"Hety said you left class just yesterday. Don't blow me off. What's going on?"

"Mother. You know, same old Laurel." I chuckled but it came out hollow, like a cough.

She didn't laugh or even smile. She didn't believe me. I could see it in the roundness of her eyes, in the arch of her eyebrows as she stared into me.

I pulled the pen out of my pocket, clicked it open and closed a few times and said, "Thanks for your concern. Is that it, then? I've got to get back to work." I stood up and stepped toward the door.

"Sy, You're up for tenure next year. Is the grant getting to you? How's it coming? I'd be happy to help. I just...don't want you to screw that up. You deserve tenure more than any of us."

"Really, I'm good." I sat back down. I tried to sound confident so she wouldn't worry, so she would stop looking at me that way. "I have at least as many publications as anyone in the department. Four were even published in *Science.*"

"We both know publication alone won't get you tenure."

"It's the budget." I sighed and returned the pen to my pocket. "Can't seem to find the time to nail it down. When it's finished, though, I'll have just the cover letter left to write." I shifted in my seat. Heat bloomed out of my chest. Alex. How would I explain the conversation to Alex? She would know. She would see it in my face.

"The budget sucks. Takes forever. All the back and forth with human resources on personnel costs and researching equipment costs. And it has to be accurate. They can see right through bull-shit. But I don't need to tell you that. When is it due?"

"Two weeks. May 1st. I'll be an altogether different person when it's done." I stood up and walked to the door. The added physical space between us, a welcome relief. "Appreciate you checking in on me. Any power you can wield to force Bradley into getting me his numbers? Maybe threaten to make him teach Basic Immunology when I don't make tenure and Yale gives me the boot?"

"Good idea. Just might do the trick." She laughed.

I left the room and returned to the lab. She was right. I needed to get my act together.

I woke up the next morning with rivulets of dried blood in chapped cracks of flesh between fingers. I scheduled an appointment with Dr. Snellen from our bedroom, before I was even dressed. I hung up the phone and thought up lies I could tell Alex as to my whereabouts. Dentist appointment? Haircut?

I went to the kitchen, poured myself a cup of coffee. "I have a therapy appointment tomorrow, from 3:00 to 4:00."

Alex sat at the dining table, eating an egg white sandwich, dressed in her gym clothes. She made a face and took a bite. "Why not save yourself two hundred dollars and talk to me about it? I know you better than you know yourself."

"I'm afraid my particular issues require the expertise of a licensed professional."

I told Dr. Snellen about Alex's jealousy and my attempts to assuage it. I told her about the increased panic attacks and the washing, that they were consuming my time, interfering with my capacity to finish the grant proposal.

"It's getting worse."

"There's a reason."

"I hate it when Alex is unhappy with me? I'm terrified I won't get tenure?"

"If she's mad at you or you don't get tenure, what does it mean about you?"

"You sure get right to the point, don't you?"

"It is the point. What does it mean about you?"

"That I'm not enough. That I'm worthless."

Dr. Snellen leaned back in her chair. "The painful feelings that go with those thoughts are probably what's fueling your anxiety. It's the feelings you're avoiding."

"What do I do?"

"Face your fears - of not getting tenure, of Alex being angry with you. Let yourself feel the anxiety. Feel the feelings you fear. And challenge the distorted beliefs that go with them."

"How?"

"It's easier than you think. Can you feel your anxiety right now?"

"Yes. It's in my chest."

"Let it come up."

"Not this again."

"You can handle it."

So, I did. I allowed the anxiety to squeeze my chest. I allowed the dizzying heat. I allowed the awful cascade of the physiological symptoms of panic. In no time, up came the feelings of worthlessness, of not being enough, that lurked in the shadows behind my anxiety. I allowed them too. Excruciating, at first. But feeling it seemed to loosen something that had been fastened down inside of me. Beliefs I held as truths about my worth revealed themselves. Then shrunk. They weren't even true. They were lies I learned to believe when I was still a child.

"What's coming up?"

"The worthlessness."

"Let it come up."

"I am."

"Good. Stay with it. If you let yourself feel it, you'll be better able to see what's true and what's not."

"It feels terrible."

"I know. But keep practicing. Keep letting yourself think the distorted thoughts and feel the feelings that go with it. Over time, the feelings will be less intense and you'll start to see the truth. Your mistakes don't make you worthless, just human."

Tears formed behind my eyes. "But what if I don't make tenure?"

"What if you don't? You'll have to deal with it, get another job. Try again. Eventually, you'll be okay again."

"Eventually."

"After a lot of heartache. If you don't get tenure, you'll have to experience the pain of it. And it will be hard. Devastating, for a while. But you'll handle it."

"I could find another job."

"You could."

"It wouldn't be as good as my job, though. We have some of the best minds and equipment in the country if not the world. I have friends here. Mother is here."

"Who knows? It might be better. It might not. You'll work it out. You always do. You always have. I trust that you'll figure it out. You should too."

She was right. I would work it out. I had hope. I left the session with a newfound determination to challenge my distorted beliefs, to let myself feel the anxiety, and to try not to be afraid of it.

I also promised myself to do everything I could to restore the relationship with Alex back to where it was before the party, before Tahiti, before the blizzard.

I tried harder. I called or texted Alex while driving to and from work, between classes and while I was eating lunch. I texted her on the elevator and between studies at the lab. When she asked who I was with, I provided a full accounting.

I bought Alex a commercial-grade color printer and a new car stereo. I doted. I obsessed. How could I make her happy? It was the question I asked when I went to bed and the first thought I had when I woke up. The first or second. It was either Alex or the grant.

But she spent more and more nights at Mother's claiming I was always at work anyway. "By the time you get home, there's nothing left of you." We barely saw each other.

One evening, seven days before the grant was due, another text from Alex. *Hi handsome, Staying at your mother's. She's wasted. Worried she might fall.* The note came with two heart emojis and a selfie of her blowing me a kiss. Her eyes, bloodshot. Her gaze, unfocused. Mother wasn't the only one who was wasted.

After a night of miserable sleep, I left home before dawn to work on the grant. I had four entire hours to myself before I was expected to meet my group at the lab. It was the longest stretch of time I had to myself before deadline.

The minute I opened the grant file, panic attack. I thought of Dr. Snellen. She would tell me to ask myself what I feared. So, I did. I was afraid of not getting tenure. I went deeper. What would it mean about you if you didn't? And there they were. The painful feelings of failure, of worthlessness. I let them surface. I stayed with them. It worked. The panic subsided.

I wiped sweat off my brow with the sleeve of my shirt. The nausea waned. The phone rang. Mother.

"Can you pick me up a carton of milk? I'm craving pancakes," she slurred, sounding like she was still drunk after a long night of consumption.

If only pancakes were all she craved.

"Could you ask Alex to pick it up for you? My schedule is tight this week. I'm wrapping up a grant application on top of everything else."

"Alex isn't here."

"I thought she stayed with you last night?"

"No, she didn't."

She probably left for the gym before Mother was even awake.

I hung up the phone and with the grant application still open on my computer, drove to the grocery store. Stanley jumped out of the windowsill to greet me when I came inside Mother's house. She was asleep on the couch. I checked her breathing then put the milk in the fridge. Apart from a half-eaten loaf of bread, a wrinkled red pepper and a box of take-out from the nearby Thai restaurant, her refrigerator was empty. Food encrusted dishes sat in a shallow pool of cold water in the sink and across the counters.

The dishwasher was full of clean dishes. I unloaded and re-filled it with dirty ones. I checked on Mother again. Still sleeping. I drove back to the grocery store filling the cart with organic kale, oranges, grapefruits, eggs, chicken breast, and broccoli. Alex's favorites. Back at Mother's I stocked the refrigerator.

The couch creaked. Slippered feet shuffled into the kitchen.

"Can you make pancakes?" she said, stinking of alcohol, her hair, matted and twisted. She sat down at the table, Stanley by her side. They both looked at me.

"I really need to get back to work."

"We want pancakes."

I pulled the milk back out of the fridge, measured flour and the other ingredients and stirred batter. I warmed the syrup. I retrieved the butter. I delivered a plate of two round, fluffy cakes to Mother.

"How come you never visit me anymore?" she said.

"I was here a few days ago."

"No, you weren't." She smeared butter on cake until it glistened.

"Yes, I was. But I admit I didn't stay long. I've been distracted by a deadline – it's this big grant I'm working on. Without it, I won't make tenure."

"Did you remember to pick up more butter?"

No, Mother, I forgot the butter.

I drove back to campus, the entire morning gone. The time I had set aside to work on the grant, spent. On the way to the lab, I pulled out my phone. I tapped the photo Alex sent the previous night and enlarged what little was visible of the background. An arched doorway. A sliver of wood trim. It looked like Mother's house.

That night, Alex met me at the door with a big hug.

We crawled into bed together, our laptops open. She slid her foot across the sheets so that it touched my leg. She was experimenting with the font on a website she created for an indie band, Flattered by Sycophants. "Which one do you like better? This one? Or this one?"

I studied the fonts she presented. "I like them both. But this one might be more flowery, over the top, like a sycophant." I was finalizing the numbers for the personnel budget as well as I could without Bradley's figures. "How was Mother last night?"

"Laurel. The usual."

"She called me this morning. Wanted milk for pancakes."

"Typical. What did you do?"

"I bought milk and made pancakes."

"Aww. Sweet of you." She leaned over and kissed me. "I don't know why she always has to bother you. She could have just told me to pick it up. I would have been happy to make pancakes."

I lost my place in the spreadsheet debating the pros and cons of saying what was on my mind. "She said you weren't there last night."

Alex stopped typing. "Yes, I was."

"I don't understand why Mother would say you weren't there if you were."

She glared up at me.

"You believe her, don't you? A notorious drunk, over me."

"I'm just telling you what she said."

"You don't trust me."

"I didn't say that."

She threw off the blankets, closed her laptop and unplugged it from the wall.

"Alex, don't."

Naked, she walked straight out of our room and into Alice's, slamming the door shut and locking it behind her.

I jumped out of bed and rushed to Alice's door. I knocked. No response. "Alex. Talk to me." I knocked again. "I do trust you. Completely." She didn't respond.

I went back to bed, too exhausted to sleep.

I heard her leave in the morning. She didn't answer my texts all day. The next week, we hardly saw each other. She spent most nights at Mother's. When she was home, she was irritable and distant. Our fight added sorrow to my stress.

28

Wide awake at 6:00 a.m., alone in bed, I got up before the alarm and shuffled to my office with a cup of coffee to tackle emails and a stack of bills before office hours. It was April 30th. The grant was due the following day at 12:00 noon. Late applications were not accepted. Automatic denial.

I opened my email. A message from Bradly with his portion of the budget proposal attached. Finally. *Have fun,* he wrote. I found three miscalculations on the first page.

I cranked out a detailed schedule, down to thirty-minute increments, of how I would use my time for the next thirty hours. I still needed to write the cover letter, provide a list of equipment costs, and incorporate Bradley's data into the personnel budget. I planned to be on campus from 7:00 to 8:30 a.m. for office hours and cleared the rest of the day to finish writing the grant.

According to my plan, I would be done with the application by that evening, get a good night's sleep then review and edit early the next morning so it would be accurate, precise and ready to send, well before deadline.

I showered, filled my satchel with every scrap needed for the day, poured another cup of coffee headed into my home office.

Twenty-five minutes ahead of schedule, in gleeful anticipation of being free of the grant, I paid bills. Phone, rent, utilities. I tore open the last envelope in the pile, a statement for the credit card I had given Alex to use for Mother's expenses.

I read the figure at the bottom of the page: $9,739.32. My heart pounded in my throat. The last several month's totals were around $400.00, all for routine purchases like groceries, toiletries and vodka.

That itemized list contained charges from restaurants, Classic Cars Auto, AT&T, Delta airlines, Hertz car rental agency, and hotels. Airlines? Hotels? I recognized the auto shop as the one Alex preferred. Several of the hotels and restaurants were from Portland, Maine. Fraud? I'd cancel the card. The next day. I didn't have time to deal with it then.

I examined the bill more closely. One of the charges was from Mojito's in Portland. Why did that sound familiar? I scrambled to our bedroom and searched for a memory cue. On Alex's side of the dresser, a match box. On the cover, an advertisement for Mojito's bar and restaurant. How long had it been sitting there? Two weeks? A month? She had recently used the matches from the box to light the candle she gave me. Did Alex go out of town on my credit card?

The bill rustled in my hand. Pain gripped my chest. My mouth went dry. I told myself to stop, to wait. It could all be addressed the next day. But I couldn't wait. I reached for the phone and called Alex. No answer. I left a message.

"Could...you...call me, please?"

I stared at the phone for a second. I should have turned it off, ignored it, ignored everything except for the grant application. But I couldn't control myself. My legs refused to let me. I collected keys, slipped on shoes and coat and drove. Drive straight to campus, I told myself. But I didn't. I drove to the Brash Barista and Books, bill in hand, where Alex said she would be working that morning.

I threw open the door to the coffee shop and strode past shelves of books and rows of greeting cards. Camille smiled from behind the counter at the end of a long walkway. "Hello, Simon." Her eyes traveled from my mine to the paper in my hand. Her smile disappeared.

I shoved the bill into my pocket. "Hi Camille. Good to see you. Alex around?"

She tilted her head, her face a question mark. "Alex doesn't work here anymore. Quit about a month ago. Got into it with the supervisor. She didn't tell you?"

"She mentioned something," I lied. My stomach lurched. Attempting to distract Camille from my reddening face and flustered mind, I said, "I'll have a blueberry scone and double espresso, please."

I found an empty table at a far corner and sat, waiting for an order I didn't want, an order I couldn't possibly digest.

With my back against a metal chair, alone in a coffee shop, the whole truth unfolded in plain sight. It landed with a sucker punch to the gut. A feathering heat whiskered up the sides of my face.

I *knew.*

Alex was a pathological liar. And I'd been played.

I stared into space. "Simon?" Camille stood, holding pastry in one hand and caffeine in the other. She set them down in front of me.

Her presence shook me out of a daze. "I've decided to take this to go. I don't need a bag. Thanks. I hope all is well with you." I wrapped the scone in a napkin, left the espresso on the table, and stumbled out of the cafe.

Certain I was going to be sick if I took even the smallest bite, I dumped the scone into the trash and walked numbly to my car parked down the block. Once inside, I turned on the ignition, flipped off the stereo and leaned back against the headrest. My hands slid down my forehead, over my eyes and stopped over my mouth.

Why would Alex lie? Why the hotel charges? I recalled multiple dates in the last month when she claimed to be overnighting at Mother's and working at the Brash Barista the next morning. Where had she actually been?

I pulled the bill out of my pocket and read through the list of charges again. It held the answers.

The phone rang. Alex. Instant nausea. I didn't have time for the conversation. I didn't think I could handle any more stress. Not that day. I told myself not to answer. I told myself that whatever she had to say could wait until tomorrow at noon.

The phone stopped ringing. Relief.

It rang again.

I answered. "I went to the Barista this morning," I said, surprised by the calm in my voice.

"I know. Camille called and told me. I quit that job," Alex said, like it was nothing.

"For weeks you've been telling me you were going there to work."

"Yeah, I figured you would disapprove if you found out I quit."

"Why? I don't care if you quit. I want you to do what's right for you." Then it exploded out of me, "What I can't tolerate is the lying. I *do* mind you charging things, like *hotels*, for example, on my credit card without asking. Truth, Alex, what's with the hotels?"

The line went dead. Disconnected? Maybe. I called her back two more times. Not the problem. No, she had hung up on me.

I shoved the transmission into drive, steered toward the university and breathed myself through another panic attack.

I pulled into my parking slot at the Anlyan Center garage. Office hours had already started five minutes ago. My phone buzzed. A text from Alex.

Your mother fell. The paramedics just took her to the ED at Yale New Haven Hospital.

I went cold. My legs turned to jelly. *Is she ok? What happened? I'm calling you.*

I called Alex three times. Each effort went directly to voicemail. She didn't respond to the text either. Now was not the time for your belligerence, Alex. I dropped the phone into my pocket and tried to run. My mind raced but my wobbly legs struggled to get me across campus to the Emergency Department.

I finally burst through the ED doors and headed straight toward reception where I came face to face with Betsy, according to her name tag. "My mother, Laurel Brust is here. I'd like to see her, please." I flashed my Yale University identity card.

"Please have a seat while I locate her, Dr. Brust."

I couldn't sit. I stood. I paced in a circle just beyond a row of the acutely sick, many in pajamas, interminably waiting their turn to be seen. I left voice messages with Alice and Oscar, communicating what little I knew.

Alice called back immediately. "I'll wrap up with my client, go home, pack, and be on my way within the hour." No word from Oscar.

After several excruciating minutes, Betsy called my name and said, over the coffee-stained counter, "Laurel Brust has been admitted to the orthopedic surgery ward. Building A, room 503."

"Orthopedic surgery," I repeated. "Why? What did she break?"

"I'm sorry, sir. I don't have any more information. Here's a map of the campus. We're here. Her building is there."

Back outside, map in hand, panic attack dissipating, I speed-walked past building after building, until I located and entered Building A. I dashed around a corner, found a bank of elevators and stepped into one. I pressed the 5 button, breathing hard, and squeezed into a space against the wall. The elevator was packed with forlorn visitors and hospital employees in blue and green scrubs.

When the elevator hiccoughed to a stop and its shiny, metal doors opened, several of us poured into a wide, sterile corridor. "Orthopedic surgery?" I said, to no one in particular. "To the right, then go left. It's at the other end of the building," said an orderly in green.

After what seemed an eternity, I quietly entered Mother's crowded, single room to find her asleep. I stared at the pitiful sight of her, grey and helpless, covered in a thin white sheet. I checked her pulse. I searched for a blanket, finding a neatly folded tan one in the closet. I covered her frail body then walked back down the hall in search of information.

At the desk, I flagged down a nurse and flashed my Yale I.D. He informed me that she was heavily sedated, catheterized, and had broken her hip. Her injury required surgery which would be scheduled as soon as she was deemed medically stable.

"Can you tell me what happened? How did she break her hip?"

The nurse peered into the computer screen, "According to notes from the paramedics, she fell. The X-ray indicates a fractured hip. That's the only information we have. We're running some labs and should have more information for you soon."

"Thank you," I said, and headed back down the hall toward Mother's room.

I stood at the foot of her bed and tried again to reach Alex. I needed information. Was Alex with Mother when she fell? Was she drunk? How did she fall? Alex didn't answer my calls. She didn't respond to my texts. I paced back and forth, my fists in a ball.

I gave up waiting for a response from Alex and flipped open my laptop. Another week of missed office hours. And how was I going to finish the grant? I had to find a way. I would write the cover letter from the chair next to Mother's snoring and the beeping, whiffing machines to which she was attached.

Two hours later, a less than stellar draft of the cover letter written, I was gearing up to work on the budget when Alice appeared.

"You made it. That was fast," I said, glad to see her delicate frame. I scooped her up in a brotherly hug.

"Thanks for holding down the fort. Any word from our long-lost brother, Oscar?"

"Not a peep."

"Shocker," she rolled her eyes. "What happened to mom?"

Bursting at the seams, finally able to unleash the horrors of that unholy day, I flooded her with a barrage of disturbing details. I informed her that, prior to Mother's fall, I had confronted Alex about charging nearly $10,000 dollars for personal items on a credit card intended only for Mother's expenses, that Alex was with Mother when she fell and that Alex was not returning my calls.

"Not good. Do you know where she is?"

"No, but I'd like to talk to her, to get some information about the fall. I'm thinking I should run by Mother's house. Maybe Alex is still there. I'll check on things, feed Stanley and pick up clothes for mom."

"Go. I'll stay and let you know if anything changes with mom."

Twenty minutes later, I pulled into Mother's driveway. From the outside, nothing was amiss. Alex's Mercedes wasn't parked at the curb in its usual place. I opened the front door and stepped inside.

Everything was in order. I expected to find something broken. I expected a mess on the floor or another indication of where she fell, the recent presence of emergency personnel.

Nothing.

I walked toward Mother's room, scrutinizing the space. Still nothing.

I pulled a small piece of luggage off the shelf in her closet and scrounged for socks, nightgowns, and robe. I collected toothbrush, toothpaste, shampoo, conditioner, body lotion, and lip balm. Wheeling the packed bag, I headed toward the kitchen to find snacks when I remembered to feed Stanley.

I stopped. Where was Stanley? He didn't greet me at the door.

29

"Stanley. Stanley."

No sign of him.

Thump. I dropped the bag and dashed into the living room. Not under the couch, not behind the curtains. I ran back to Mother's room. He wasn't under her bed. He wasn't in the closet. He wasn't downstairs.

I bombed up the stairs, opened the door and peeked into Alice's old room. He wasn't on the bed. He wasn't under the bed.

"Stanley."

I opened the door to my bedroom. There he was, curled up, sleeping, in the middle of the floor. I walked over and scratched behind his little orange ears.

He was stiff. Cold. Rigor mortis.

Stanley was dead.

I flinched, withdrawing my hand.

The door to my room had been closed, right? I retraced my steps. I opened it. How did Stanley get inside? The doors to the upstairs rooms were usually closed. Maybe Alex put Stanley in here, out of the way, while the paramedics worked on Mother. Made sense.

But. Why was he dead?

I sat on Oscar's twin bed, the one closest to the door, and stared at Stanley. I swallowed, hard, against the lump in my throat. I blinked back tears and got to work.

From the recycling bin, I scrounged a Bianco Di Napoli Whole Peeled Tomatoes box. It was firm and large enough to transport Stanley to the vet for cremation. Mother would want it that way.

Stanley was her favorite in a lifetime of pet cats. I lined the box with a blanket, lifted his weightless body into the box and covered him with another blanket. I carried him out to the car, and placed him carefully in the hatchback.

I went back into the house to finish packing for Mother's hospital stay. While my body was busy with these tasks and my mind made plans to drop off Stanley's remains, a pit formed in my gut. I had to talk to Alex.

I jumped in the car and fled to my apartment.

Speeding, I raced past the university on side streets while Stanley's boxed body and Mother's luggage slid, in balletic unison, colliding with each other and the walls of my car as I careened around corners.

I arrived at my street, screeched to a halt in front of my home, and parked haphazardly. Breathing hard, I glanced around in search of Alex's car. It was nowhere to be seen.

I ran across the lawn and leapt up the flights of stairs, two and three steps at a time. Trembling, I stood at the portico of my home and fumbled for the key. My shaky hands struggled to fit it into its slot. Finally unlocked, I pushed the door open.

My apartment was trashed.

Entering gingerly, I heard the crunch of grainy bits beneath my step. Years of studiously collated, highlighted and tagged research articles, once in meticulously and systematically organized stacks in my office, were flung across the living room. I took a few more steps inside realizing, in agony, that the material under foot, splayed across the entrance of my home, were pieces of the shattered Venus of Willendorf statue.

The enormous ficus had been pulled, with what must have been enormous effort, from its home in the turret into the center of the room and upended onto the Persian rug. Its metal stand left a ten-foot-long gash in the hardwood floor. The doors to both balconies gaped as a cold wind scuttled the papers.

I poked my head into my office. The desk and shelves were bare, drawers empty. The sculpture of Alex, missing. White papers and beige file folders carpeted the floor. Pens, pencils and multicolored thumb drives were scattered across them like confetti.

I ran down the hall, stopping to scan dining room and kitchen. The butcher block was empty. She had taken all my knives. Alice's room appeared untouched. In our bedroom, drawers and closets stood open. Alex's clothing, gone. The spaces I had made for it, empty.

Back in the living room, I closed the balcony doors and sat down in the center of the sofa, surrounded by a mayhem constructed of my most cherished material possessions. A thick, constricting depression wrapped itself around me like a straitjacket. I couldn't move.

For the longest time, I sat, immovable. My despair hypnosis was temporarily interrupted by chimes, an incoming call from Alice. I accepted the call without speaking.

"Simon? Are you Okay? Did you find Alex?" I barely registered the sounds that came across our wireless connection.

"No," was the only word I could force from my throat.

"You sound strange. What's wrong?"

"Everything," I said, flatly, and hung up. I turned off my phone and resumed torpor, barely breathing.

Ninety minutes later, the need to urinate forced me to surface from the catatonia. Cramped and stiff from sitting in one position for so long, I hobbled across the debris-strewn room, like an old man, just out of bed in the morning.

I relieved myself, washed my face and trekked back across the ruined summary of my life. I opened the door and left the apartment without a single move to tidy.

I drove Stanley's body to his veterinarian's office.

When I opened the door to the clinic carrying a box, both receptionists stopped what they were doing.

"Oh no," one of them said.

"Yeah. This is Stanley Brust. He might have been murdered." I swallowed against the persistent lump. "I'd like the vet to determine cause of death." From a medical standpoint, I could have done the examination myself. But I didn't. I couldn't bear the thought.

"Yes. Of course. I knew Stan. He was so sweet. Here's some tea," the other receptionist said, taking the box from my arms, handing me a steaming mug. "Have a seat while we get some paperwork going. We'll need a couple of signatures."

"Do you want a full autopsy?"

"No. Just an exam. And I'd like to have him cremated."

"Of course. We'll take care of everything."

The kindness of the receptionists and the warmth of the tea thawed my frozen mind enough so that I turned my phone back on and, paperwork completed, drove back to the hospital.

I parked in the lot at Mother's building and sent Hety a text while walking to the building. *My mother is in the hospital. I won't be in today. Please let everyone know.*

My phone rang. Hety. I let it go to voicemail. She left a message. I listened to it on the elevator.

"*Sorry to hear about your mom. I hope she'll be alright.*" Pause. "*There's something...I want to run by you. Please call when you have a chance.*"

What now? An issue with a student? Someone complaining about a grade? The never-ending saga of broken equipment at the lab? I switched my phone to silent and walked down the hall to Mother's room.

She was still sleeping. Lines of worry creased Alice's forehead as she shifted to one side of the oversized chair/undersized loveseat to make room for me. I opened a bag of almonds with sea salt, pilfered from Mother's kitchen, and poured several into her open hand. I tossed a couple into my mouth.

"How's it going? Any communication?"

"Nope. She's been out this whole time."

"Any word from the surgeon?"

"Yep. Dr. Russo thinks she'll be ready for surgery tomorrow morning. She's recommending a full hip replacement."

Mother shifted under the tan blanket. She rolled over and slowly, slowly pushed through her medicated haze. "Simon? Alice?"

We greeted her with sunny explanations of her whereabouts, her diagnosis, and her impending surgery. Despite our best efforts to calm and soothe her, perfected by years of practice, Mother had a sour disposition.

Alcohol withdrawal. I chastised myself for failing to inform the nurse at the desk that delirium tremens in room 503, Building A, was a strong possibility.

Sooner than I knew it was appropriate, I asked the medicated, alcohol-deprived brain of my mother one of the many questions that were shrieking from my amygdala, cramping my guts, and running amok in my frontal lobes, "What happened?"

Befuddled, my sober-and-not-happy-about-it Mother appeared to search her memory. The sincerity of her efforts made obvious in the way her watery, jaundiced eyes darted from one crusty corner to the next, the way she ever so slightly tilted her head, and in the pursing and expanding of her eyebrows.

"Mom, how did you fall?" said Alice.

"Were you alone?"

"Was Alex with you?"

"Are you in any pain?"

"Mom?"

She fell back to sleep.

Alice looked at me, seeming to comprehend the distress that the unanswered questions and the somnolence inflicted upon my already fragile state. She waited, without a word, until I was ready to talk.

"Let's go find the infamous hospital cafeteria," I said. I wasn't hungry, but I needed to walk. I needed air. "On second thought, let's get out of the meatloaf and Clorox flavored air of the hospital. Let's go to McClanahan's."

On the way to a fresher and homier environment, we stopped by the nurse's station to inform the staff of Mother's brief and irritable foray into consciousness. We also exposed her long-term, unsavory love affair with booze.

But our disclosure wasn't necessary. Her blood work had already ratted her out. She had a morning blood alcohol level of .141, well beyond the legal limit of .08, and elevated liver enzymes. They were fortifying her with B12, thiamine and fluids through the hanging bags of yellow liquid attached to her vein.

I walked away from the unit plagued with guilt for disclosing a truth I had long been taught to minimize and conceal.

30

The doors to Building A slid open. A grassy blast of spring hit me in the face, unsullied by the wheezing exhales of the ailing, their excrement, and their unfortunate diets.

As we walked to the pub, I spilled the untold, offensive facts of my day. For the next two hours I talked and talked. I didn't eat my food. I couldn't drink my beer. I told her everything. Alice was the perfect receptacle, empathic without judgement, interruption or question.

Due to the sisterly psychotherapy, I began to feel restored enough to function on some fundamental level. Clinging to the bottom rung of Maslow's Hierarchy of Needs, far from Self-Actualization, I scarfed cold food and warm beer.

Sated. Silent. Alice's arm hooked around mine, we returned to the hospital and our broken, sleeping Mother. I considered encouraging Alice to sleep at my apartment but I didn't want her to stay alone until I changed the locks. Anyway, I doubted she would agree to leave. We both stayed the night in Mother's room, leaning to either side of the faux love seat, not sleeping.

In the semi-darkened, beeping, shuffling night, my grief-warped mind finished the personnel budget and started the equipment budget.

I also made plans. I decided to finish the grant and my academic duties, settle Mother and Alice, and then leave town, alone.

I would cancel backpacking plans with Father. I couldn't be with him and process the gloomy crevices of my mind. I didn't know him well enough to disclose the details of my love affair with Alex and her blindsiding betrayals. I would be terrible and preoccupied company. He wouldn't understand. And he wouldn't want to hear about it.

I canceled my flight to Geneva and booked one to Denver. I would call my father and apologize. He'd be just as content to hike the Matterhorn without me.

When it was still black outside, we were all awake, including Mother.

"How are you holding up, Mom?" said Alice.

"I'm fine. In good hands," she said. Her tone was calm but she had fear in her eyes.

Maybe she was trying to sound optimistic to shield us from her fear. What a nurturing and unfamiliar gesture, I thought.

The next couple of hours flew by with visits from doctors and nurses, preparing her for surgery, checking her vitals. I didn't ask the questions burning in my throat. We didn't disclose the grim truth about Stanley.

"See you on the flip side," I said, at 7:55 a.m., when they wheeled her away, down the hall.

"I'll make your favorites, crab cakes and potatoes au gratin, when we get home," said Alice, waving goodbye.

She smiled from the gurney and waved back at us.

Back on the love seat, Alice opened a book and I opened my computer to work on the grant. It was due at noon. I had less than four hours to finish what would normally take at least eight.

My phone buzzed. A text from Hety.

Sorry to bother you. Could you call me?

I was such a jerk. I forgot Hety. I set my laptop down and ducked into the hall to return her call.

"Hi. What's up?" I said.

"How's your mom?"

"They just wheeled her away for surgery. Full hip replacement. She's in good spirits."

"Wow. Please wish her a full and speedy recovery from me."

"I will. So what can I do for you?"

"The reason I'm calling.... Alex showed up at my house yesterday. Asked if she could stay with me for a while. Said you two had a fight and you kicked her out. She told me not to tell you but I wanted you to know. I didn't want it to cause problems between us."

My stomach lurched.

"I appreciate you telling me. I didn't kick her out. That's another lie. Hety, I wouldn't...She's..."

"We're friends."

"She just looks like a friend. I've seen some disturbing behavior from her."

"I'm not worried."

"Well, I am. Might not want to let her get too comfortable."

"She's pretty comfortable already."

"I can come by if you need me."

"No. I'll handle it. Just take good care of your mother."

By the time we hung up, I was in the throes of another panic attack. The audacity. Alex had no shame. I paced the halls of Mother's wing. I had to pull myself together. I had to finish that grant.

I returned to Mother's room, sat down on the loveseat and went back to the laptop.

"Holy shit. What happened to you?" said Alice.

"Alex."

"What did she do now?"

"She moved in with Hety."

"No way. Hello, boundaries?"

"Apparently, hers are made of stick figures and matches."

For the next three hours, I forced myself to focus through symptoms of panic and rage. I finished a haphazard guesstimation of equipment costs and a less than mediocre cover letter. My stomach queasy, I pressed the send button at 11:57, just under the deadline. It was the shoddiest, most incomplete, most important grant application I'd ever written.

"Congratulations!" said Alice.

"Then why do I feel like throwing up?"

"You'll be fine. I'm sure you get every grant you write."

"No, I don't, actually."

My sister caught me up the on details of her life. All the while, I tried not to think about Alex, about what would happen to me if the grant was denied, where else I might find such gratifying work, and how much I would miss my colleagues.

"So, I was thinking, I might ask Sam if he's game for an open relationship."

"Why? Why would you do that?"

"I met someone else. Very cute and sexy," she said, buttering two halves of a chocolate muffin taken from Mother's accidental breakfast tray.

"Too much information," I said, shaking my head. "I have nothing against consenting, open relationships. But what do you have against Sam? Smart, good sense of humor, motivated, able to tolerate and even *distract* Mother when the conversation goes south. That one, alone, makes him a keeper in my mind. And he listens to The Rolling Stones and David Bowie."

She extended me half of the muffin. "Yeah, I know. He's a good guy."

"No thanks." I couldn't eat. "You're just floating around, trying not to be vulnerable, meeting bits of need through a bunch of different people. You feel safer spreading yourself thin, like the dog in Seligman's learned helplessness experiments, to avoid pain. But, the way out, the open gate, is to face your fear of abandonment. You have father issues."

"No, Dr. Freud, I have brother issues. Okay. I'm sure I'll regret this question, but what is learned helplessness?"

"Never mind. Something I studied during my psychiatric clerkship. Seligman did some interesting research in the late 60's, explaining why people give up, stop trying. It'd be considered unethical by today's standards. Anyway, you're just afraid Sam will leave you, so you try not to get too attached. You think that if you have other irons in the fire, it won't hurt so much if he leaves. Not true. It'll still hurt."

"Thanks for the dire prediction." She bit into the muffin. "That's not all of it. One person can't meet all of your needs."

"True. But you're avoiding the underlying issue. What if they do leave? What does it mean about you? What about dad leaving? What did *that* mean about you? The thing you really fear is that they left because you're not worth staying for. You avoid those feelings. If you dealt with them, who knows what dating would look like for you."

"Oh, god, stop." She wiped her face with a napkin. "I see your point. You think I should hang in there and see where it goes with me and Sam." She paused. "I might. I might not. But I'll think about it. Promise. So what deep dark fears are you harboring about why Alex screwed you over the way she did?"

"Same."

She laughed. "How did you get to be so enlightened?"

"Months of therapy."

"Really? I didn't know."

"It's not the sort of thing I'll advertise."

Dr. Russo flew into the room, her white coat flapping like a superhero's cape. "Ms. Brust's surgery went very well. If all goes as anticipated, she'll start walking later today, be discharged in one to two days, and undergo physical therapy for the next six to eight weeks. She'll be back in her room soon. You can expect her to be groggy and in and out of sleep for the next few hours." She left as heroically as she arrived.

"Good thing we didn't have any questions," said Alice.

I stood up and kissed the top of her silvery head. "I'm going to run some errands. I'll be back in a few hours. You okay staying here without me?"

"Of course. Get out of here." She stood and gave me a hug. "I've been hoping you would leave so I can binge watch *The Good Place.*"

I left the hospital to clean the apartment, shower, change the locks, and run by the office. Emotionless, I swept up the remains of the Venus of Willendorf, collected the academic papers and placed them in one chafingly unorganized stack on top of the desk in my office. I returned files to drawers and placed books and artifacts back on shelves.

Probably dead, another casualty, I returned the ficus and its ball of exposed roots to an upright position and returned it to the turret. I swept up the burial mound of soil it left behind, in the middle of my father's rug, vacuumed floors with a compulsive thoroughness, and scrubbed clean the entire apartment. Sheets, clothes, and towels were all washed with overflowing cups of detergent.

I scheduled the repair of the long beige gash carved into the floor by the plant stand. It matched the wound Alex left on my soul. I couldn't look at it. I ran to the attic, shook the dust out of mismatched rugs and covered it.

Standing in my sterilized living room, I pulled the phone out of my pocket and scrolled for Alex's number. I stared at it for a minute then put the phone back in my pocket. Seconds later, I took it out of my pocket again and called Alex. No answer. I didn't leave a message.

I called Dr. Snellen to see if she could fit me in before I left town.

Around dinner time, I strolled into Mother's room with a bucket of KFC, mashed potatoes and coleslaw. Mother was alert, sitting up in her watercolor robe, bolstered by pillows, chatting with Alice. She had just returned from her first walk on her new hip and appeared more refreshed than Alice, who had dark circles under her eyes. Her clothes were rumpled and her hair stuck to her head. I piled food onto three paper plates and handed one to Mother.

"Did you run by and feed Stanley or is Alex taking care of things?" she said.

Alice and I exchanged glances. "I'm so sorry, Mother, Stanley's gone. I found him dead in my old room. His body is at the vet's for cremation," I said.

Tears shimmered in her eyes, then in my sister's eyes. I wiped up the glob of mashed potato that had fallen onto Mother's tray and bit the inside of my lip, unwilling to tap into my anguish. It wasn't time.

She didn't ask about the details. I distracted her with news from the vet that Stanley's ashes would be available for pick up in a few days. The remainder of the evening was somber. Mother drifted in and out of sleep. I tended to as many responsibilities as possible from the screen of my laptop. Alice left, newly minted keys to my apartment in hand, to spend a much-needed evening and overnight alone in my apartment.

"If Alex comes by, don't answer the door and call the police," I whispered, so Mother wouldn't hear.

"Roger that."

I stayed overnight next to Mother. From my partially upright position on the ill-conceived loveseat/chair, I kept an eye on her vitals. She appeared to sleep soundly. Numb, awake most of the night, I analyzed, I organized, I compartmentalized everything that had happened over the last couple of days.

Shortly after dawn, lips cracked and crusted with dehydrated drool and last night's mashed potato, Mother rolled over in bed, facing me. She tried to speak.

"You alright?"

Trapped in the desert of her throat, words failed to escape.

I grabbed the hospital cup on her food tray, filled it with water and helped her sit up enough to take a drink. When we both settled back down, she stretched toward me again, eyes wide, and croaked, "Alex."

"Alex, what?"

She coughed. I raised the head of her bed and repositioned her pillows. I helped her take another sip of water. She leaned back against the pillows and rested. Then her lips moved.

"Alex tripped me."

31

Heat stung my ears and the sickly feeling that had been lurking in my guts returned with authority. "On purpose?"

She shook her head and whispered, "I don't know."

She coughed again and stared at the ceiling. I was glad she didn't witness the sweat erupt across my forehead or the look of horror in my eyes. She took a long drink of water on her own. She set the cup down on her tray. She inhaled. She exhaled.

"We were in the kitchen. I was reading the newspaper. Alex got a few calls. She stepped into the hallway so I couldn't overhear. Seemed upset." She coughed, and cleared her throat. "She was making me toast for breakfast. I told her I wasn't hungry. I didn't eat it. That seemed to really make her mad. I finished my coffee and got up to go take a shower. At the same time, Alex took the toast from the table. That's when it seems like I might have felt her foot under my foot. I don't remember much after that until the paramedics put me in the ambulance."

I listened while images of the event played in my head. I was the one on the other end of the line with Alex that morning. I was the one who upset Alex. It was my fault.

"That's horrible. I thought you two were getting along."

"We do get along. I thought we did," she said, her voice gaining strength.

"We should call the police."

She looked confused. And sad. "I can't believe Alex would trip me."

"I can't either." She betrayed Mother, too. "Where was Stanley when this happened?"

"He was sitting on the floor next to me. Maybe I fell on him. Oh, no. Do you think I hurt Stanley?" she said, as a group of doctors, residents, and nurses filed into the room for morning rounds.

I wiped dried sweat off my brow with a scratchy hospital tissue and tried to look professional. I tried to listen to their assessments of my mother and her hip. I tried to ask the right questions. But all I could think was that it seemed unlikely that Mother fell on Stanley. He'd run out of the way. Maybe the paramedics or their equipment got Stanley. Even if she did fall on him or if they somehow hurt him, how'd he get upstairs, curled up like that? With the door closed behind him.

The rest of Mother's day was spent eating, napping, and walking on the new hip. She improved rapidly and was discharged on schedule. I settled Alice and Mother into her house the next morning.

I brought hot green tea, the remote and another pillow to where she rested on the couch.

She grabbed my arm and said, "I don't want the police involved."

"Okay. It's completely up to you. If you change your mind, let me know. Get some rest. I'll be by tomorrow." I patted her crooked, hand, feeling more warmly toward her than I could remember feeling in a long time. "I'll pick up groceries. Let me know if you need anything special."

I left her house and drove to my appointment with Dr. Snellen. I needed that session. I stood in her waiting room, shifting from one foot to the other, too edgy to sit. At 11:02, her office door swung open. She popped out, took one look at me and hurried me inside.

"What happened?" she said, foregoing the usual pleasantries as we both took our seats.

I told her everything. Righteous indignation, rage, banished from consciousness for the better part of a week, exploded from the cracks in my armor. I listed each betrayal in chronological order.

I covered my face with my hands and shook my head. "I'm such an idiot. A fool."

"We all get fooled. You saw the signs. Your panic attacks tried to show you what your mind didn't want to see. You had doubts. You ignored them. That's the recipe for anxiety."

"We just clicked. That's a big part of why it's so confusing. It felt right."

"The click. It's the first sign of trouble."

"I thought it was the first sign of a soul mate."

"It can be. Based in my experience, though, that click is the sound of pathologies colliding. Like when a selfless person meets a selfish person, click, perfect match. Perfect maybe, but not in a healthy way."

"There were so many red flags. I blew them all off. Why would I do that to myself?"

"Why would you? For legitimate reasons that probably run deep, Simon. You were vulnerable."

"Vulnerable how?"

"Concussion for one. Your demanding schedule. Alcohol will do it, too. They all disconnected you from your feelings. Most importantly, it's the emotional experiences from your childhood, your unmet needs that made you vulnerable to Alex."

I listened. *Unmet needs.*

"As small children, we have basic emotional needs. We need to feel heard, accepted, validated. If those needs aren't met when we're young, some will spend their entire adult life trying to find someone who will meet them. It can lead to a repetition compulsion where we choose the same type of people and have the same kind of unsatisfactory relationships, over and over again."

"Repetition compulsion."

"It's unconscious. Trying to get others to meet our unmet needs can lead to unhealthy choices in friends and romantic partners. If we didn't get those basic needs met as children, unfortunately, we have to figure out how to meet them ourselves as adults. No one can do it for us."

"Okay."

"Over time, if we work hard on it, we can free ourselves from the needs that drive poor choices."

"How do I work on it?"

"Start by identifying the needs. Bring them into consciousness. You'll have fewer blind spots in relationships when you do. Then, meet them yourself. Stop looking outside yourself for it. It's not out there. Other people might meet them now and then. But the opportunity to have those needs met by someone else during the critical time period has passed by the time we're adults."

"What are my unmet needs?"

"Think about it. On a deep level, what did you get out of being with Alex? What made you stay?"

"I will think about it."

I left her office less angry, leaving space for more complicated feelings to emerge. And I finally felt hungry. I hadn't eaten all day.

I drove home, threw keys and satchel on the floor and walked directly into the kitchen. I opened the fridge, fished around a tall carton of half-and-half and bottles of water for the glass container with a blue lid preserving left-over steak and baked potato. Nothing. I checked all the refrigerator shelves and the cold-cuts drawer. Still nothing. Strange. I could have sworn I put it in there. Maybe I left it at work.

I cracked open a fresh jar of peanut butter and plunked two pieces of multigrain bread into the toaster. Seconds later, toast sprang from its slats, crisp and golden. I slathered each piece with yellow butter and brown peanut butter, combining the two into greasy waves. I carried dinner into my office and ate in front of the computer.

For the next five days, with discipline, detached persistence, and minimal sleep, I finished grading and prepared a new set of data for analysis at the lab. Every evening, I visited Mother and Alice.

I kept to myself, sure the entire department had by now heard about the messy end to my relationship with Alex. I assumed Hety was being discreet. But the gossip would get out the minute people showed up at her house for the next party. I reminded myself to check in with her the next time I saw her.

At the end of the week, our research group met in the department lounge for breakfast. Summer break had officially started and I was on vacation for the next two weeks. The room was loud, full of mingling students and professors including Roberto, Bradley, Gen, and my residents. I kept an eye out for Hety but she wasn't around.

I was the last in line at the buffet, putting together a burrito with scrambled eggs, potatoes, and pico de gallo when Bradley sidled up behind me. He grabbed a plate.

"Let me know when I can move into your office," he said.

"If I don't get this grant, there's a good chance that neither of us will have an office. And you won't be able to charge the university for your suite at the Edinburgh conference, either."

"I'll survive. You, not so much."

Roberto appeared between us, picked up a napkin and said, "If he doesn't get this grant, Bradley, I'll blame you."

"Won't be my fault."

"I'll still blame you."

Roberto steered me toward a small table, away from Bradley. We sat down across from each other. We hadn't spent any meaningful time together in months.

"You showed up just in time. I was about to dunk his face into the sour cream."

"That's what friends are for."

I stared down at the burrito on my plate. I had been harboring an unjust anger toward him since that day on the elevator when I felt like he was criticizing Alex and our relationship. I had been avoiding him.

"You're a good friend," I said.

"Fill me in. What's been going on with you these days?"

I told him about Mother's fall, her surgery and current status.

"Sounds like she's on her way to a full recovery. And how are things with the naturist?"

"Turns out you were right. I guess I couldn't see the difference between being cared for and being controlled. We broke up." I kept the ugliest details to myself.

"I'm sorry to hear that. How are you doing?"

"I don't know. Fine. Haven't had time to deal with it, yet. Hey, what's happening with the adoption process?"

"Don't tell anyone yet," he leaned across the table, "but I think we're getting a baby. The mother is smart, delightful, due in two months. She's a freshman at the University of Connecticut. Philosophy major. How perfect is that? And the biological father, also a student, is out of the picture. Gave up his paternity rights. We don't anticipate any trouble from his side of the family."

"Best news I've heard in a long time. I'm happy for you. I'm sure Bob is ecstatic."

"He's already working on announcements. I'm building a bassinet."

"Lucky kid. You'll make great parents. Maybe I'll even babysit, sometimes."

"I can't picture it."

"I might. When they're twelve."

"Yep, you're going to be a big help."

"Uncle Simon."

My phone buzzed through the pocket of my sport coat. I pulled it out and looked.

Roberto rolled his eyes. "What does your mother need this time?"

"It's not her." I returned the phone to my pocket.

"What? Why is your face turning red?"

"It's an email from the National Foundation for Cancer Research. It's about the grant."

"Open it."

"No. I think I'll wait until I'm alone so no one sees me cry." I stood up to leave.

"C'mon. Just open it. You'll be fine. And I have a Kleenex."

I pulled the phone out again and sat back down. I stared at it.

"No. I really think it would be wise to wait until I'm in a place with no sharp knives."

"The knives in the lounge are all plastic. Open it."

I held the phone in my hand and looked around. Most of the students and professors had already eaten breakfast and left the lounge. Gen and her research group sat at a table on the far side of the room. They were all preoccupied with the screens on their laptops.

I opened it.

32

We regret to inform you that your grant application has been denied.

I read and reread.

"What does it say?" Roberto said.

"Denied."

"What?"

"I didn't get it."

"No way. That's impossible. Give me that phone."

I handed it over. "Pretty concisely worded rejection from the National Foundation for Cancer Research."

He read the email, shaking his head in disbelief. "Apply for others. There's got to be some options before your tenure dossier is due in the fall." He slid the phone across the table to me, face down. I returned it to my pocket.

"I've checked everywhere. It's the last cancer-specific grant offered this year. Well, there are a couple others but together they add up to less than two million. I need five million. I'll apply. But even if I get them, it won't total the ten million I need for tenure. It's over. I'm over. I'm not going to make tenure."

"That's insane. You've published as much as anyone in the department. Your work has led to more successful immunotherapies than anyone else's."

"Doesn't matter. The funding requirements are quite specific. And I haven't met them."

Roberto leaned back in his chair, his hands clasped together on the top of his head. Pain clutched at my chest. My mouth watered. Nausea. I needed to leave before another panic attack set in.

"I'm out. Don't worry, I'm fine. I'll call you when I'm back in town." I stood up and sped out of the room, leaving behind an uneaten burrito and a dear friend. I would miss him when I changed jobs. I ducked into the stairwell. I didn't want to see anyone.

I blinked back tears all the way to my car. My phone buzzed again. What now? It was a text from the vet's office, *Stanley's body is ready for pickup at your convenience*. Perfect timing. The day was already ruined, might as well go collect my dead cat.

"I'm here to pick up the remains of Stanley Brust," I said in monotone to the receptionist behind the counter.

She typed something into the computer. "Are you Simon Brust?"

"Yes."

"There's a note in Stanley's file from Dr. Cavendish. She wants to meet with you. Give me a minute. I'll see if she's available."

I waited.

Dr. Cavendish peeked out from a back hallway and gestured for me to follow. We entered a small office with no windows and dark wood paneling. The desk was cluttered with unkempt stacks of paper. She closed the door and invited me to sit.

"I'm glad I caught you. I'm so sorry for your loss. Stanley was such a sweet cat. I examined him. His neck was broken. Probably died instantly. He didn't suffer." She held my gaze.

I looked away at the framed degrees and licenses on the wall. "Could it have been caused by a fall or an accident?"

"Perhaps. Where was he when you found him?"

"Curled up on the floor, like he was sleeping, in the middle of a bedroom." A sea of pain threatened to drown me. I beat it back behind walls.

"Could he have fallen from something and landed where you found him?"

"There's really nothing to fall from in that room. He might have been hit by equipment from the paramedics that worked on my mother. He could have gone into the room and died of his injuries. But the door is usually closed and...thank you, Dr. Cavendish." I stood and grabbed the door knob. I needed to escape that closet of an office.

"Would you like me file an animal abuse report?"

"I don't know if that's necessary. Let me get more information first."

"Of course. My assistant will bring Stanley's ashes to you," she said, with that look people make in these situations.

I drove home with the silver urn containing Stanley's ashes next to me in the passenger seat. At red lights, I threw out a hand to protect it from tipping over.

I couldn't wait to get out of town. Tomorrow, I would fly to Colorado and launch a backpacking trip across an ocean from my father's.

I ran up the stairs to my apartment with Stanley's urn to call my father and disclose the itinerary change. I had put it off too long. But I wasn't telling him about the grant and the inevitable loss of tenure. He was the last person I wanted to tell. He would never forgive me.

I pulled a heavy wad of keys out of my pocket and slid the newest, shiniest one into its slot. There was no friction as I turned the key. The door was already unlocked.

"Brust, you're losing it," I said out loud, flogging myself for failing to lock the door. Another failure. I walked straight into my office, set Stanley's ashes on my desk and called my father.

"Are you packing your hiking poles?" he said when he answered.

"I'm calling with some bad news."

His voice cracked. "Your mother?"

"That too. Sorry, I should have told you sooner. She fell and broke her hip. Had hip replacement surgery. She's doing great. Up and walking. Recovering at home with Alice."

"Oh no. I'm sorry. Do you need anything?"

"I don't but I'm sure she'd love to hear from you…"

I listened. He didn't respond, ignoring my reference to Mother and his responsibilities as husband and father and decent human being, again.

"Maybe you could call her?" I pushed it.

"I don't think she'd want to hear from me."

"Yes, she would. She asks about you, constantly. You just stopped all communication with her when you left. She doesn't understand. I don't understand it, either."

He went quiet.

I did too. I waited him out. I let the tension build. I hoped he felt uncomfortable. I wanted him to think about her, about the situation he left us in.

"That's between me and your mother," he said.

He was impenetrable. A fucking fortress.

"Then why am I always in the middle of you two?" I paused, hoping it would sink in. "Anyway, the reason I'm calling. I'm not coming to Geneva. I can't hike the Matterhorn with you. I apologize for the late notice. There's just...too much going on." The words came out harder than I meant them.

His voice dropped an octave. "I understand. But I haven't seen you in a year. Maybe you could visit later this summer?"

His tone. Disappointment dripped from it. I felt bad, guilty. Why? I didn't do anything wrong. Don't anger your father. You'll never see him again. Enough tiptoeing. I had been doing more than my share of the work to maintain our relationship all these years. And I was done playing the messenger between him and Mother. It wasn't my job. It never should have been my job.

"Actually, Dad. I'm not flying to Geneva to see you again until you come to the U.S. to visit me. It's your turn. It's past your turn." I hung up the phone. Sadness hung off my bones.

In less than one week from Mother's fall, hours after discovering I was denied the most important grant of my career, and ten minutes after the only assertive conversation I'd ever had with my father, I numbly organized piles of camping gear in preparation for my solo trip.

On the top of my bed in neat rows lay sleeping bag, packets of dehydrated food, waterproof coat and pants, water purification and consumption systems, tent, map, GPS, alcohol stove, shovel, headlamp and sleeping mat.

I meandered into the kitchen, searched cupboards and finally the pantry for the flask Alex brought on our walk in the blizzard. There it was. I pushed away the memories it unleashed. Over the sink, I poured tequila through a funnel into the flask.

When the flask was full, I carried it down the hall and added it to the stack of gear on my bed. I stared at it. Then I picked it back up, carried it to the kitchen and poured the tequila back into the bottle. I couldn't afford the weight. And I didn't want it.

I scrounged for woolen base layers. The nights would be cold in Colorado. I opened the bottom drawer of my dresser and felt around under sweatshirts. I dumped the contents on the floor. My travel money, nearly $1,800 in cash, gone. Pain gripped my chest, again. I spun out of my bedroom in a trembling fit of rage and headed to the attic to collect my backpack.

I stormed up the steps, grabbed my backpack and headed back down the stairs. Wait. Something was different. My favorite bicycle, the one Alex rode, the green Cannondale CAADX Carbon Tiagra cyclocross, usually parked next to my backpack, also gone. I hadn't noticed it when I scavenged rugs to cover the scratch on the living room floor. How did I miss that?

Pacing back and forth in my living room, I added the bike and the money to the ever-growing stack of disillusionments, losses and betrayals that Alex had perpetrated against me. I couldn't let her get away with it. It wasn't right. It wasn't fair.

I called the police.

Thirty minutes after filing a complaint with the police department's non-emergency number, a cruiser slid up to my curb. I took two and three steps at a time to get to the door downstairs and let her in.

Detective Sanders nodded and took notes on a narrow, spiral pad. She said few words as I displayed the damage to my floor and shoved into her hand the papers from the vet, confirming Stanley's suspicious death by broken neck.

"You think Alex Argyle killed your cat?"

"Possibly. It's hard for me to believe. But when you consider the way Stanley was found, nothing else makes sense. I would like you to investigate."

As requested, I didn't mention the likelihood that Alex also tripped my mother, caused her broken hip and forced her to undergo surgery and a long recovery fraught with ongoing pain and medical appointments. She surveyed the attic while I composed a list of stolen items, vet and flooring repair costs and unauthorized credit card charges.

"I reported the credit card charges as fraudulent but haven't heard a determination from the bank yet," I said after she completed the inspection and we were back in my living room.

"You *gave* Alex the credit card?" She looked up at me from her note pad.

"Yes, but I specified that it was only to be used for my mother's expenses."

"Uh-huh. You specified. And you'd been living together? Romantically? For several months?"

"Yes."

She scribbled notes. "And Alex had been working for you?" A look of incredulity flitted across her face.

"Yes. Paid in full," I said. She thought I was just another jilted lover seeking revenge.

"Do you know where I might find Alex?"

"Yes." I swallowed. Hety. I hadn't had a second to follow up with her.

Cramps twisted my guts while I provided Detective Sanders with Hety's address, Alex's email and phone number.

She left my apartment. I fled to the bathroom and emptied the contents of my bowels into the bowl. Beads of sweat rolled down the back of my neck. I turned on the faucet, leaned over the sink, and gaped at myself in the mirror. How did you get yourself into this mess?

I teetered back to my bedroom, hovering over the camping gear. I wanted answers.

Camille. Maybe she could provide some insight into the sadistic workings of Alex's mind. I flipped through my list of contacts. I didn't have her number.

I left my apartment, jumped into my car and drove the short distance to the Brash Barista and Books.

When, at last, I made it to the front of the line, I said, "Hi, I'm looking for Camille Benoit?"

"She's not working today," said an unfamiliar face with a small mouth and big, black glasses.

"Do you happen to have her phone number?" Maybe he would take pity on me.

"I can't give out that information."

"Of course not. Fair enough. Thank you." I returned to my car, disheartened. I googled her name. She came up in connection to the Millicent Warner Gallery with a New York address and telephone number. Had she moved?

Undeterred, I searched my spatial memory for directions to her home and drove. I suspected that if she was home, she wouldn't be impressed with an uninvited guest at her door. Disregarding rules of etiquette and my overpowering tendencies toward introversion, I pressed on, using the commute to formulate a list of questions to ask about Alex.

Thirty-five minutes later, I was standing on a cement porch, knocking on a beige door. I leaned against the metal hand rail. I knocked and waited. And knocked and waited. The Beatles songs,

I'm so Tired followed by *Blackbird,* emanated from inside. The white album. Music I imagined Camille might play. I knocked again, harder this time. No answer.

Crestfallen, I walked back to my car and was about to duck inside when the front door cracked open. Camille stepped onto the porch.

She was barefoot, wearing grey men's boxer briefs and an orange tank top. Her hair had grown out in swoops and flips that nearly brushed her chin. Her wiry legs, translucent, were free of tattoos. I admired the flames reaching up her arms and neck while my mind wondered where the fire began. Her loins? No. I didn't know her well, but that didn't seem like Camille. Her heart? To reflect her passion for art? Reasonable hypothesis.

"Simon? Hi," she waved. I slammed the door shut and hurried over to her. "It's so nice to see you." She stood on her tip toes and gave me a warm hug. She smelled crisp, like paper. "Been downstairs, folding laundry. Music's blaring, didn't hear you." She beamed a welcome like she'd been expecting me all day.

"I apologize for just showing up like this. I would have called but I don't have your number. Any chance you have time to talk?"

"You came at a good time. Come in. I'm just doing laundry." We stepped inside.

"I have some questions about Alex that I'm hoping you might be willing to answer. Things exploded between us."

"Oh, no. I'm sorry. Are you okay?" She surveyed me as if trying to get a read on my mental state. "I'm not surprised. When I saw you at the Barista, that look on your face…I wondered if Alex was up to her shenanigans."

I followed her into the living room, fixated on her slender feet as they compressed the nap of multicolored, hand-woven rugs and flexed across the hardwood. Her place had changed. Swirling white marble abstracts and nudes of various sizes on tall and short stands still filled every corner and lined every wall. Again, I was rendered mute by her talent.

It was the color of the walls. No longer white, they were terra cotta, like the setting sun.

"It's Tiki Torch. What do you think? I just finished painting last week."

"It glows."

She laughed. "I think so too."

"Sit. Anywhere." She lifted two brimming, plastic laundry baskets off a fuzzy burgundy couch and dropped them to the floor and glanced up at me. "I'm thinking we might need wine for this conversation."

"Agreed."

She disappeared into the kitchen. I sat on the floor, legs extended, with my back against the sofa. The position made me feel too young, like I was a kid in college. I scrambled off the ground and sat on the couch. I crossed and uncrossed my legs. Bangs and clanks came from the kitchen.

"Need some help?" I shouted.

"No. I've got it, thanks."

What was I doing there? I tried to come up with an excuse to leave. Before I could hatch an escape plan, Camille reappeared bearing a platter of charcuterie, a bottle of Beaujolais, and two tall wine glasses.

She set them down carefully on a coffee table made of gnarled tree. "I'll be right back." She returned with plates, silverware, napkins, and corkscrew, added them to the collection, then fiddled with the stereo. I uncorked the wine as Billie Holliday blared into the room.

Camille turned the music down and poured us each a glass of wine. With a knife and fork, she filled two plates with thin slices of prosciutto, yellow and white cheeses, humus, green olives and crackers. She reached over the table and handed one to me. "Dig in." She plopped into a leather chair across from me, took a sip of wine, chewed an olive and peered at me. Her face said, whenever you're ready.

"So, I stopped by the Brash Barista, hoping to find you. The person at the counter said you weren't working and, you'll be reassured to know, refused to disclose any of your personal information." I stacked cheese and meat on a cracker. I took a bite and returned it to the plate, my stomach, uncertain.

"Big glasses?"

I nodded.

"My replacement, River. Friday's my last day. I'm launching a full-time career in art. I completely terrified, by the way. But I landed a show in Manhattan at the Millicent Warner Gallery. Kind of a big deal. Starts in June. I'll be there for four weeks. The Barista hemmed and hawed about giving me that much time off, so I took a great leap off the cliff of reliability and predictability and put in my notice."

"I suspect you're headed for a soft landing. Congratulations. It is a big deal. I looked you up, trying to find your number before I drove here. Saw your name listed with the gallery. I suppose I should buy another one of your pieces while I can still afford it. Especially since mine is missing."

"No. Alex did *not* take the sculpture."

"She did. Among other things. She wrecked my place. Tripped my mother. Probably killed her cat."

"No way. Oh my god. What a psycho."

"I know. I miss the sculpture. My eyes were drawn to it while I worked. Seemed to capture how I felt about grant writing."

"I've seen Alex's temper. She triggers easily. I was worried she'd flip out on me when I asked her to move out in September."

My face went hot. September? I met Alex in September.

33

"Would you feel comfortable telling me what happened?"

"I let Alex move in, about two years ago, so I could work from home. Beautiful body to draw, well proportioned, toned, long, sensuous lines."

I could hardly hear Camille's words past the buzzing in my ears.

"I know the one." A vision of Alex's naked body shoved itself into my mind, against my will. I tried to shake it out.

"Sorry. You're fragile." She hopped out of her chair to refill our wine glasses. She threw a few more crackers on her plate and sat back down.

"I thought having a model at home would save me from driving back and forth to the studio. More efficient, you know? And sometimes I like to work late, when the studio is closed. I also felt sorry for Alex, who was pretty much living in the Benz when we met. That was the deal. Cheap rent in exchange for modeling. The arrangement worked great, at first. Over time, though, she started paying the rent late, then paid half, then she just quit paying. But that didn't bother me as much as the fact that she just wouldn't show up for drawing sessions. It started interfering with my work. She'd just go missing. Wouldn't answer my texts."

"Go missing. Sounds familiar." Like Mother said at Christmas.

"Incommunicado for hours. Disappeared in the middle of the night. Alex has some questionable contacts. Micah's been arrested for forging checks or something along those lines. Gabe's addicted to coke or meth. She was vague about it all. I'm pretty sure they steal mail from people's boxes, hoping to find credit card numbers, bank account information, so they can try to hack into it."

"Explains the mail scattered all over the back seat of her car. Alex said it was junk mail collected from dog sitting." Long exhale. "She never mentioned Gabe or Micah."

"Hold on. What did you just say?" Camille took a sip of wine. "*Dog sitting? Alex?* That's hilarious." She burst out laughing then coughed, catching wine with her hand as it spilled from her mouth and ran down her chin. "Can you seriously picture Alex, dog sitting?" She wiped her chin with a napkin.

"Not when you say it like that." We both cracked up.

"Scooping up dog poop with a baggy? Alex? She wouldn't lower herself." Her shoulders started to shake from peals of laughter. She made poop scooping gestures with her hand. She clasped her stomach and hunched over. The image she created of Alex and the contagion of laughter sent us both into fits. We couldn't stop. Every time we settled down, Camille made another shoveling motion that set us off again.

"Whew. I haven't laughed like that for a long time. Micah and Gabe are the slackers Alex hangs out with when she vanishes into thin air. Doing criminal shit, I guess."

I wiped my eyes. We were quiet for a few minutes.

"You know, I felt like she got me. I thought what we had was the real deal. Special. I guess it was all lies. And I fell for it."

"Oh, don't be so hard on yourself. I was completely buffaloed, too. Alex is *good*. She's a charmer. Smooth talker. Pours on the compliments and gifts. *You're so smart. You're so pretty*. Convinces you of your fabulousness. And, even more so, of her fabulousness. Knows just the right things to say." She tapped her temple. "She knows how to get inside your head. So sexy and fun. It's easy to let things slide and go wherever the pied piper, Alex, is leading."

"That's it, exactly." I had one more question. I hesitated to ask it. I swallowed a mouth full of wine and mustered the nerve.

"Did you two ever sleep together?"

Camille grabbed a sesame seed cracker from the platter and used a knife to smear it with a scoop of hummus. She added a slice of prosciutto and took little nibbling bites until it was gone. When she finished chewing, she stood up.

"I need a cigarette. Let's go for a walk."

"You smoke?"

"Shhhh. Not in front of marble. They'll turn yellow just hearing the word."

We collected in the doorway. I waited while Camille stepped into a beat-up pair of leather clogs and threw on a men's saggy, brown cardigan with leather elbow patches and big buttons.

"My smoking jacket."

"Never mind. Really. Don't answer that question. It's none of my business." We walked in the street next to parked cars. "For some sick reason, I would like to know."

Camille pulled a pack of Lucky Strike out of one sweater pocket and a lighter out of the other. She glanced at me. "Listen, doc, I smoke four a day. It's a French thing. Part of my heritage. Don't give me any shit about it." She tapped a cigarette against its packaging, lit it and took a long drag, "Of course we had sex," she said, exhaling.

I waved the smoke away. "Oh, sorry," she said. She moved the offensive object into the hand farthest from me and blew in that direction. "I suppose I don't need to tell you this, but Alex is very seductive. Sleeps with everyone." She took another drag. Smoke curled out of her nose. "Probably not easy to hear, but it's true." We walked in silence. Two adolescents zoomed past us on scooters.

"I need to hear it. Is Alex bi? Pan sexual? Queer?"

"Maybe. But I never thought her behavior had anything to do with sexual or gender identity. Alex is an *opportunist*. It seemed to me that her seductions were less about sexual desire or gratification, more about manipulation. And power. She uses sex. Like it's a key to open doors. To get things. Or like a passport to gain entry into a new adventure, access to worldly goods."

"Alex told me you never slept together. Why lie? I wouldn't have cared." We walked in silence for a block. "This whole disaster started for me just like it did for you. I felt sorry for her, no father figure, single mom, working odd hours. I was trying to help her."

We returned to Camille's house, climbed the porch stairs and went inside. I settled into my place on the sofa. Camille grabbed the wine bottle and was about to fill my glass.

"No thanks. I'm good."

She filled her own and carried it to where she stood at the window.

"More lies." She shifted her weight, displacing black waves of hair. I couldn't see her face. "Alex's father is a retinologist. Mom's a pediatrician. They both live in California. Alex was raised in a stable household. Her mom's brother is in jail for larceny, though. Maybe it runs in the family. Her parents divorced when Alex was around 16. I've met them both at different times when they were here in town visiting Alex. Seemed nice enough. Got the sense Alex was quite the handful as a teenager. Arrested for shoplifting. Set her father's Mercedes on fire. He doesn't speak to Alex much, probably because he's been lied to so many times, bamboozled out of money and a whole bunch of other chicanery. He implied as much during his last visit, about a year ago."

The room shriveled, its edges gauzy, as the truth rained down on me like golf-ball-sized-hail. Camille walked back across the room, sat down in her chair, pulled knees to chest and searched for my eyes. I felt her pity. My stomach careened.

"Alex only cares about Alex. We're not her only victims. Where do you think the Benz came from? The laptop? The speakers? Nice clothes?" she said.

"Idiots like me. And you. Add a Tahitian pearl, new tires, a bike, a sculpture, cash, credit card charges to out of town *hotels*, my trust, my dignity, and a bunch of other stuff to that list."

"I think she *enjoys* lying. It's like a sport. She has fun seeing how much she can get away with, how many lies she can get people to believe."

"Con artist? Antisocial Personality Disorder? Psychopath? In medical school, during a psychiatric clerkship, I read that their brains don't function like normal people's brains. Less blood flow to the prefrontal cortex. Makes them impulsive, less capable of empathy," I said, cramming unwanted emotions into the numb oasis of intellect and reason.

"Sounds like Alex. Sprinkle on some unbridled narcissism and you have the complete picture. She has to be the best, have the best, designer everything, knows all the right people. Well, she says she does. And she talks too much. She never stops talking. About herself. She's the hero at the center of every story. Drove me nuts."

"You could've filled me in before I moved the little villain into my house."

"I suppose I owe you an apology. Truth is, it took me a while to figure it out myself. Couldn't really get my head around it until Alex was gone. Anyway, you wouldn't have believed me. I saw how smitten you were."

My face went hot again. Pain stabbed my guts. I was going to be sick. I excused myself and retreated into Camille's black and white mosaic tiled bathroom. I turned on the faucet and let cold water run over my hands. I rinsed my neck and face, dried them with a towel and returned to the living room. I was done talking about Alex.

I wandered the sculptures, stopping to examine an abstract of two entwined bodies. One body started where the other began.

"So tell me about your tattoo."

"Basically, I'm obsessed with fire. It has intelligence. An organic will, a purpose. It *tries* to spread. It *wants* to engulf. It seems to *know* where to go to find fuel."

"I agree. It's alive. Creates entire weather systems to support itself. So, where does it start? The fire."

"Ha. Brave of you to ask. Most people want to but they don't have the nerve. Not where you might imagine. Starts at my stomach. Fire in the belly. It's about my drive to create. I can't *not* make art. It has a life of its own."

"Just like fire." And I couldn't not research cancer. I winced as the cramps in my guts returned. I inhaled, trying to breathe it away. "Well, I suppose I better let you get back to your laundry." I collected my plate and the nearly empty bottle of wine and delivered them to the kitchen. Camille picked up the platter and followed me.

"Thanks for being available. For being honest. I needed the truth. You've been a friend to me," I said at the door, wrapping Camille in a hug.

"Sorry to shatter your illusions," she said into my chest. "Hey, come see my show in New York."

"I might just do that. Go easy on the Un-Lucky Strikes."

"Yeah, yeah."

I drove home in a dust storm made up of Alex's lies colliding with the facts I had learned from Camille. After getting lost for the second time, I put my address into Google maps and let it guide me home.

Once back inside the apartment, I avoided thinking about the details of our conversation. I avoided thinking about the details of my life. Instead, I methodically filled my backpack with everything I had laid out on the bed. I strapped it on and walked around. I weighed it: 36 pounds. I was ready. I crawled into bed.

I couldn't sleep. My legs flailed, sheets and blankets kicked to the floor. In the quiet of night, the implications of my conversation with Camille forced their way into consciousness. I was a failure. I lost my job. I fell for Alex's lies. I had not only hurt myself, but everyone around me. Mother. Hety. Gen. How did I not see through it? I was really screwed up. Around 1:00 a.m., I finally slipped into an agitated sleep.

Around 2:30 a.m., I startled awake. There were sounds in the hall, a presence in the doorway. I bolted upright and swung a fist at the air. Then, a familiar snicker, "It's just me," said the darkness. A figure stepped inside my bedroom. Alex.

34

"How did you get in here?"

"The door was open."

"No, it wasn't."

"You're right. I have a way with locks."

"That's what I hear. You're no longer welcome in my home." I leapt out of bed, vulnerable in my grogginess and underwear. I strode toward her in the doorway and flipped on the light.

Her hands reached for my waist. "I'm so sorry, Simon. I really crossed the line." She pulled me toward her. "Please. I love you."

I twisted out of her grasp. I walked to the closet, stepped into a pair of sweats, threw on a t-shirt and marched past Alex, out of the bedroom, headed directly for the front door.

For the first time, I didn't believe her. And for the first time, I didn't *want* to believe her.

"You say that word. But you don't mean it. It's just another one of your lies. You don't love me. You used me. I'm not sure you're even capable of love."

She followed close behind. "Simon, *stop*. That's not true. You know we're made for each other. We're perfect together. You'll never meet anyone like me, who loves you as much as I do."

"I hope I don't." I opened the door and extended my palm, an invitation for her to leave. Out of the corner of my eye, I noticed gaps and disarray near the stereo. Alex had removed the fancy speakers while I slept. They were nowhere in sight. Probably already downstairs in the Mercedes.

"You just came for the speakers, didn't you? Please take anything else you may have forgotten when you destroyed my home. Perhaps you'd like another one of my bicycles. I hope you enjoyed the leftover steak."

Alex's expression transformed from pleading innocence to sinister. I braced myself.

She approached me slowly, the muscles in her neck taut. "You're crazy, you know. Pathetic, actually. A loser. Your father's ashamed of you. Your students hate you. I didn't use you. You used *me*. You still owe me money for all the nights I spent babysitting your mother."

"I don't owe you anything. And I want you to leave Hety alone. I'll tell her everything you've done. I've already filed a report with the police."

"She won't believe you and neither will the cops."

"What if they do?" I said, in complete calm.

Alex walked out the door.

I closed it and locked the useless lock, turned off the lights and returned to bed, unable to sleep. Not shaken. Not angry. Just awake.

I saw Alex for the cancer she was. She couldn't hide it from me any longer. I couldn't hide it from myself.

At dawn, I showered, drank two cups of strong coffee and ate a bagel with cream cheese, tomato, and salt and pepper. At 6:30 a.m., I hoisted the bulging backpack into the car and buckled Stanley's urn into the passenger seat.

On the way to the airport, I stopped by Mother's house. I barely recognized the clear-eyed, fully dressed woman that greeted me at the door. The remnants of the mother she was and could have been. I entered the house holding Stanley's urn. The sight of it set off a chain reaction of tears.

Through the sadness, I perceived a tension between Mother and Alice. Understandable, given Mother's likely cravings and the fact that my sister had moved every ounce of alcohol, including mouthwash and cold medicine out of her house and into my apartment.

Currently without booze for longer than she had been since the long-ago year in my youth, she wasn't interested in long-term sobriety. Without my sister's knowledge, I was later informed, she eventually figured a way to have a fifth of vodka delivered to the house while I was gone.

Over another cup of coffee, I disclosed to her that Alex charged up the credit card intended for her expenses and that, when confronted, Alex flew into a rage. It was me who Alex was talking to on the phone before Mother fell. My words had upset Alex that morning. I also told her that Alex ravaged my apartment, stole money, a bicycle, a sculpture, and might have killed Stanley.

The confession poured out of me like a mud slide, oozing, black, and suffocating. Mother stared, without speaking. She didn't move. I didn't stay to clean up the mess of my words. I left abruptly, failing to make them breakfast, failing to pick up a few groceries, as promised. I escaped to the airport early, desperate to get out of town.

I strolled the halls of Tweed, New Haven, aimless, turning in and out of shops, unzipping and zipping sale-rack luggage, comparing the virtues of noise cancelling headphones, flipping through pages of books and magazines without registering titles or words, until it was time to board.

My flight departed and landed on time.

Brown sparrows darted through the tented peaks of Denver International Airport. I took the train to baggage claim, plucked up my backpack and followed signs for the shuttle to the Hertz rental car lot.

I heaved my backpack into the trunk of a silver Yaris, plugged in my iPhone, set music to shuffle and began the six-hour long road trip to Durango.

On U.S. Route 285, somewhere past Conifer, electric violin. David Bowie's voice, *With your long blond hair and your eyes of blue, the only thing I ever got from you was sorrow.* I hit the off button and drove the remaining distance in silence. Thanks, Alex, you ruined music for me, too.

I ruminated about my last session with Dr. Snellen. Unmet needs. What did I get out of the relationship with Alex? She brought light and energy to my otherwise staid existence. She was fun and funny and her intelligence was unique, abstract, philosophical. She was creative. Fluid. Open. We talked about everything.

Snellen said to go deeper. Okay. I give more than I receive in romantic relationships. My relationship with Alex mirrored my relationship with Mother. Ruby, too, maybe. Not Gen, though. With her, conversations about everything except cancer research stayed on the surface. More like my relationship with my father.

My phone vibrated. It was Gen.

"Hello?"

"Simon? Are you there?"

"Gen?"

"Hello?"

Disconnected. No service. I threw the phone into the passenger seat and cursed the mountains and rural Colorado for its lack of utilities, displacing feelings that threatened to explode out of suppressed corners of my psyche.

I checked into a seedy hotel in Durango, the kind with rows of rooms, sagging exterior air conditioners, and concrete encased banisters and stairwells. I slogged to my upstairs room, catching a glimpse of something that scooped a dollop of sour out of my disposition: I had a stunning view of the Animas River.

I'd spend two nights at the hotel, acclimating to the altitude before hiking into the Weminuche Wilderness.

According to my phone, Gen called twice while I was in transit. In the messages, her speech faltered. What was that about? More bad news. I threw my backpack on the bed, scrounged for minimalist toiletries and brushed my teeth. Behind me, through grimy, open curtains, the sun was setting, orange and pink.

I stepped out of my hotel room, stood at the guard rail and watched the river for a few minutes. When darkness fell, I sat down on the plastic chair just outside my door and returned Gen's call. I hadn't spoken with her since I fled the lounge.

"Sy, how are you holding up?"

"Fine," I lied. "You?"

"Roberto told me about your mom's fall. How's she doing?"

"Yes. She fell, broke her hip, got a new one, and is currently recovering at home with Alice."

I wanted off the phone. I was about to wrap up the conversation by regaling the glories of my outstanding river view when emotions clouded my judgement.

"Alex probably tripped my mother, caused the broken hip. She also destroyed my apartment. Oh, and is blaming me for all of it," I blurted.

"I'm confused."

Long silence. "Alex and I were living together until a week ago."

More silence. "You two? A couple? I thought Alex was just helping with your mom."

"She's the reason we're no longer friends with benefits. How do you not know this? You know everything. No detail gets past Dr. Genevieve Hale," I said, a hostile force behind my words.

"I heard rumors. Lots of rumors. But you know how it is with the talk in the department. Everyone is hypothetically sleeping with everyone else. I didn't believe it. And I assumed you would tell me if it were true. Why didn't you tell me? Wow. I guess I didn't want to see it. I'm just...surprised you would *date* Alex. I mean, she's charming. She can dance like nobody's business. But there's something.... off about her."

"Understatement. Please, elaborate."

"I don't know. She's slick. Definite slime factor. Why didn't you tell me you were together?"

"She asked me not to."

"What's up with that?"

"I don't know."

"I think I might know." She hesitated.

"Just say it."

"The night of your party, remember? I went to the pantry to find your decanter."

"You already told me. You were on the ladder. She wouldn't let go of your ankle."

"Yes, but I didn't tell you everything."

My breath came faster. "What?"

"She finally let go of my ankle. I climbed down the ladder and was back on the ground with the decanter..."

"And?"

"She *kissed* me."

A sickly void yawned in my guts. "I don't know how to respond to that."

"I'm sorry. I should have told you at the party."

"Why didn't you?"

"I was embarrassed, I guess. Afraid I led her on. That I did or said something to make her think I was interested."

"It wasn't your fault. You didn't do anything wrong. I've got to go. I'll call you when I'm out of the woods." I started to hang up.

"Simon, *wait*. The reason I called..."

35

My heart pounded in my throat. "Let me guess. I'm to vacate my office and leave Yale immediately. I've been banished from the university and the streets of New Haven?"

"No." She paused. "Quite the opposite."

"You're killing me, Gen."

"The department received a ten-million-dollar endowment today. In your name. You were principal investigator on research that directly led to a cancer treatment that saved the life of the eight-year-old daughter of billionaire Harold Savoy. You'll more than meet the requirements for tenure."

The information settled into deflated places in my shoulders and chest and pumped them full of air. I could keep my job. I could continue my work.

"You really know how to torture a person. Did you ever consider starting this heinous conversation with that news?"

She laughed. "I was worried about your mom."

She provided the details about the endowment and we said our goodbyes.

I opened the door to my room and sat on a grungy chair by the window. I couldn't sit still. I went back outside and walked the path by the river in the dark to the edge of town and back.

I'd been preparing myself to leave Yale. I'd investigated a position expected to open at Duke and investigated other Immunology programs that studied how cancer hides from the immune system. But I didn't have to think about it anymore. I didn't have to worry about it. I was staying.

Back inside the hotel, I flipped through cable channels. Too many commercials. I turned the television off, washed my face and crawled into bed.

Awake in my room in the middle of the night, the rosy afterglow of the endowment faded. I found myself asking the same tired questions. Why? Why would Alex try to wedge her way between me and two people so important to me?

She *wanted* to *hurt* me. She took what she could from me and tried to position herself into a better situation. With my people. Gen was independently wealthy and a figure in the community. Hety had access to mounds of money and would have fewer expectations and demands on Alex's time and whereabouts than I did. Alex didn't care about me. She only cared about what I could do for her.

I decided to evaporate into the Weminuche Wilderness the next day. I would suffer the altitude. I needed to be off the grid, away from everyone and everything. Away from distractions and demands, the usual flood of emails and phone calls and questions from students. Unreachable. I needed to figure myself out.

I flicked on the lights, sat up in bed against two flimsy pillows and consulted my map and the Internet.

With the tip of my pen, I traced a path. Starting at the Needle Creek trailhead, I'd hike to the Chicago basin the first night. I would take the Johnson Creek Trail to the Vallecito Creek Trail and connect to the Continental Divide and the Elk Creek Trails. At the Elk Creek trailhead near Silverton, I'd meet the train for the return trip to Durango.

It totaled at least 50 miles of hiking with substantial elevation gain, more if I climbed any of the 14,000-foot peaks in the Chicago Basin.

I'd finish in five nights and six days. According to travel blogs, most people did it in four. But I was an emotional wreck, out of shape and not acclimated to the altitude. With my iPhone, I reserved round-trip tickets on the Durango and Silverton Narrow Gauge Railroad.

As for the second week of vacation, I hadn't decided. Maybe I'd hike a portion of the Colorado Trail. For now, I just wanted to be gone. I fluffed unfluffable pillows, clicked off the bedside lamp and pulled up the covers.

The late-night planning session took my mind off the Gen con- versation. But the second it was dark again, her words and the pit in my stomach returned. Alex tripped Mother. Alex kissed Gen. Alex was living with Hety.

I squeezed my eyes shut. The images kept coming.

Alex betrayed me and the most important people in my life. Banished from consciousness for the better part of a week, anger reappeared, landing with a mallet's blunt force. I stewed all night.

As soon as yellow light illuminated the space behind the hotel curtains, I tossed the thread-bare polyester sheets and comforter off my naked flesh and went straight into the last shower I would take for nearly one week.

The day was shaping up to be exactly as predicted, sunny with an afternoon high of 68 degrees. Headachy, I checked out of the hotel, backpack slung over one shoulder, and wandered Main Avenue in search of a carbohydrate and fat laden breakfast.

At the Lone Spur Café, I forced myself to eat an entire Denver omelet (when in Rome), two strips of bacon, a stack of buttered toast, and chugged as much potable water as I could pour down my gullet.

Bloated from the altitude and too much breakfast, I left my waiter a hefty tip, used a modern toilet one last time, and headed down the sidewalk in the direction of the train station.

On the way, I pulled over to a bench, sat down next to my pack and called Hety.

"How are you?"

"Good. Not sure I can say the same for Alex."

"What do you mean?"

"The police came by yesterday. Questioned her on the porch for about twenty minutes."

"Hopefully they cuffed her and took her downtown."

"No. I wish. I'm not sure what happened. She didn't say much about it. But I asked her to move out after they left. It didn't feel right to have her living here. She sat on my couch and refused to leave. My parents came over and asked her a bunch of uncomfortable questions about her plans for the future. She's gone now."

I bit the inside of my cheek. "I'm sorry I exposed you to this mess. My mess."

"It was good for me. In a way. You know I needed to grow a backbone."

"Mission accomplished, Hety. You took care of business. I'm impressed. Did she say where she was going?"

"Nope. Some guy, Gabe, I think, came over with a truck. They loaded it and the Benz and drove off."

"So, she's just...out there."

"Somewhere."

"On to the next sucker. Wish I'd sorted it out as quickly as you did."

"Yeah, something about her felt off."

"Well, I'm about to disappear into the woods. Glad you're okay. Well done. See you in a couple of weeks."

I threw on my pack and found the train depot down the street a couple of blocks. I pushed my way through the crowd in search of the correct platform. Five bleary eyed backpackers standing in a line against the wall reassured me I was in the right place. We idled, acknowledging each other without words, awaiting permission to board.

Hety did the very thing I failed to do. She listened to her sense that things weren't right. And acted accordingly.

My phone rang. Detective Sanders. Of course.

"This is Simon," I said, instantly hot, a familiar quiver in my hands.

She informed me that Alex's story was quite different from mine. Her tone, sharp, sarcastic, conveyed that she didn't believe me and worse, that she believed Alex.

Alex told the Detective that I was the one who destroyed the apartment in a jealous, controlling rage that erupted when Alex tried to break off the relationship. I allegedly took advantage of Alex by not paying for work she had done at Mother's house. In fact, I still owed her several thousand dollars for the overnights. The credit card was *given to* Alex, the bicycle was a gift, and the sculpture was *of* Alex so it rightfully belonged *to* Alex.

"Alex denied killing the cat. She bawled her eyes out when she found out he was dead," Detective Sanders said, like it was proof of Alex's innocence. "Due to the nature of your relationship and the fact that you gave the credit card and the other items to Alex, you don't have a case."

My legs went weak. I was about to hang up when some force within me, perhaps the injustice of it all, made me press on.

"I didn't *ask* Alex to overnight with my mother. It was never part of our agreement. She *volunteered.* She usually stayed because she was too drunk to drive or as a cover for running crimes in the middle of the night. You should investigate. Alex Argyle is a hacker, pilfers people's mail with the intention of stealing credit card numbers. She's probably involved in identity theft. Check the back seat of her car if you don't believe me. Talk to her former roommate, Camille Benoit. B-E-N-O-I-T. She could corroborate," I said to what seemed an uninterested ear on the other end of the line, already moving on the next case, chalking up my complaint to another lover's quarrel.

"I'll make a note of it, Mr. Brust."

I hung up and slid to the ground. Anger and regret swirled around inside of me. The emotional cyclone was interrupted by a nudge from a wooly backpacker who pointed to the train.

"Time to board."

I willed myself to stand. To walk. The train departed the station at 8:45, scheduled to arrive at the Needleton Stop at 11:15. With a whistle, the steam train clanged out of Durango.

I lurched and swayed with its movements. A steal bar in the seat back beat a bruise into my spine.

In less than 40 minutes, we were in the forest. I couldn't appreciate the scenery. I hardly noticed the mountains. I stared out the open window perceiving little but the tight fist of anger that lodged itself in my chest. It was laced with shame.

The Alamosa River somehow lured my attention away from the internal torture chamber of my mind. The power of the milky green drew me to it, pounding its relentless path through the canyon.

Just before the Needleton stop, an announcement. "Backpackers, you have five minutes to retrieve your packs and disembark."

I scrambled to find my pack in the open luggage car, afraid I wouldn't offload on time. But I did.

I leapt off the train, the only form of transportation and civilization for miles. As it jogged back into motion, surprised passengers gawked out windows at the scraggly group it was about to leave behind, in the middle of nowhere.

We backpackers formed a huddle, exchanging plans and routes, tips about the area. Everyone seemed eager to begin their journey into the woods. Needle Creek, shallow and wide, shimmered in the noon-day sun as we tramped across the bridge toward the trailhead.

I hung back and paused in the center of the bridge. I wanted to be last in the line of hikers. I wanted to be alone.

I had about six miles of hiking and 3,000 feet of elevation to tackle before I would set up camp. Most of daylight was already spent. Cool, pack riding comfortably, I made good time. The well-marked sand and rock trail followed the creek, swollen with early summer snow melt.

Within 60 minutes, the trail steepened. My thighs burned. I hauled myself and the pack up and up. Sweat trickled into my eyes. My back ached. I loosened straps and tightened others without stopping.

Four hours later, sloppy with fatigue, I banged the toe of my boot into a rock. It sent me hurtling forward then down, toward the ground. I caught myself. Lesson learned. I focused on the trail, taking one heavy step at a time.

The physical activity and the time alone weakened my defenses. Feelings and thoughts that had been shoved away began to creep out of the shadows.

36

Mother laying in a hospital bed with a broken hip. Stanley's dead body curled up as if he were asleep. Discovering hotel charges on my credit card. I relived it all. Every detail. I hashed and rehashed.

How could I have believed the lies? Did she ever love me? Was it fake from the beginning?

I picked up a stone and hurled it into the stream. How could she treat me like that? How could anyone treat anyone like that? I threw another. She didn't love me. At best, she tolerated me. She just used me.

Daylight waned. I sat on a boulder and chewed handfuls of granola, slurped the last of the water. It was time to find a campsite. I passed several. Too small. Too close to the trail. I forged ahead and was rewarded with a spacious, forested site on the creek far enough away from the trail to provide complete privacy. It boasted an outcropping overlooking a small waterfall and a narrow trail that wound down the steep embankment to the creek.

I unclipped the pack, peeled myself out of the straps, and set it down on a flat rock. Cold mountain air startled the sweat on my back. I scouted a flat area for the tent, unfurled my shelter into its center then scuffled down the trail to the creek.

I crawled across grey and yellow boulders, edges worn smooth by erosion, like the temperament of the aged. In the center of the stream, I plunked the water purifier's straw into its green-blue depths and pumped. The temperature dropped the moment day turned into dusk, a stern warning from Mother Nature.

I gulped filtered water until I had my fill, pumped again and then climbed the short, steep trail back to my gear. I lit a fire in the alcohol stove with small sticks and dried leaves and boiled water, first for a cup of green tea, then for dehydrated vegetable korma. Due to the altitude, the korma took forty long minutes to cook. Impatient, starved, I blistered my tongue on the first bite.

I leaned against a fallen tree, warmed by the stove. Alex's shoves during the blizzard, why did I let it go? I took her back. What an idiot.

My gut knew. I *knew*. Her behavior was aggressive. I ignored my intuition again in Tahiti when she went to the bar without me that first night, flirted with Parker and stayed all night at the party. She convinced me that it was no big deal, that it was my fault. That my *feelings* were *wrong*. Unjustified. Why did I disregard what my gut knew?

The ground beneath me hardened in the cold mountain air. I put out the fire, unzipped the tent and crawled inside. Cocooned in my sleeping bag, I lay awake. Why couldn't I see it? See her, for who she was?

Early the next morning, by the light of my headlamp, I made black coffee and ate a protein bar. I pumped fresh water, dismantled the tent, and re-stuffed my backpack. I was back on the trail in the grey light before dawn.

Within a mile, the landscape changed. Trees became bushes, stones morphed into grass. I entered the Chicago Basin, a flower speckled valley tucked between three, soaring fourteen-thousand-foot peaks. Mentally, I wasn't in any shape to climb them despite the promise of their names: Sunlight, Wisdom and Mount Eolus.

I was exhausted from two nights without sleep and sickened by the emotions finally released from their cages. I tramped straight through the basin, eyes on the trail. Even the grazing mountain goats couldn't shake me from the memories, the questions.

Before nightfall, I found a campsite on the Johnson Creek Trail, about a mile shy of the intersection where I would turn north. It was small, just off the trail but close to the creek.

I set up the tent and pumped water from the stream. I made tea, ate the rest of the granola for dinner then crawled into bed and collapsed.

I was awakened by a snort. A bear! I flicked on the headlamp placed next to my pillow and felt around the tent for the bear spray. I listened for movement. The forest was quiet. I drifted back to sleep, bear spray in my hand.

I heard the snorts again. I kicked off my sleeping bag, shoved feet into boots and with the headlamp on, and crawled outside to check the perimeter. Nothing had been disturbed. The food canister was still buried. No sign of a bear.

I sat on a log and took in the stars. Too cold to be outside, I went back to bed deciding to stay awake until sunrise, just in case. But I fell asleep.

Snort.

I burst out laughing. Congested from the altitude, I had been awakened by my own snores. I was the bear.

The laughter tripped a switch. I started sobbing. Tears formed wet spots on my pillow. Alone in the Weminuche, I wept. The anger was gone. Sadness had taken its place. I missed the Alex I thought I knew. The relationship I thought we had. I missed Stanley. I grieved for Mother and Hety and Gen, for what I put them through. I grieved for myself, for the panic attacks, for nearly losing my chances at tenure.

When I finally drifted off to sleep, I slept and slept, until the heat of a late-morning sun forced me awake.

I stayed put for another night. I scrounged sticks, built a fire, and spent the day hydrating and napping.

By late-afternoon, fed, rested, physically restored, I poked a stick into the fire and conjured plans to hire a housekeeper and grocery shopper for Mother. Maybe a student or an agency.

But she could do it all herself. Why was I always scrambling to do her basic household tasks when she could do them? She was only 64.

It was the commitment I made when I was just a kid to take care of her. So she might think I was worth something? It just kept us both trapped in dysfunction. My efforts had only made her worse, more dependent. All these years, I'd only been making it easier for her to drink.

No. I wouldn't hire anyone. She could, if she wanted.

I went to bed early and slept all night.

In the morning, I slipped into my backpack and made my way the short distance to the Vallecito Trail and headed north. For hours, I hiked, gaining elevation on the steep, rocky trail. My legs ached. Blisters erupted on the tip of a middle toe and on the balls of both feet. Worse, the ankle injury reappeared.

I limped off the trail and into the forest, freed myself from my pack and sat on a log. I yanked off boots and socks, reached into a zippered pocket and removed three Band-Aids and a tube of Neosporin. I greased the inflamed patches of flesh, then covered them. I scrounged for the roll of Ace bandage, wound it around my ankle and swallowed three Motrin. The socks were cold from sweat when I pulled them on again. My ankle refused to go back into its kennel. I loosened the boot laces and squeezed it inside.

Back on the trail, the pack felt heavy. One foot in front of the other.

How was Alex able to fool me? I was vulnerable. Snellen said I got something from being with Alex. Something that ran deep.

I scouted a camping site for the night, wandering into an alcove by the stream, surrounded by trees. It was a reasonable distance from the trail with a level area big enough for the tent. It would do. I dropped the pack, walked straight to the creek, pulled off my boots and socks and soaked my blistered feet and swollen ankle.

I smeared fresh Neosporin on blisters, covered the red welts with clean Band-Aids and re-wrapped the ankle.

I unpacked, pitched the tent, and boiled filtered water. With a belly full of rehydrated chili, I wandered back along the creek and scrambled up on a boulder. I reclined, merging with the hot, stony surface while an afternoon sun warmed my face. I closed my eyes. Trees creaked. Water gurgled. In the distance, hawks. I stayed on the rock, listening to the forest, until a blue dusk stole the heat.

In the morning, I ate, packed and set off early. I had to cover twelve miles if I was going to be on time for the train's short stop the next day. I hiked as hard and as fast as the blisters and ankle would allow.

As I pushed my body north, mile after mile, over rocks, up the steep trail, I came to terms with myself.

In that hallowed ground, where the unconscious becomes conscious, I confronted my own contributions to the Alex fiasco. Something injured inside of me was responsible. Unmet needs.

The childhood lack of support, Mother's drinking, constant criticism, and Father's emotional absence left me starving for approval and acceptance.

My needs made me a sucker for Alex. She sensed it, too. She could see them and used them to manipulate me.

She knew I craved conversation beyond cancer research and provided intellectual stimulation. She validated my thoughts and ideas, early on. It was better than any drug. She noticed that I was overwhelmed with work and offered to help Mother. And she did, for a little while. I was so relieved to have the help. She perceived that I needed approval and showered me with praise. Like Camille said, she knew how to get inside.

I ignored the warning signs because I wanted, I *needed*, what Alex was serving. It explained the panic attacks. They were trying to alert me to the truth. But I didn't want to see it. Anxiety is the avoidance of emotion.

Alex's true identity was hidden behind her charm, seduction and lies. I decided, too early, that I knew who she was, a normal cell. But she was a cancer cell disguised as a normal cell. The longer cancer cells go unseen, the better they are able to hoodwink the immune system.

I would continue therapy with Dr. Snellen. She helped me see.

I picked up the pace. Tears mixed with sweat in salty streaks.

When I unclipped the pack for the night, I was physically exhausted and sore but emotionally strong, self-assured. I let it resonate while I pounded tent stakes into the ground.

I found a still cove in the creek and stood next to it in the sand. I peeled off every stitch of clothing, grimy and pungent from compounding days of sweat, and tossed them onto a nearby rock. Wanting to be fresh for the train ride back to Durango, I lowered my body into the mountain stream.

Pebbles on the creek floor dispersed under my weight. Teeth clenched against the cold, I lay on my back in the water and submerged for a moment, resurfacing like the newly baptized.

I dried myself with a micro-towel, plunged the dirty clothes into the creek and scrubbed them with stones. I hung them in a tree. With any luck, they'd be dry by morning.

From the bottom of my pack, I scrounged a clean shirt, socks and a pair of pants I'd been saving. Still naked in the cool of evening, I pumped water, heated it, and finished bathing with soap and sponge. I dressed, clean and in clean clothing.

I ate every morsel of dehydrated stew, two huge helpings, scraping up gravy with a spoon. I drank cup after cup of hot tea until my insides were warm and my lips less shriveled from dehydration. I sat on a tree stump and warmed myself by the flames of the alcohol stove.

I wouldn't have any more panic attacks. And if I did, I knew how to manage them. I would ask myself what I was avoiding. I would deal with whatever feelings were bothering me.

That night, I slept soundly, waking in the same position I was in when I fell asleep. I dreamt I was flying over calm seas. I dove into the water and swam with the fishes. How would Jung interpret it, I wondered. I made a note to look it up when I got home.

I broke camp on yet another cloudless morning. My last day in the Weminuche. The final six-mile leg of my journey. I stepped on the trail and headed in the direction of the Elk Creek train stop. My gait, steady. My pack, lighter.

Thank you, Alex, I said out loud to the trees.

Despite the torment she caused, I was grateful to her for exposing me to my less inhibited side, to the possibility of a deeper connection, to the pleasures of cohabitation, and to the things I ignored.

At the train stop, five hikers stood in a circle. I approached and said hello. They greeted me with the warmth of shared experience.

I left the group and climbed on a flat rock at the creek's edge. I took off my pack, leaned against it, and waited for the train with a clear view of the horizon.

Acknowledgements

Stuart Horwitz and Madison Utley from Book Architecture, thank you, for swooping in at just the right time. Their detailed critiques grounded me when I was adrift in the void. To Janet Steen, my editor, thank you for the gentle guidance that helped me hone and add subtlety. Thank you, Barbara Spindel, for recommending Janet. To the Women's Fiction Writers Association and Barbara Josselsohn, thank you for matching me with my critique partner, the hilarious, warm, and astute, Jennifer Sinclair. Thank you to Kristofer Delaney for the awesome cover design.

Thank you to Valerie Brodar, the book's most dedicated reader and most persistent champion. Valerie is a meticulous and insightful editor whose compassion sustained me through periods of hopelessness and whose friendship is one of my luckiest finds. Thank you to Myra Spindel, Psy.D., for asking, for reading, and for listening. Her emotional generosity is a rare and much appreciated gift. Thank you to Brian Bain, M.D., who offered to edit a terrible early draft and, afterwards, still wanted to be friends. His observations lead to an alteration that improved the story line.

Thank you to Clark, whose comment about antigens sparked an idea that lead to this book. He endured unending ruminations with Zen-like kindness and his steadfast support provided me the psychological freedom and space to write.

M. E. Delaney is a psychologist specializing in trauma and anxiety disorders. *Plain Sight* is her debut. She is finishing a children's book and writing a second novel.

www.ingramcontent.com/pod-product-compliance
Lightning Source LLC
Chambersburg PA
CBHW041747310726
48978CB00011BB/340